SORRY YOU'RE LOST

Also by Matt Blackstone

A SCARY SCENE IN A SCARY MOVIE

SORRY YOU'RE LOST

MATT BLACKSTONE

FARRAR STRAUS GIROUX
New York

Farrar Straus Giroux Books for Young Readers
175 Fifth Avenue, New York 10010

Printed in the United States of America by
RR Donnelley & Sons Company, Harrisonburg, Virginia
Designed by Roberta Pressel
First edition, 2014
1 3 5 7 9 10 8 6 4 2

mackids.com

Library of Congress Cataloging-in-Publication Data
Blackstone, Matt.
    Sorry you're lost / Matt Blackstone. — First edition.
        pages cm
    Summary: New Jersey seventh grader and class clown Denny Murphy has just lost his
mother, his father is uncommunicative, he is in trouble with his teachers, and to top it all off,
his best friend has a scheme to get dates for the end-of-year school dance.
    ISBN 978-0-374-38065-6 (hardback)
    ISBN 978-0-374-37121-0 (e-book)
    [1. Grief—Fiction.   2. Middle schools—Fiction.   3. Schools—Fiction.   4. Fathers
and sons—Fiction.   5. Dating (Social customs)—Fiction.   6. Popularity—Fiction.
7. Conduct of life—Fiction.]   I. Title.   II. Title: Sorry you are lost.

PZ7.B5332Sor 2014
[Fic]—dc23
                                                                        2013021215

    Farrar Straus Giroux Books for Young Readers may be purchased for business or
promotional use. For information on bulk purchases please contact Macmillan Corporate and
Premium Sales Department at (800) 221-7945 x5442 or by email at
specialmarkets@macmillan.com.

To JAMIE and MARLENE —M.B.

SORRY YOU'RE LOST

FIRE

October 13th

There's a gum wrapper at my feet. Juicy Fruit. I wish I knew who dropped it so I could tell him not to litter at my mom's funeral. The room is musty and smells of lemon. My starchy shirt and stiff suit are drenched in sweat. The priest tells me it's time. Not for telling people to pick up their gum wrappers, but time for the service. Time to speak. For *him* to speak. We declined the chance. Like this:

Dad: "You want to say anything at the service, Denny?"

Me: "In front of people?"

Dad: "Yeah."

Me: "Well then, no."

Dad: "Me neither. Don't think I'll get any words out."

We sit in the front row. The priest is able to get words out of his mouth; they just aren't any good. He keeps using the word "essentially" to cover up the fact that he has no clue what to say because he has no clue who my mom is.

Was. She's now past tense, like anything else that happened yesterday: the news, the weather, the ball game.

"Susan Murphy was a loving mother and wife," the priest says. "Essentially, she was truly a model citizen." I want to interrupt him and stand up and shout, "NO ONE CARES THAT SHE WAS A MODEL CITIZEN. No one cares that she was a member of the PTA. That's not why we're here. We're here because she was mine and now she isn't."

He continues. "She loved her tea. Essentially, she loved tea in the same way she loved her friends and family. She was always there for them in their time of need. She was a hard worker and an avid reader. She was truly a loving and lovely woman."

There he goes again, reading the CliffsNotes—*The Life and Times of Essentially Susan Murphy*—and man, I want to run onstage and shake him and scream, "You don't know her! She was the best! She *is* the best. The best at telling my dad to swallow a bottle of chill pills, the best at making me do math homework, the best at waking me up on time for school after I fall back to sleep the first three times, the best at packing my favorite cereal, the best at carpooling to soccer practice without saying anything *too* embarrassing. (Though she did once call me Honey Bunches of Oats. In public. At school, in the hallway. And everyone heard. *Everyone*. And she did once write on my lunch box, 'Enjoy the Honey Bunches of Oats, My Honey Bunches of Oats.') But

4

she's still the best! The best at making soup when I'm sick. The best! Don't you know that?"

I almost stand up and do it. Rush the stage, I mean. I even raise my heels and flex my calf muscles, but there are over fifty people sitting behind me and sweat is leaking down my neck and my skin is on fire. It's hard to rush the stage when you're on fire.

I peek behind me. Manny's in the fourth row, wiping his eyes. I don't recognize anyone else. Because I don't want to. That way I won't feel bad when I bust free, which is what my legs have been screaming for me to do: LEAVE! RUN! GET ME OUTTA HERE!

Manny would know how to get home from here. He's my best friend, not because I like him a whole lot or because we have much in common, but because he's always been there, like some prehistoric insect that survived the test of time. If I told Manny my scheme, he'd push his thin-rimmed glasses up his skinny nose, twirl a strand of his gelled hair, raise his pencil-point eyebrows (he says he raises his eyebrows when deep in thought because his intellect is "highbrow"), rub his chin, and say, "Indeed, it is quite a flabbergasting conundrum: How can one elude one's family and/or bamboozle the guards? Some might say that we must let the question marinate to allow the maximum amount of brain juice to saturate this meaty dilemma, but not I." [Cue the scheme, the mathematical computations on our average speed and distance required to cover, the risk analysis on driving without a license—five years before you're even *eligible* for a license, a second reference to ushers as "guards," a timed escape at the "changing of the guards," and a request for a "nominal monetary reward" for his "infrastructure of knowledge."]

If you're wondering why Manny talks funny, it's because he thinks he's smarter than everyone else, and he probably is. Manny doesn't ever blend words by using contractions. That would be too informal and improper. He once saw someone wearing a T-shirt that read "Nobody's perfect. Except me." Manny fell in love with the shirt but disapproved of the contraction, so he had a shirt specially made that read "Nobody is perfect. Except me." He wears it nearly every single day. He's probably got it on now underneath his black suit, not that it really matters what he's wearing. Not that it matters what anyone's wearing or doing or saying or thinking or chewing.

Though I really wish someone would pick up that Juicy Fruit wrapper.

The car is black and the seats are black, but as I look out the window, it feels like any other day. The sky is light blue, the leaves are orange and yellow, the air is crisp and cold like an apple from the refrigerator, the roads are clear, and the restaurants we pass are still open for business. The red Mc-Donald's sign beneath the golden arches brags of billions served. Though I'm not the least bit hungry, I'm aware that it's lunchtime. I want to pretend that it's a regular ride home, but my dad isn't driving. He's sitting next to me, staring out the window, his whole body clenched like a fist. I realize that mine is, too. I tell it to relax and stop sweating, please stop sweating, but it doesn't listen. I want to tell the driver with the stupid black hat to turn on the stupid air-conditioning, but my mouth isn't working. Unfortunately, the radio is. The whole way home all I can think is, *That song is ruined. And so is that one. And that one. Now that song is ruined, too.*

When we pull into the small driveway, my body is still on fire.

At least there's no music in our house—if you don't count the murmured sound track of visitors. They're gathered in the family room. Though I'm not sure they're family. And even if they are, I'd trade them all for my mom. For just one more year or month or day or afternoon with her. I take a peek down the hall and notice most of them are strangers.

I also notice that I smell. My black suit is a damp towel and my white shirt is a soaked, stinking mess. There's so much I want to say, want to write down, but first: *Dear Old Spice deodorant, I'm glad we recently met each other. I thought we had a good thing going. A real solid relationship. But you're a traitor and you're weak and I smell.* I know I shouldn't think about it, but thinking about it makes me not think about it. Why we're here, I mean. Why I'm on fire.

1

Neighbors and old friends and people claiming to be my cousins hug me. "I'm sorry for sweating on you," I tell them. They say their thoughts and prayers are with me, but nothing extinguishes the fire. Not their hugs or their platters of food or the pile of phony sympathy cards written by some guy with a waxy mustache sitting in an attic that smells of mothballs. That's the way I picture it anyway. The image isn't comforting. And neither is the one in my family room. A play-off baseball game is on. The Phillies just blew a save in the bottom of the ninth, and the people on the brown velvet couch are muttering under their breath, grunts and grumbles and groans, but they manage to shove chocolate chip cookies and apple cake and corned beef sandwiches in their mouths. They talk politics and baseball and tell jokes like "You heard about the constipated accountant? He couldn't budget." This from someone claiming to be my uncle twice-removed. I think I get his joke but it still isn't funny.

What *is* funny is that the guy's got mustard on his mustache. Not the brown spicy kind with seeds; the yellow one, bright as a highlighter, a neon blob on the side of his mouth. Each time he takes another bite, the mustard quivers. I want to laugh because "mustard" and "mustache" sound similar and anything stuck in a mustache is funny, especially yellow mustard, but I can't cry and I can't laugh—at this or the next joke from Uncle Mustard's son, Cousin Mustard, aka My Long-Lost-and-Should've-Remained-Lost Cousin: "Why couldn't the pirate get into the movie? Any guesses? Anyone? It was rated Arrrrrr."

Saw that coming a mile away, but didn't have enough energy to stop it—or the next, from Uncle Mustard: "Last week I met this dog that could talk, I swear. I asked him what's on top of a house and he said, 'Roof!' I asked him what's on the outside of a tree and he said, 'Bark!' I asked him what's the feel of sandpaper and he said, 'Rough!' And then I asked him who the thirtieth president of the United States was and he scratched his head thoughtfully and said, 'Calvin Coolidge?'"

Someone tells Uncle Mustard to wipe his mouth. "Hey, it is what it is," I hear Uncle Mustard say, though I'm not sure whether he's talking about the mustard or why everyone's gathered here. I want to ask him and hear him lie, tell me what he thinks I want to hear, and I'll slash through, cross out, slice through all the phony bologna (though I know he's eating corned beef, not bologna, and it's not phony bologna, it's real bologna, and it's already sliced). I want to get to the real truth about whether these people even care, but Uncle Mustard is already walking away and I don't want to yell.

I turn my attention to my dad, who, instead of greeting guests at the door, permits entry, his wide body stepping aside with a curt nod. He looks like a bouncer. He must think uncle impersonators will barge in and steal the corned beef. You can steal a lot from my dad (not that I do) and he won't notice, but steal his *food*... cue the sirens, call the authorities. It's best to alert someone before the explosion, as it's tough putting him back together again.

My dad greets Manny at the door and allows him entry. Manny's eyes look red under the rims of his glasses. "I am sorry," he says. "She was a great lady and mother. To me as well. Please accept my condolences."

My dad nods. "Come in," he says, then blocks the door with his body once again. I'd tell my dad to stop being a bouncer and join the, I don't know, party / sports bar / competitive corned beef fest, but he's better off where he is. Neighbors and these strangers don't know their boundaries.

"Sure looks like there'll be plenty of leftovers... can feed a whole fleet... or just your dad. Take care of the old man, will ya?" "Playin' any sports, Denny?" "You should talk to someone." "Really sorry about, you know... ever been to Maine?"

And then someone says, "It's really heartbreaking for me, too," and all I hear is *I'm leaving, I barely knew her, I've stayed too long.*

There are sweat stains under my arms. Thanks, Old Spice. There's a mustard stain on the carpet—not from Uncle Mustard. This one's brown and probably spicy and definitely making a wet circle the size of a quarter on top of the fabric. At the crowded dining room table, the smell of sour pickles, the sound of crinkling cellophane. Neighbors and aunts talk about the SATs, how the test is hard and rotten and so are the tutors. I should feel grateful I still have about five years before I take it. But I don't feel grateful. I hope whoever is in charge of Thanksgiving cancels it next month.

Someone fills a glass at the sink without waiting for the cold water to cool down. I should tell them it's warm.

My bouncer dad eyes the corned beef. The neighbors are buzzing in my ear again and it's making me dizzy: "If there's anything you need, Denny, you know where to find us." "Following the Phillies?" "Man, you're in the seventh grade already?" "Do people at school know?" "You look snazzy in that suit." "It must be so tough." "Make sure you keep busy." "It is what it is." "How are you coping?" "Seen any movies recently?" "What are you up to later?" "Sure looks like it's shaping up to be a lovely day outside." "Such a lovely service this morning, wouldn't you say?"

The sweat stains under my arms are swelling, and there's so much I want to say to these people, shout to these people, write down for them to read and reread so they'll never ever bother me again, but all I can think is, *Dear Old Spice deodorant: You suck.*

ROCK STAR

3 1/2 months later

Aloha, goddess of mathematics!" I give Mrs. Q a gummy smile as I walk into a packed math class. "Aloha!"

I live in New Jersey, not Hawaii, but I love me some Aloha. Love the sound of it. Who doesn't? Come on, everyone loves the sound of "Aloha," even teachers, and people with really bad taste, like teachers. Ah, those gods and goddesses of literature, mathematics, and other fine subjects . . . If I were a teacher, I'd *love* to be called a god or goddess. And to be told how good I look.

"Wow, Mrs. Q, did anyone ever tell you that you have really nice earlobes?"

I don't have ~~a whole lot of~~ any experience whatsoever with pickup lines, but that's my favorite one, not that I'm trying ~~too hard~~ in any way to come on to Mrs. Q on this February morning. Though I do mention, as she reaches instinctively for her earlobes, that she looks aces, which is an awesome word that means awesome.

She shuts her eyes and bites her lower lip. "Denny, please sit down."

Teachers just don't know how to take a compliment. They really don't. They get all paranoid that you're using some kind of teenage-coded sarcasm to make fun of them, which of course is unfounded and ridiculous and downright insulting.

And usually true. (I *might've* once told last year's sixth grade science teacher that his lectures were "whack," horrible, lame. Chuckling nervously, he said, "I'll take that as a compliment, Denny. Being whacky is a good thing." Couldn't agree more.)

In this case, Mrs. Q really *does* look aces. Her skirt is nicely pressed, her hair pulled back in a ponytail. And you already know about those magnificent earlobes. Plus, her skin is as smooth as butterscotch pudding, but it'd be a whole lot smoother if she weren't a rookie teacher. How do I know she's a rookie? Because she's young and pretty, and her breath smells like coffee, her eyes droop like old flowers, and the bright orange poster on the outside of her door says, "You are entering the Learning Zone."

It really says that. The Learning Zone.

When the class gets rowdy, which is pretty much whenever I drop by these days, she points to the poster to remind us that we've entered the Learning Zone, as if the reason we're talking is simply because we've forgotten what zone we're in.

"Denny, please take a seat."

"Mrs. Q!" I gasp. "*Take* one of your seats? Heavens, no! Good heavens, no. I am not a thief. A borrower, sure; a lender, certainly. But a thief? No, ma'am."

Her seats don't exactly have street value. The desks and chairs are attached, like foldout trays on an airplane, or an armrest, or a skimpy one-piece bathing suit. Not that I wear skimpy bathing suits or anything. Seriously, I don't. I mean it. (Right now I'm wearing a green long-sleeved T-shirt and baggy jeans. *Not* a skimpy bathing suit.)

I glance at the rest of the class beyond Mrs. Q. Smiling faces, as chipper as a Sunday afternoon. And why not, for they're all enjoying my morning performance, except for Sabrina, who sits in the front row and always asks for extra math homework. But everyone else is chipper, especially my Rockafella crew: a small group of devoted homeys who never fail to laugh on command. We're not a gang, we're not even friends. I don't have many of those not named Manny, not that I discriminate based on name. I'd happily befriend someone *not* named Manny but ... anyway, the Rockafellas respect my craft, my art of faking it. To steal a word from my dad, the Rockafellas and I are colleagues. We may not be friends, but we work together. In harmony.

From the right side of the room, they're warming their golden pipes, feeling out the rhythm.

"What what?!" cries Billy D. He isn't asking a question.

"Wicki wicki wicki!" shouts Doug E. He's spinning an imaginary record.

"Yup yup," says Sean. I don't know his last initial. Or anyone's last name. They're just my harmonic colleagues. *Wicki, wicki, wicki, pop-u-lar-ity, hee-hee.* Just a little sample of our hits.

One of the Rockafellas screams out, "DO-NUTS! DO-NUTS!" which is sort of my name. Manny named me. Not because I like donuts or I'm shaped like one or because my middle name sounds similar to donuts, like Dontz or Domus. Not because my first word was "donut" or because I dressed as a donut for Halloween when I was too young to know any better.

Manny named me Donuts because I once beat him in a donut-eating contest during an elementary school field day event. That's it. That should have been it, but he got so bitter at my victory that he posted flyers all over the school with my face below my new name. Donuts. I took down as many flyers as I could, but the damage had been done. I was renamed. Born again as a pastry. I wish I had eaten slower. Or had a stomachache that morning. Or not come to school. But I came, I ate, and in those two minutes, everything changed forever. It reminded me of that famous

Robert Frost poem, "The Road Not Taken," where a split-second decision changes the course of your life. You've probably read the poem because it's so famous, but in case you haven't, it goes like this: "A group of goofy kids gobbled donuts in the back of the school near the broken fence. I swallowed four, Manny only three, and that has made all the difference."

Donuts . . . the name is a blessing and a curse. I mean, it's not exactly a selling point for the ladies. Seems nobody wants to squire a Donut about town, which makes sense, I guess. I probably wouldn't make out with a girl named "Funnel Cake." In general, you don't want to be labeled a pastry—unless you do what I do. Lets me be the dancing Rockafella, the Jolly Man, Jolly Olly.

Anyway, I'm at the front of the room jollier than a Jolly Rancher with a very important decision to make: where to sit, front or back. The front is my stage, spotlight and all, where I mark my territory and proclaim "Donuts was here," just in case the social worker asks whether or not I came to school and inquires about my state. (Not New Jersey; I mean how I'm doing, if I seem sufficiently cheery.)

The only bad part about the front is that Sabrina, the girl who asks for extra math homework, is always perched there, with her book open—to the right page, no less—and her hazel eyes focused solely on the day's lesson. Because her straight black hair covers her right eye like a curtain, I can't prove that both her eyes are focused on the board, but if her grades are any indication, she doesn't get distracted by sideshows such as myself. Still, that doesn't stop her from rolling her eyes—the visible one, the left, I mean—and grumbling about me needing to grow up, which I don't really mind because it's pretty much true and Sabrina's face is pretty pretty—I mean, it's pretty much pretty. Well, very pretty. It's fair in color, and even though she's not wearing any lipstick or any other makeup, her full lips look glossy. Not as glossy as a picture, but glossy like, nice. And she's got this small stud on her nose that is cute at all times of the day except when she's blowing her nose. Oh, and she wears a Batman band on her left wrist and she wrote on her bag in whiteout and pen—names, dates, poems, lyrics, jokes, a Batman logo—and nothing goes better with math than Batman and graffiti.

Still, her grumbling is a turnoff, and I must admit that her presence has, at times, impacted my performances, the way a kid chokes when his parents attend his baseball games. But over time, through repetition, I've learned to ignore my critics because critics are like banana peels. They try to make you slip, and they all stink.

"Denny, please sit down." Mrs. Q says this in soothing tones and offers a pat on my shoulder, a common move from the goddess of mathematics (especially since she found out about my mom). It's chummy and casual, a sub-tle nudge in the right direction that, for her purpose of leading a lesson, is for me to park in the back.

17

"You know, Mrs. Q, I've been thinking, when you're a baby, parents can't wait for you to speak and walk around. In elementary school, you're encouraged to talk, communicate, and explore the classroom. But then you get to middle school, where they tell you to sit down and shut up."

"Denny, I need you to please stop distracting everyone."

"I'm participating."

"This isn't the way to participate."

"But it's the only way I can, and I gotta participate somehow, especially when I'm in your class. When I'm in the Learning Zone, I try to give one hundred percent, one hundred percent of the time, which, as goddess of mathematics, I'm sure you realize is the most I mathematically can give at the highest frequency mathematically possible."

I have a keen sense of when I'm losing my audience, and I know, as I look around the room, that though my classmates remain chipper, I've lost them.

Except for Sabrina, rolling her eyes and sighing with such gusto that her hair leaps to the side of her face. The class is knee-deep in talk of the seventh grade dance and I am lost in the sauce: "Which group are you, like, going with?" . . . "What do you mean, you don't know yet?" . . . "I know Jimmy just, like, *has* to go with Jenny, because they're, like, hooking up, but even they're going in separate groups" . . . "Which group are you in?" . . . "Who's in your group?" . . . "I wish the day was here already" . . . "You don't even know what you're, like, *wearing*? I mean, HEL-LO?"

Hello. Whoever invented middle school dances should have the following written on their tombstone: HERE LIES THE DESTROYER OF MANKIND. AND WOMANKIND. BUT THE MAN LYING HERE IS NOT KIND, SO PLEASE LEAVE ROTTEN FLOWERS AND MOLDY PIZZA CRUSTS.

"Okay, class . . . okay . . . up here . . . class . . . please . . . please listen up." Mrs. Q plugs in a dinosaur—an old, dusty overhead projector at the front of the room—then raises her right arm in the air to get our attention, swaying it from side to side like they do at rock concerts, lighters in the air. But lighters are banned from middle schools. So she just waves her arm. "Listen up. Up here, everybody. We have an interesting lesson ahead of us today, but first let's review last night's homework."

I let my eyes wander so as not to be noticed, but it's hard not to look at something when you tell yourself not to, so after four seconds of avoiding Mrs. Q's gaze, I take the slightest peek. Our eyes meet and it's hopeless. "Denny, please come to the front and do the first three problems from last night."

Crap. Doesn't she know that showtime is over?

"Come on up, Denny. You can do this."

I don't know why Mrs. Q believes in me. Maybe because she's a rookie teacher and doesn't know any better. Maybe because she heard about my mom from the sixth grade teachers. Maybe Mrs. Q sees something of herself in me, something deep, something you'd see on a greeting card: "I am you, you are me, together we can be." No, forget that. She believes in me the way parents "believe" in a clumsy kid on the soccer field: she doesn't have a choice. She's being drowned out.

It's raining seventh grade dance: "What are you doing after?" . . . "Which after-party are you going to?" . . . "Hold on, you don't *know* what you're doing im*med*iately after *the dance*?" . . . "You mean, like the *second* after, or like *after* after?" . . . "You don't *know* what you're doing after? You're just gonna sit on your couch and watch movies with your parents . . . L-A-M-E-O, and Lame-O is your Name-O."

No, Lame-O is YOUR *Name-O,* I want to shout at everyone except Mrs. Q, but it probably sounds lame because it is. Comebacks always sound better in your head.

Mrs. Q tugs at the clunky projector, lines up a flimsy Xeroxed sheet of problems, and watches them flicker on the front board. The bulb is running on fumes and looks like it will die any second.

"Denny, go ahead. Class, listen up!"

I grab a blank notebook and trudge to the front of the room, toward the sound of the rumbling projector. Mrs. Q hands me a skinny black marker. The projector's blinking light hurts my eyes. I say a silent prayer that I don't do anything too weird or embarrassing or just plain dumb; that even though the marker in my hand isn't permanent, what I write won't do any permanent, irreparable damage to myself, others, my family, especially my mom, or my reputation, which is already damaged as it is.

I scribble an eight . . . a three . . . a plus sign . . .

I roll the marker in my hand and look at the projector, then at my blank notebook, then back at the projector. My current English teacher and role model and hero, Mr. Morgan, taught me that when struggling with writer's block, I should write what I know.

I don't know math. So I write what I know. "Hit it, Rockafella!" That's what I write, three words in a sloppy hand. My Rockafella crew drops the beat: "Boom chicka boom chicka chicka chicka boom. Boom chicka boom chicka chicka boom boom . . ."

Finally, laughter from the dance fanatics. Even Sabrina cracks a tiny smile.

Boom chicka boom chicka chicka chicka boom . . . What Mrs. Q doesn't realize is that we really *are* at a rock concert. That I'm a rock star. That the school is my stage.

From the back row, clapping, encouraging chants, a thumbs-up. My audience in Mrs. Q's class wants a show. What am I supposed to say, "Thanks for the memories but after such a prolific year so far, show's canceled"?

The robot dance is my specialty, in which I jerk my body from side to side and karate chop the air in a halfhearted impersonation of a robot. *What what, boom chicka boom chicka chicka chicka boom. Yup yup, boom chicka boom chicka chicka boom*

boom. I'm not half bad at the caterpillar either, which requires leaping into the air and hitting the ground chest first, with my body slinking like a caterpillar. But because my Rocka-fella crew throws those "chickas" into the beat, it's only appropriate to bust out the chicken dance. The hand motions are fairly boring—flapping beak, wings, tail feathers, followed by four claps—but the refrain is joyous and liberating. *Du, nun, nun, nun, nah nun, nah nun nun, du, nun, nun, nun, nah nun, nah nun*. I think you're only supposed to spin in circles or do-si-do your partner like in a square dance, but I'm in a classroom with lots of space, and a concert begs improvisation anyway. I mean, if concertgoers heard the same exact thing at a concert that they could hear on a CD, they'd stay home. So it's obviously necessary that I throw in a few wild elbows, spin up and down the aisles as my classmates sprinkle me with laughter—sweet, sweet laughter—and chant my name like a rock star: "DO-NUTS! DO-NUTS!" A few pats on the back, a few light punches in the arm. "DO-NUTS!" I go up and down the rows of armrest desks and continue my show, which is good clean fun, appropriate for any audience, except for maybe Mrs. Q, who flails her arms so wildly that I can't tell if she wants us quiet or if she simply wants out of there, to spread her wings and soar out the window.

Or maybe she's doing her own version of the chicken dance. That's obviously what she's doing, and since Mrs. Q is joining in so graciously, I take my performance to new heights. *Yup yup, what what, boom chicka boom*. New Jersey's own, Bruce Springsteen, the ultimate performer and my dad's favorite rock star, would be proud of my next move. My dad . . . not so much, but Bruce would. In the front corner of the room, near the door, I spot an empty chair with an unused armrest desk. A perfect stage.

I tell myself not to. Then I think of my mom—what she'd want me to do, what kind of man she'd want me to be—but there's no going back. I try, I really do, but after welcoming everyone to the revival, ratcheting up those good vibes, and working up a good sweat, it's hard to say, "Well, I've come this far, might as well turn back now."

Bruce Springsteen would understand. He would completely understand why I leap onto that unused armrest desk. He would sympathize with me finding myself atop a plank of wood that so closely resembles a surfboard—an uncanny resemblance, absolutely uncanny—that I can't help but pretend to surf. While shouting "Aloha!"

Bruce would get that I'm not surfing for surfing's sake. That it's all a parody, a demonstration really, to raise awareness for Hawaiian stereotypes. The ignorance of those who think that *all* Hawaiians surf . . . shame on them!

Bruce would so totally get that I'm also trying to prove a point about the unsteadiness of armrest desks. That I'm merely drawing attention to the fact that Mrs. Q, as goddess of mathematics, deserves far better classroom equipment than an old overhead projector. That Mrs. Q doesn't have a Smart Board is an outrage! An outrage!

Mrs. Q, for her part, seems to understand the purpose of my demonstration, as her chicken dance has greatly increased in intensity, but she stops dancing altogether when I leap off the armrest desk.

I don't really leap. I actually sorta fall. Into the trash can. A small, green, round, metallic (and hard) can. I don't really fall *in* the trash can. It tips over on the floor. With me inside. My feet, I mean. It's up to my knees, really—the side of my knees (now that I'm on the floor). I try to transition into a caterpillar/worm dance to make it seem like I fell on purpose, but I banged my wrist on the way down and, well, I'm still in a trash can.

So, yeah, I fell in the trash. There's a whole lot of laughter, and not the good kind. Too much finger-pointing, too much covering of mouths. And eyes. And faces. And people looking away but peeking back to see if I'm still in the trash.

(I am.)

"Thank you, everyone, thank you, *South Jersey*!" I announce, then I make peace signs with my fingers (which is hard to do while you're lying sideways) and shout, "God bless you! And may God bless the United States of America!"

Bruce Springsteen would totally get the sign-off. Any rock star or president would completely understand. But I'm not a president and I'm not a rock star.

And I'm not the kid in the trash.

THE HALLWAYS OF BLUEBERRY HILLS

From the cold classroom floor, as I finally dislodge my feet from the can, I glance up at Mrs. Q. Her eyes are red, her lips parted. I take no pleasure in this. I want to punch myself in the face, but it's hard to punch yourself in the face with your brain screaming, "No, you idiot, stop!" and plus, everyone is watching, including Mrs. Q. I want to make her laugh, make her smile, comfort her, pull flowers from my pockets, but it's too late for that, and I feel itchy, like red ants are crawling up my leg.

They keep going. I can't stop them. I have to get out of here. But then someone throws a blue Bic pen across the room and I shout for him to mind his manners and treat the goddess of mathematics with some respect. Because I mean it. I even retrieve the pen and throw it back at him so he learns never to disrespect Mrs. Q. "Behave! Show some maturity! She is a great teacher who deserves your utmost attention!" I shout, but my messages are getting muddled and I know I'm being a hypocrite and I need to leave. I point out to everyone that "Aloha means hello *and* good-bye" and then I reach for my cell phone and head for the door. Mrs. Q tells me to sit down and put my phone away, and I want to at least listen to one of her orders and make her feel better and set a positive example for the immature pen-thrower, so I put my phone in my pocket as I walk out the door. Cheers of "DO-NUTS" follow me into the hall-way, where the walls are covered with posters for the seventh grade dance in April. *Get your tickets for the dance on April 3rd—or forever be a turd.* Even though the words are nicer, that's how the posters make me feel.

Once it's safe and I'm sure I'm alone, I pull out the phone and put it to my ear. "Hello? Hey, Mom. How are you? I'm messed up—I mean, I messed up. Again. I know. I. I'm sorry. I'll try. Yeah. I'll tell Dad you said 'hey.' Talk to you soon."

I close the phone and bring it down to my side. I really do feel better. Not well enough to go back to the Learning Zone, but better. I think of giving Manny a call, but then I remember that my mom's phone doesn't work anymore.

I'm trying to remember the exact date my dad discon-nected her phone service when someone tugs me on my arm. I look up to see Chad Watkins, his brown hair combed to the side, light and bouncy like an Herbal Essences commercial.

"Hall pass," he says. "Now."

An eighth grader, Chad's the goalie and captain of the soccer team, which is a really big deal in a state as backward as New Jersey. Chad wears shorts to school, even in the winter, which show off his bulging calf muscles. He really does have big calf muscles, but they *could* be implants. Bulging calf implants. At least that's what I tell myself. (And that the thick hair on his legs must be a result of either the implants or steroids.)

I only mention his hairy bulging calf implants because they're always on display. Everyone knows that Chad has worn shorts to school every single day since he got here, and you know he only does it for the streak, like it'd be some world crisis if he took a day off. His reputation would never recover, which you can tell matters to him a great deal because he has a crescent-shaped mark above his left eyebrow that looks too clean and convenient to be a real scar.

"Hall pass," he repeats. "Show it to me. Now."

Like most students, I've gotten acquainted with Chad in the hallways. I mean, my arms, shoulders, chest, and stomach have. Chad isn't a hall monitor but he owns the halls, and you're supposed to thank him if by some chance every single time he punches you, like it's some great honor that he reached out to you or something.

It'd be one thing if Chad was just some thick neck who dropped out and sold batteries in his garage, so you could sorta feel bad for him as he pummeled you, but his grades are good. Top-of-the-class good. And even though he's already got his life carved out in front of him, he remains treasurer of the student government, which supposedly makes him a swell guy for helping when he doesn't have to, like he's doing everyone such a great service by counting the school's money.

And because he's so smart, he eats healthily. You'd figure he'd gnaw on red rope licorice or beef jerky all day, but he eats carrot sticks. Baby carrot sticks. That's what he's eating now with his right hand. With his left, he's poking me in the chest, demanding a pass.

I obviously don't have one, nor do I feel like taking any crap after a performance that made me want to punch myself in the face. Maybe Chad will do it for me.

"Your mother," I say. It's the only thing I can think of.

Chad reaches into his bag and pops another carrot stick into his mouth. "I'll ask one more time," he says, crunching the carrot between his teeth. "Hall pass."

"And I'll tell you one more time. Your mother."

His nostrils flare. "Where are you supposed to be?"

"You're not hearing me. I'm supposed to be with your—"

I don't see his fist until the air has already escaped from my body. I grab my stomach and crumple to the ground, my face against the hallway floor, breathless. I gasp, gasp, but my lungs are shut, can't breathe, at all, not a single pull, of air. Breathless. Not like it is in a freezing cold shower where there's some air, but like it is in space, where the atmosphere isn't made for human lungs, so unless you're wearing some souped-up space suit, you'll die instantly of asphyxiation and shrivel into a raisin. As I lie there in the middle of the hallway—already half man, half raisin—I reach into my pocket for my phone. *Mayday,* I want to say, *Help me,* but I can't speak because I don't have any air, because the atmosphere is out of whack and I don't have a space suit or space shoes, or at the very least a space helmet. And last time I checked, they don't stock space helmets in the halls of Blueberry Hills.

That's the name of my school. Blueberry Hills Middle. It sounds like a maple syrup factory or some organic meadow where bluebirds sip from fountains and children frolic in the grass with corduroy overalls rolled up to their knees.

Blueberry Hills. It may sound real nice, it may even look nice from afar, but up close, our school is a carton of berries with a few pretty blue ones like Sabrina on top and piles of purple ones with moldy white cottontails underneath. Those blueberry hills aren't so smooth, either. They're worn with jagged rocks that trip you up if you get careless and complacent and start to find your stride. With a student body of over eight hundred in grades six through eight, kids can't help but fall through the cracks. The hills are sloped, the fall steep, the ground like concrete. You don't skin your knees at Blueberry Hills Middle. You break them. And then there's the lousy one-piece desks, the old teaching equipment, Chad, the stupid dances . . . I guess you could say that permanent, irreparable damage to students is what we're known for, and that a local meteorologist named Bobby "Tornado" Thompson went here, which is why the Jersey school board is considering shutting us down. For the permanent damage to students, not "Tornado" Thompson. That dude is legend.

The same can't be said of our school's test scores (low), lunch food (mostly untouched), or mascot. It's a Flying Dog. With big old ears and slobber coming out of his mouth. His job is to get students to sing and bark along to the official song: "Who Let the Dogs Out?" Yeah, it's like that.

Still, Blueberry Hills—it sounds delicious. Sounds like a picnic in the park with a blanket full of homemade sides that everyone eats from buffet-style. In fact, the first thing I learned about Blueberry Hills was that it really *is* a buffet. At orientation last year, the gray-haired director of student activities stood at the front of the auditorium, held the microphone against his bottom lip, and after clearing the phlegm in the back of his throat, boasted, "Blueberry Hills is a smorgasbord, or as you young folks like to call it, a buffet. You better have room for seconds, thirds, even fourths!

We offer football, tennis, basketball, baseball, soccer, student government, yearbook, chess, checkers, drama, tutors, computers, a recycling club called Recycle or Die—they got to pick their own name, see—and then there's art club, French club, Spanish club . . . heck, if you don't find our smorgasbord to be filling enough for ya, you can start up your *own* club."

Manny tried to start a debate club—"found and charter it," as he put it—but nobody came to the introductory session. Still, Manny wanted a varsity debate jacket with "Captain Manny" or "Mr. Perfect" stitched across the front lapel. When the director of student activities refused to pay for it, Manny stormed into the principal's office to file a formal complaint, a restraining order, and any other legal action he could take. The principal, Mr. Softee, whose real name is Mr. Soffer but everyone calls him Mr. Softee because he's soft on student punishment, nodded with his fingers over his mouth. After Manny had concluded his speech, Mr. Softee said that he admired Manny's tenacity and would love to talk further. Then he couldn't hold it in anymore and burst out laughing.

"I will be back—with signatures!" Manny cried, slamming the door behind him.

He tried to recruit my help, but no way was I gonna risk my cred for a few lousy signatures. Can you imagine the hit I'd take roaming the hallways with a clipboard in my hand

and a Captain Manny bumper sticker on my butt? The bumper sticker read "Help me pass this important legislation, or I'll pass gas." His idea, not mine.

The hallways at Blueberry Hills Middle are as wide as the organic maple syrup meadows the name sounds like. It's best to picture the hallways at my school like three-lane highways on each side. Not like in elementary school where you only think the hallways are so huge until you visit years later and can barely fit two people side by side. Or how you used to think your backyard was so huge it could swallow you whole, until you wake up one day and realize it's little more than a patch of grass you can cover in four seconds flat. I haven't timed how long it takes to walk the width of the Blueberry Hills Middle School hallways because that would be weird even for me, but I can say confidently that the wide hallways do wonders for Manny's business schemes.

(Before Manny's boycott of contractions, his favorite expression was "Don't be a scammer hater." Postboycott, it became "Do not be a scammer hater." Either way, what he meant was to get out of the way of his "perfectly designed schemes executed to nothing less than perfection." His words, not mine. But you gotta hand it to him, some of his scams are A1. A+. Aces. Last year, he told his science teacher, Mr. Halbright, who hung posters of Albert Einstein around the room, that not only was he Einstein's great nephew twice-removed, but also the proud and humble owner of an Albert Einstein autographed beaker. "It is a family heirloom, destined for eBay," he confided to Mr. Halbright between classes, "but if you fancy it, I can procure it from my mother's safe." Mr. Halbright, a constant sweater—perspiration, not the clothing—could barely contain himself. He wiped his wet face with his starchy sleeves as Manny took him down: "Swear to me, Mr. Halbright, that our transaction will remain confidential." Mr. Halbright swore. He is now one hundred dollars poorer. He also owns a glass measuring cup signed by one Emmanuel "Manny" Templeton.)

This year, it's candy. And oh how business is booming! He makes more now than ever before: over $55 a day. A *day*! According to Manny, "Business must change with the times. Record shop owners were smart to get out before the iPod. But candy is timeless, as timeless as good friends and, so I have heard, fine wine and cheese. Well, cheese ages well but it does get moldy; however, candy is eternal, like diamonds, unless you keep it in your pocket for too long. Or sit on it, spit on it, or melt it. But no refunds, that is my policy, for the customer is never right."

"Hey, Donuts!" he shouts across the wide halls, wearing a tan fishing hat, the floppy brim all the way around his head. "Wait up, my good friend!"

At least he isn't selling me candy. How do I know? Manny's candy sales are discreet. He sells it like a ticket scalper. It's supposedly against the rules for him to sell candy on school grounds if it's not for an official fund-raiser, but there's no rule against buying candy, so instead of asking if anyone wants to purchase candy, he wanders the halls murmuring, "Anyone *selling* candy? Extras anyone? Anyone got an extra bar? I only need one."

I keep walking. You have to be in the mood to talk to Manny—especially now, when he's zigzagging through the halls shouting my name with his book bag on his chest. He carries it that way for easy access to his candy. "Easy access" meaning he doesn't have to remove his book bag, but the access is anything but easy. He smuggles candy like I imagine a kingpin smuggles drugs through an airport: a combination lock at the zipper; a layer of ragged clothing at the top, the smell alone a deterrent from searching any farther; underneath, a pencil case crammed with packs of M&M's; hollow highlighters stuffed with Jolly Ranchers, Atomic Fireballs, Warheads; folders of candy straws; a five-subject notebook with all the paper torn out and boxes stapled to the dividers with a surgeon's precision, filled with five varieties: Skittles, SweeTarts, Sour Patch Kids, Swedish Fish, and gummy worms; and underneath that, a three-ring binder linking a hole-punched box of Butterfinger. I haven't even gotten to the bulk of his profits because I haven't mentioned the fake bottom—three-quarters of the way down, a long piece of Velcro around the perimeter. Tear *that* off and you find the real treasure: two more boxes of candy, forty-eight bars in each package.

"Donuts! Hold up!" Manny barely moves his arms when he walks, so he moves like a robot—and with his ban on contractions, he talks like one, too. He just sort of beams himself down the hall, which, as a fan of *Star Trek*, is a source of great pride. For Manny. I don't get it—the *Star Trek* obsession *or* the trapdoor backpack. I can't help but shake my head as he approaches me and begins the laborious process of removing his bag that, even with Manny in the seventh grade, is heavier than he is by thirty pounds—at least until the end of the day if sales are good. And sales are always good.

He's breathing hard by the time he pulls his bag off his chest, adjusts his glasses. His "Nobody is perfect. Except me" T-shirt hangs loosely, for Manny's all elbows and bones. His lack of shoulders makes his neck appear long and looped like a fishhook, or a clothes hanger, or a question mark.

A cute brunette with a ponytail walks between Manny and me. Instead of offering candy, Manny tips his fishing cap, thumb and index finger against the front brim, bends slightly at the waist, and says, "M'lady . . . good day, m'lady."

("M'lady" is the exception to his ban on contractions. He says it's bad to formally remove charm from an expression when he's trying to be most charming. I know about the m'lady rule because he tries it a lot. And gets rejected a lot. Like now.)

To prove she's not his lady, she makes a gagging noise, rolls her eyes so far back I worry they'll get stuck. Then she makes an "L" sign with her thumb and index finger and shoves her hand into Manny's chest. I think about telling her it's dangerous, that it's easy to jam your fingers that way, but she storms off before I can get it out. Laughter fills the halls. Manny rubs his chest as he stares furiously into my eyes. As always, he probably has a vital question for me.

"Donuts, I am glad I caught you. I have a vital question to ask you."

See. Told you.

"Not now, Manny."

He smirks. "I heard a flabbergasting rumor just recently. Did you break your wrist falling off that desk in Mrs. Q's class?"

My face goes red. "How did you—"

"Hear so quickly? I am well connected to the social pipeline in this neck of the woods. Though I may not be the foundation of the pipeline, I am an integral part of it, and information is prone to leak out to all its integral parts."

Manny is far from an integral part—except maybe in candy sales—and he knows it better than I, but it's not worth arguing with him. When Manny starts debating, he doesn't stop until he's right and you're bloody and beaten and admit that you're scum and he's royalty, that you're dumb as nails and he's smarter than Einstein. Some days even *that's* not enough. Some days, when he's really on his game and his ego oozes like melted cheese, he won't shut up until you proclaim that he's more powerful than God. But even *that's* not enough. "Which God are we talking about?" he'll ask. "Let us debate the merits of organized religion."

So I leave it alone.

"Thank you," I hear over Manny's shoulder. "Thank you." "Thank you." Chad's pounding everyone in their arms, one by one. "Thank you." "Thank you." "Thank you."

Then me in the right shoulder. Smiling, he says, "Your meat is sour."

"That makes no sense," I tell him.

Chad ignores me, takes a step back, cocks his fist, and decks Manny in the arm.

"Muchos gracias," Manny says. *"Merci, arigato, danke, spasibo, grazie—"*

Chad grins. "You're welcome, *m'lady.*"

When Chad's out of earshot, Manny rubs his arm. "Flabbergasting . . . the audacity of that brute. Well, at least my meat was not sour. What a buffoon. And speaking of buffoonery, did you break your wrist dancing this morning?"

"No."

He shrugs. "Okay, now that we have gotten that insignificant detail out of the way, there is something I must discuss with you. But first, follow me to the Warehouse."

The Warehouse is Manny's locker, where he stores extra candy boxes and wrestling memorabilia. His eyes are fixed on the inside of his locker, where he has taped a photo of WWF wrestler Mr. Perfect, looking mean and muscular in a yellow leotard matching the color of Mr. Perfect's signature blond locks, oiled up and curly, resting on the championship belt draped over his right shoulder.

"Again?" I say. "Again with Mr. Perfect?"

Manny adjusts his glasses, tucks the wiry frames behind his big ears, and declares, "As the greatest Intercontinental Champion known to man, Mr. Perfect was the greatest wrestler on any continent, which, of course, is the very definition of Intercontinental."

"I know, I know," I mutter.

"Do you? Do you really know?" Manny traces his finger along Mr. Perfect's veined forearms. "If you knew about the raw power of Mr. Perfect, you would have a picture of him taped inside your locker."

Even if I did, it wouldn't compare to Manny's shrine: coins, an autographed photo, a plastic figurine, a cheap plastic thermos Manny uses to drink gross things like tea and coffee, a wad of gum Mr. Perfect (supposedly) spit out and swatted into the crowd, a used white towel Manny scored on eBay, and a leg from the busted wooden stool that Mr. Perfect (allegedly) bashed over the head of a fellow wrestler.

"He used it, you know," Manny says.

"Used what?"

"Do not insult my intelligence. I sensed you looking at my stool."

If I had pronounced that sentence, Manny would've

screamed it from the rafters—"Can you believe Donuts thought I was looking at his stool!"—but I let him continue.

"Mr. Perfect used that stool in the prime of his badass-ness, which is a word that I copyrighted with the Library of Congress so do not even *think* of stealing it."

"Wouldn't dare."

His eyes still glued to Mr. Perfect, Manny whispers, "I need to talk to you."

"If you want me to leave you two alone, I can—"

"It is not funny, not in the least bit," he hisses. "This is an urgent matter." He grabs my shoulder, clawing with his fingers and nails as if his life depends on it.

"You gotta take it easy, Manny. It's not Game Seven of the World Series."

"I live every day like it is Game Seven of the World Series, especially today." He looks both ways down the hallway. His eyes are so wide and panicked they appear three-dimensional, like those of a cartoon character in midair before its plunge from a cliff.

"We are not safe here," he breathes. "What I have to tell you is highly classified."

I sigh. "If it involves Mr. Perfect, I'm out."

"Shhhh." He peeks to his right. "This does not involve Mr. Perfect. But it does involve a perfectly designed scheme that I will execute to nothing less than perfection."

"But of course you will."

"This is classified, Donuts. It could impact our whole nation, or at least"—he releases my shoulder and spreads his fingers into a *Star Trek* salute—"*our* nation. We are not safe here."

Even for Manny, it's a bit over the top. "Oh no!" I cry. "Planet Xenon needs us!"

"That does not qualify as *Star Trek* vocabulary, nor is the sarcasm appreciated, especially given the enormity of the plan I shall unfurl. Now, I urge you to flank me—"

"*Flank* you?"

"Follow me as we depart for our desired destination."

When I ask him where he wants to go, he explodes: "To the lunchroom, *Donuts*!"

You'd think by the way he stresses my name that I'm a donut-hoarder, which I'm not—I weigh 117 pounds, if you must know—but compared to Manny, I'm a Siberian elephant. I don't know why my elephant self is from Siberia, but everything sounds bigger if it's from Siberia. For example, which sounds bigger: a husky or a Siberian husky? I only mention it because by point of comparison, I'm the Siberian friend.

But compared to my daily pranks and performances, Manny's scheme is so big there's no room for it in America. It belongs only in the land of large huskies.

It belongs in Siberia.

THE PLAN

The lunchroom is filling fast, the heavy air filled with the smell of oil. Grease, salt, a deep fryer . . . yup, french fries, again. I feel my face breaking out before I eat a single fry, before I get on the lunch line, before I even stand up. I touch my cheek. No zits yet, but they're coming. I can feel them like an old lady feels the weather in her bones. I don't need to be an old lady to forecast the weather in the lunchroom: it's hot, thick, sticky, and sweaty with a likely chance of cliques and cruelty.

Manny takes a swig of coffee from a yellow Mr. Perfect thermos and pulls out a deck of magic cards. "I will deal first," he says, seated across from me at our lunch table. I call it our lunch table because we're the only ones sitting there. It's not an overly long table, so it's not like we're complete outcasts, but the table certainly isn't meant for two. Mr. Softee helped install smaller, circular tables to give the lunchroom a more "café feel," which I appreciate, but would it kill him to lower the humidity? Foolishly, I put my elbows on our table. And now they're stuck.

"We need to talk of a matter of vital, flabbergasting importance," Manny says. "But first, look at your cards. It is not a difficult game. It is simple math. Addition, subtraction, and data analysis. To conquer this game, you do not need to be a math whiz; *I* am, but you do not have to be. Still, my mathematical skills do contribute to my domination in the world of Merlin the Magical Wizard."

Manny peeks above his magic cards at a passing brunette so far out of his league—out of his orbit—he should be wearing a space suit. "Good day, m'lady," he says, tipping his fishing hat. She pretends not to notice.

So does he. "What cards do you have?" he asks me.

I don't feel like playing, so I try to change the subject. "You don't know anything about girls."

"More than *you*," he fires back. Staring at cards of sorcerers, dragons, and balls of fire, he clasps his hands together, plotting his next move. "At least I kissed a girl."

"She was your cousin!"

"But she *was* cute, you have to admit that."

"And she *was* your cousin. Besides, she was wishing you a happy birthday. That's why she kissed you on the cheek."

"Okay, fine. She only kissed me on the cheek, and thank god for that. Incest runs rampant where she lives. I would not want my kids to have six tongues anyway." To prove the point, he loops his fingers around his eyes, swings his jaw from side to side, and rolls his pupils back so all I can see are the whites of his eyes. *"Blarrrrrlllll!"* he yells, twisting his tongue. *"Blarrrrrlllll!* Quick, Donuts, use Merlin's magic dust to bring me back to human form. Come on, this is really hurting my eyes. *Blarrrrrlllll!* Summon Merlin's powers, do it—do it now! *Blarrrrrlllll!"*

I toss my cards on the table. I fight an urge to switch tables . . . but where am I gonna go? "You're wasting my time, Manny. What'd you have to talk to me so badly about? What was so vitally important?"

Manny sighs, collecting my cards. "You have the patience of an antelope. I bet if I gave you a book entitled *Patience* you would not finish it. I see now that I must begin." He packs his cards away, then locks eyes with me. As he opens his mouth to speak, his body stiffens. "You have been through—a lot—together—me, too—a distraction—what we need." Out of character for Manny, his words trip over themselves. He stares for a moment at his shaking hands at the edge of the lunch table. "We need a distraction, have been through a lot, need a distraction. You especially."

I know what he's talking about, but I don't want to talk about it. Her. I don't want to talk about her. To him or anyone else. I know he misses her, but not like I miss her, and I don't want to talk about her.

I smile and say in my chummiest voice: "So what's this plan you want to tell me about?"

He shuts his eyes. "You do not have to—we can talk—"

"So let's talk. What's the plan, Stan?"

"We need a distraction because—"

"Yeah! The man with the plan! The Manny with the Plan-ny. Tell me!"

He nods thoughtfully. "Okay," he says, and begins.

"My candy enterprise has expanded. You may have noticed a surge in my sales and a spike in my popularity—or as I like to call it, my compatibility quotient. It seems that the brown-haired beauty who just walked by has yet to receive the memo, but my compatibility quotient has recently risen at least two degrees. Alas, you also may have noticed—unless you are keeping something from me—that we both lack companionship for the dance, do we not?"

"Not?"

"You are still devoid of a group, an after-party, and a potential female dancing partner, yes?"

I nod.

He takes another sip from his thermos. "I am going to solve our problems, Donuts. By nature, I am a problem solver—my math teachers would agree—and I am going to solve our problems. Well, *my* problem first, and then yours, if we have time, which we probably will. It is like those airplane videos, where the flight attendant instructs you to put on your own oxygen mask before assisting anyone. Safer that way. Selfish perhaps, but much safer."

A freckled sixth grader clutching a notebook approaches

our table. He isn't there for me. I should be used to this by now.

Manny greets the kid with a smile. "Big test today, I hear. If your grade were a pizza pie, this test is a rather large slice, yes?"

"Yeah, unit exam. Environmental science. Thirty percent of my final average."

"Wow, that *is* a rather large slice. Nervous?"

"Well, no. I mean, yeah, I mean, it's a big test."

Manny looks both ways (on both sides of the lunchroom). "The scene is safe," he whispers to me (apparently I'm in training), then reaches into his bag and says to his buyer, "Have no fear, eat a Three Musketeers."

The kid slips him a dollar and tears open the wrapper before returning to his seat. Manny must see my mouth agape, for he grins and says, "It is all in the delivery."

"But he didn't even tell you what he wanted . . ."

Manny shakes his head. "You tell the customer want they want. One of the many lessons I have learned along the entrepreneurial superhighway."

"But how'd you know there was a science test today?"

"It is simple. Because I am an integral part of the social pipeline, I have access to copious quantities of information which I use to my financial advantage. That is what I have been telling you, Donuts. Unlike you, I have made something of myself, and made quite a large sum of cold, hard cash—or as I like to say, 'freezing firm cash'—but however you refer to it, it is still money. Money that I will use, and, perhaps, *we* will use but only after I secure it for myself—see, that airplane motto once again—to help us acquire dates to the dance."

"You mean go with a *group* to the dance, right?"

"Negatory. Why follow the masses in their groups when we can bask in the spotlight of the dance floor with dates in our arms? I am talking about dates. Not the dried fruit, either, though they are delicious and nutritious and great for your colon. I am talking about live, human dates. Can you imagine how our compatibility quotient will skyrocket with actual dates? This is what I have been needing to explain to you: my plan."

It's easy to get sidetracked by Manny's blabbering, so it doesn't hit me at first. It comes in pieces. Money, plan, dates, dance . . . "Wait, Manny, you want to—"

"That is affirmative. I am raising money to boost our compatibility quotients and increase our chances of landing live, human dates."

"Wait, we're *raising money*—"

He reaches across the table to cuff my mouth. "Quiet, you ignoramus." His hand tastes like chocolate chip cookies.

I try to say sorry but his hand muffles my speech. All I can muster is "sry."

"Can I trust you enough to remove my grip?"

I nod, so Manny lets go, then sighs. "I refuse to go down in the annals of this school as a bona fide loserasaurus, a math whiz who can count the girls he has danced with on no hands. As a rising entrepreneur, such negative attention would be an insult to my brand." He pauses. "My motives are clean here, I assure you. I simply would like a date, especially for the pictures. Pictures are key, Donuts, because unlike you or me, they are as immortal as diamonds and candy that has not melted or been sat on. You see, pictures, like our reputations, will last forever. If we are successful in our venture, everyone until the end of time or at least until we get to high school will know we squired eighth graders to the dance."

"Eighth graders!"

"That is affirmative. The general public will not know nor care to know anything about our candy enterprises. All they will see is a picture and pictures do not lie. They may not tell the whole story, but they do not lie."

"But, Manny, where are you gonna get a date?"

His eyes dart around the lunchroom. "Here, at our school, fine academic institution that it is. I hope you can taste my sarcasm." He licks his lips to exaggerate the point. "Of course, after all my work, I shall only select the most elite specimens. By 'elite specimens,' obviously I mean"—he clears his throat—"babes, honeys, beauties, sweeties, and/ or sweetie pies."

He sounds lamer than that lamest parent calling the lamest pair of jeans *dungarees*. "But, Manny, how are you gonna convince the—"

"Babes, honeys, beauties, sweeties, and/or sweetie pies."

"Right, how are you gonna get them to go with us? I mean, you. I mean—"

"'Us' is fine, Donuts. I will shoulder most of the sales in the first month until we get a rhythm, and until I land a date for myself. I will always be the boss and C.E.O. of our candy enterprise, but we are in this together. Now, for the record, we are not *buying* dates; that would be loserasaurus-esque. We are *enticing* them. We are *raising* money to sweeten ourselves as dance commodities: a limousine, a gourmet meal, a fine suit, concert tickets—whatever it is, we shall indeed increase our chances of getting a whiff, however brief, of the sweet scent of popularity."

"Will it work?"

"*Have you never seen a music video?* What year do you *live* in?! Every guy in a music video gets the girl because they all have something to offer: a fresh ride, a boat, an after-party in the hotel lobby. We may not have boats or after-parties in hotel lobbies or babes, honeys, beauties, sweeties, and/or sweetie pies lined up yet, but think of raising money now as a way of stocking our ammunition for battle." He scratches his chin. "Someone wise once said, 'Love is a battlefield.' Well, we shall be prepared for battle. I am talking big enough profits to give our image a metamor-phosis: our hair, our shoes, our clothes, our swagger, our jewelry. Maybe some rapper bling. Really tasteful, though.

I do not know if you have noticed, but I could use a new wardrobe."

I steal a glance at his "Nobody is perfect. Except me" T-shirt. "Hadn't noticed."

"Most important, Donuts, the more we raise, the more we can offer: access to the hippest of after-parties that are so hip only hippopotamuses are allowed in. Only the hippest of hippopotamuses . . . or is it 'hippopotami'?" He scratches his chin. "Yes, hippopotami. The hippest of hippopotami can certainly splurge for a red carpet to walk on at the dance, a forest of rose petals, a designer dress designed by a designer for our dates, a meal prepared by an Iron Chef, a helicopter tour of New Jersey, a ride to and from the dance in a Ferrari, a Bentley, a Lamborghini—"

"Could we eat tortellini in our Lamborghini?"

He rolls his eyes. "Teachers say there are no stupid questions . . . they are lying. But I will answer it anyway. We can eat whatever we like. Filet mignon, caviar, escargot, tortellini, you name it, we can have it—offer it, I mean, as reason for live human female beauties to dance and take pictures with us. Speaking of such . . ." He pauses, then scans the lunchroom premises. "You can sense her, correct?"

Of course I do. Allison Swain, an eighth grader. Allison is aces. That is a universal law. The sky is blue. The grass is green. Allison Swain is aces. Allison's hair, a light auburn, bounces with each step she takes across the lunchroom. Those green eyes, full lips. Three freckles on her left cheek in the winter, six in the fall, nine in the spring, and twelve in the summer.

She's my neighbor, always has been. Her lawn is always cut. Her wallpaper is pink. She drinks skim milk. Her family gets the newspaper delivered every morning, but she only reads the front page. She used to wear pigtails, pink T-shirts, and pump sneakers. Once I spied on her in her backyard among a row of plants that curve like garter snakes, but I don't think she saw me, at least that's what I tell myself.

Manny elbows me. "You are drooling," he says. "And it smells terrible. I think your saliva is infected. I recommend a doctor visit to check for rabies."

Allison stops next to a crowded café table filled with eighth graders, kisses everyone there, smiles like a Cheshire cat, and takes a seat at the end of the table next to Chad Watkins, his hair bouncy and full-bodied, his calf muscles bulging underneath the table, his right arm resting on the shoulders of Allison's blue and white cheerleading uniform.

"They are dating, you know," Manny says. "Heard it through the social pipeline."

"I should talk to her," I say, pretending Manny's gossip and Chad don't exist.

"Well, *that* sounds convincing."

"I mean, I—I will. I'll ask her to the dance. Without bribery."

"I think that might be the most flabbergasting thing you ever said. I swear, the older you get, the more your brain shrinks. By the time you are forty and wrinkled, you will not remember my name. You will call me up on the phone and say, 'Hello, there. I don't know who you are or why I'm calling you, but hello. Hello, there. Hello.'"

"Manny, I'm telling you, I can get her to go with me without bribery. We're neighbors, after all. I'll start small . . . baby steps. I should buy her lunch."

He grins. "First, buying someone lunch is bribery. It is nutritional compensation for a kiss, not that our cafeteria food is nutritious or proteinaceous in any way. No one in their right mind would eat the swill they serve. I need not remind you of that time I found a crusty red fingernail in my hamburger." He gags. "It was in my mouth, Donuts, in my mouth! It was wretched, truly an abomination that should have been the end of my cafeteria food career. I should have thrown in the napkin and retired that very afternoon. But no, I went against every fiber of my being and gave it a second chance. That is when things got hairy." He gags once more.

I can't help but laugh. "It wasn't *that* bad, Manny. It was only a single hair."

"There was enough hair on my hot dog to clog a shower!" he cries. "The hairnets those lunch ladies wear are obviously defective, but I did not sue because my conscience is the size of a whale and my compassion spreads over continents. Besides, I had nothing to gain. Lunch ladies have even less money than I do."

Chad picks his shirt up to show everyone his abs. They're all very impressed, especially Allison, who goes in for a touch. She lingers too long for my liking.

"Listen to me, Donuts. Buying Allison lunch is a terrible idea. Or anyone at her table. Especially that brunette Anna Harden, with the purple headband. Ooh, baby, shiver me timbers." (He shivers. Anna is a close second to Allison, with athletic firepower to boot. After college, she'll either be a professional lacrosse player or a model. If she asks me, which she ~~probably~~ definitely won't, I'd suggest model. Better to preserve those pearly white teeth.) "Look at them, Donuts." He means Anna's table, not her teeth. "There must be something in the water. Wait, is that . . . no, I thought they were drinking Fiji Water. Just Evian. Oh well, still something magical about that table. I bet if you pick anyone and put them there, they will turn into a goddess"—he scans the room—"yes, even no-neck Ingrid or Pippa with the long stockings or Sabrina."

Manny nods his head at a table to the left, a few over from ours, to Sabrina, from the front row of Mrs. Q's class, now sitting with five girls chatting away about something, their books and notebooks open. Dark hair falls over Sabrina's eyes as she puts her elbows on the table, sips Cherry Coke, and nibbles on rat poison or the lunchtime equivalent: bologna on white bread. But Sabrina doesn't seem bothered by her lunch, her work, the humidity, or the gossip, or the fact that Cherry Coke has long gone out of style. Immune, she seems, to it all. No dual Donuts-like personality, no self-consciousness. Just her, what she wants to eat, what work she wants to complete, what shoes she wants to wear—a pair of faded blue Converses with no laces—and when she catches me staring, she doesn't look away. Slow jazz music isn't playing in the cafeteria or anything, but when our eyes meet, she rolls hers and, well, that's the end of that.

"What's so awful about her, anyway?" I ask.

He looks around before answering. "She beat me in a debate. Nobody beats me in a debate. I cannot believe that emo girl beat me! You should have seen it. I mean, I am glad you did not see it, but it was quite a sight. It was torture, plain and simple." Manny buries his face in his hands and groans.

"Is it safe for me to speak?"

Through his hands, he mutters, "I have concluded my recap of this unfortunate incident. I certainly will not be accompanying her in a sports car to the dance."

"Well, I'm getting on the lunch line. Maybe I'll invite Allison or Sabrina. I could introduce them to—"

"Stop." He sticks his arm out like a crossing guard. "Stop right there. You want them to meet the lunch lady? Are you kidding?"

"Her name is Marsha and she's a nice lady." I push past him.

"Not so fast, Boston Cream," he says. "When you have returned from the garden of grease, we will reexamine my plan."

HIBERNATION

Before I even reach the lunch line, I hear someone shout, loud enough to wake up the aliens on Mars: "HEY, DONUTS MADE IT OUT OF THE TRASH CAN ALIVE!"

My face goes crimson. Then neon red. I look behind me to see Chad pointing at me, one arm around Allison.

My heart is like a battering ram being rammed against a chest made from a door, and my breath is like a dog's that just ran out the gate and took off down the block. I can't find it—my breath, I mean. It ran away. But all skilled performers know that timing is everything and that keeping one's composure is important, even when your breath runs away. "Thank you—everyone!" I shout. I reach for my chest and gasp for air. "From the bottom—of my heart, I appreciate your concern. The lesson is—to never dig for DONUTS—in the trash can! I am glad—to report that I've already made a full recovery!"

Before anyone can say anything else, I dash to the lunch counter where Marsha is salting fries. Her spiderweb of a hairnet is ripped in two places, but she tries (unsuccessfully) to straighten it out when she sees me approach. "Hey, sugar! Everything okay, baby?"

I can't help but smile. "Hi, Marsha, what's on the menu today?"

The menu is the same every day. That's the joke. Though she's heard it dozens of times, she throws her head back and howls. "Baby, you sure know how to make a lady laugh!"

"I'll be here all week."

"You promise not to run off with another woman and never come back?"

"I promise."

"In case you do run off with a woman, a word to the wise: Women are relationship beings. Men are not."

I ask her if the pizza tastes good.

"There you go, changin' the topic," she says, and chuckles. "But you'll find out someday. A woman will tell you she wants to talk. Again. But hear me, baby: all she needs is attention and love. And to be reassured that you ain't goin' nowhere. Oh, you'll see."

"Pizza, please. Got any left?"

"Tell you what, 'cause you made me laugh, two slices for the price of one. Don't tell nobody about this or else I won't be here to give advice, if you catch my drift."

"Caught it."

"Great catch! Now here you go, pizza and fries, made with you in mind." She passes me a tray of food. "Hey, whatcha doin' the rest of the day?"

I haven't memorized the rule book on the student / lunch lady relationships or anything, but this feels out-of-bounds. "Uh, bye, Marsha," I mutter.

"See ya, sugar. Have a blessed day."

"Same time, same place, tomorrow?"

She cracks up again, even louder than before.

I head back to our café table and Manny immediately starts ripping into me for eating cafeteria food. The fire bell interrupts him, which isn't a bad thing (I can only take Manny in small doses, even when his schemes work to my benefit), but I still haven't eaten lunch and my head is pounding and I barely slept last night. Above the clamor of chairs and café tables being shoved, a white-haired lunch aide shouts, "Single file, people! Move in an orderly fashion!" Good luck to her.

Evacuations are a free-for-all. And a fantastic stage.

"Hurry, people!" I holler. "Get on your horse!"

Murmurs of laughter, music to my ears. "It's a real fire, people! We must evacuate the premises at once! Not a second's delay. It's a matter of national security. The president told me himself!"

Up ahead, Allison and her crew blend into the masses. I jump as high as I can to get a better look, like I'm on a pogo stick. On the fifth leap, I land awkwardly, twisting my ankle. Pain shoots to the side of my foot. "AH! EVACUATE!" I hop over to the side and steady myself against the wall, which is rough like sandpaper and sticky—something under my right hand. I lift it. Purple glitter, of course. From another dance sign.

I wipe it on my jeans. Wipe it, wipe it again. Then check my ankle. Something about rubbing glitter on my twisted ankle really gets to me and I wonder what would happen if I just tipped over. Fell over. Like a falling tree: timberrrrrrrr . . . and lay in the hallways while everyone else was outside at the all-important fire drill. The third one this month. (February is supposed to be so short, but it never seems to end.)

There aren't too many things in this world worse than having to stand in line during a fire drill, watching your breath and shivering without a coat. Too much time to think, to remember how she wouldn't let me leave the house without a coat ("Put on your coat, honey, it's cold outside") and a hat and a neck warmer (but she wouldn't let me get a face mask like I wanted to because it made me look like a villain in a superhero movie, which she said was a bad thing). How we'd heat up hot chocolate with marshmallows on snow days. How she'd tell me to run my hands in cold water again after I spilled my hot chocolate again. How she'd let me use a whole carrot from the fridge for a snowman's (really long) nose. How she'd tell me how happy she was when *she* used to get snow days. How she'd tell me she was jealous of me.

I just suddenly feel so heavy. Like I ate a dozen donuts filled with bricks instead of jelly or cream and now they're stacked on my shoulders. I know it doesn't make sense, but that's how I feel during this stupid fire drill, and all I want to do is lie down and count sheep and pretend I'm a hibernating animal like a bear or a badger or a bat or a snail or an earthworm so that I can disappear for a few months. You'd think hibernation and high school would go hand in hand like peanut butter and jelly, macaroni and cheese, Batman and graffiti, Bruce Springsteen and the E-Street Band. But you can't hibernate in middle school. Trust me, I've tried. The nurse shakes you awake, like you're a maraca. And there are just too many people keeping tabs on your progress.

Except during fire drills. They make you wait in lines, but it's not like they take attendance. Nobody would even notice, except for Manny, who grabs my arm. "Stick with the plan, Romeo," he says, "and your days of being a crash test dummy for female attention will be long gone. As we improve our compatibility quotients, they will flock to us like a flock of geese. Good-looking geese, of course."

Something about the way he says it makes me want to fall down—no, the whole scene. My gimpy ankle, the flock of geese, the bricks on my shoulders, the lunch line announcement, the purple glitter on my jeans, no more hot chocolate . . .

I'd pull out my phone but Manny is too close. He's always too close. Like I said, the whole scene, depressing. No other way to put it.

THE NATURAL SCHMOOZER

Let me get something clear: I don't *actually* think my mom's on the phone with me. She doesn't say anything. Doesn't give me advice. She just . . .

It started soon after she died. Twenty-four days later. I was at a party. It was the biggest, baddest party, only for the coolest cats in the class and I was a Bengal tiger. (Hear my ROAR!) Okay, fine, it was a pizza party. In school. And there were blue streamers and pink cupcakes and I stood by the food table, alone, thinking about her. Kids in my class had already stopped asking me about her, stopped giving me cards, stopped telling me they were sorry. They had decided, I guess, that everything was back to normal, and they didn't want to upset me by bringing it up. They had decided that at parties like this they wanted me to be happy, to have a real party instead of a pity party. Maybe they just wanted the lie—that everything was okay—to make themselves feel better. Or maybe they just forgot and thought I had forgotten, too. I hadn't. A part of me wanted them to check on me, and another part of me wanted them to ask about her, but the largest part of me—most of me—didn't because it didn't matter. Nothing they said could bring her back, and I liked thinking of her the way I wanted to think of her without anyone telling me to stop or think of her differently or just keep busy. Gotta keep busy, people said, so that I wouldn't think of her so much and feel so bad. A history teacher came by once to ask me if I was okay. "Yes," I told her. "Great," she said.

When my mom was first diagnosed with cancer, I learned the word "malignant" and heard the word "spread" and knew the word "hope" was a mirage, a fantasy that would only make things worse. But then I learned the word "remission," and the doctors loosened their ties, cracked bad jokes (said her blood type was B-positive, so we should be optimistic, too), and they increased the odds of her survival to fifty-fifty, like she was something to wager on in Vegas. I slept well and ate well and celebrated on the inside. My kidneys shook pom-poms, my liver did an Irish jig, my small intestines did the worm. The future was bright with a likely chance of sunshine—and then it was over.

As I stood near the food table amid the circus of pizza-scarfing and flirtatious smiles, I kept reminding myself it was over, that she no longer had fifty-fifty odds, that there was no longer any reason to be optimistic, that remission was no longer in the cards. I'd wonder who'd pick me up from school and then remind myself it wouldn't be my mom. I'd look at the pizza and wonder who was making dinner tonight and remind myself that it was over, over, over, over, over. She wasn't coming back.

And all that reminding, having to actively remind myself again and again that she was gone, made me feel as small as the ants on the classroom floor nibbling on a stray piece of mozzarella cheese. Made me want to step on those ants (I did), and step on myself and throw a whole pie in a student's face for complaining about his mom's curfew rules and another pie in my teacher's face for organizing this stupid party (I wish I did), because I was alone, with no one to talk to, and it looked really bad, it must have, and there was that long table of food but you don't want to be the only person snacking, and everyone was talking but me, so I tried to blend in. I pulled out a cell phone. And spoke. And blended in like a banana in a blender, and what a brilliant acting job it was. It was truly an impressive banana performance. I even laughed a few times. And it worked. I was less alone. No longer a lonely banana.

Sometimes I feel that she's with me and sometimes I don't. I just talk into the phone, and it makes me feel better for a minute, like the chicken dance in Mrs. Q's class, which is a great way to burn calories. Not everyone agrees with that statement—my dad, for one—which is why I'm taking the long way home. The long way, meaning "the wrong way," or "the complete opposite direction of my house."

Instead of walking along the main drag in town, where the split-level houses look cloned and franchised like food chains, I make a right out of the school, which takes me past McIntyre Funeral Home and its white sign and white awning and white siding and misshapen black cars. Past the Little League baseball field with its grass frozen over. Past the Rock 'n' Roll Diner, its jukebox on full display through the window, which gets me thinking of Bruce Springsteen and, for some reason, his hair: he has lustrous locks, thick in the front, thicker in the back. A mullet, I think. My haircut doesn't have a name, but it's oily, misshapen, and has angel wings on the sides of my head. Some people may call it an angel haircut, but I haven't yet met those people.

It's only five o'clock, but it's almost dark. Like some pesky freeloading guest, winter has come and never left. (Leave already, February, you're no longer wanted.) Some of the trees have tiny buds, but most of them look like bald, hunchbacked old men.

When I'm a block away from my house, I hide behind a bald tree and peek down the block to see if my dad's rusty green Buick is parked in the driveway. Of course it is, right on schedule. He's a salesman at some fancy antiques store where they sell old clocks for thousands of dollars, so he's always well aware of the time. And now, at precisely 5:10 p.m., it's nearly time for him to make mad, passionate love to the object of his desire. I've seen it more than I should, and it's embarrassing and hideous and wrong. At first he takes it slow, nibbling on the outside of the legs and thighs, but then he loses control and his mouth becomes a ferocious tiger and his fingers get shaky and violent. He doesn't come up for air until he's good and satisfied and full. He barely ever wipes his mouth, not until the end.

He sure loves his fried chicken.

I take a few more minutes, allowing maximum time for him to complete his meal before finishing my trek home.

My house, like everyone else's on our block, is a ranch. There are no horses or farmers at my ranch. My house is called a ranch because it's a one-story house with a basement. The laundry room is in a long, dark corridor in that basement. There's only one light in the laundry room, which you can't turn on until you're halfway through the darkest part of the darkest room in the house.

When I was younger, I hid there in the shadows. No windows or candles. Black as night. I sat cross-legged on the cold floor and invented games. When my mom came down to do laundry, I hid behind an old wooden dresser, and when her footsteps reached the bottom of the stairs, I pretended to be a ghost, a hideous ghost, from generations past. My mission was to scare to death the humans who moved in on my property. They had to pay for their sins in the worst possible way. Starting with this lady of the house.

My mom's bare feet swished across the floor as her fingers felt their way through the darkness. In the middle of the room, she groped for the light switch, but right before her hand could find the switch, I leaped out of my hiding spot and, ghost that I was, screamed as loud as I possibly could, "BOO!"

The laundry room isn't used anymore. My dad won't go near it. Every few weeks, he drops off our clothes at the laundromat. He doesn't cook, either. Twice a week he loads up on fried chicken.

When I was younger, my mom ran the kitchen with two golden rules: you can't mix sugar cereals (a Trix and Lucky Charms combo was a no-no), and no fried chicken. She forbade it from entering the house, citing my dad's high cholesterol.

"Please, honey," my dad would beg.

"Oh, stop groveling," she'd say. "I'm doing you and Denny a favor."

In place of my mom, I got fried chicken and a week full of leftovers.

I open the front door. The microwave is humming, which can mean only one thing. My dad hasn't eaten yet. Crap.

He's at the kitchen table in a red-collared shirt washed so many times (by the cleaners) that it now looks like dusty brick. His skin is pale and stubbly, his cheeks a faint red, as if they've been washed a few too many times as well (but they haven't; he could use a shower). His unblinking eyes are stuck on the television. He doesn't even hear me come in until I drop my backpack in my room. "Time for dinner!" he shouts.

Really not in the mood. For the food or the company.

Not sure which sounds worse, actually: leftover chicken from four days ago, or watching my dad devour another chicken leg and then wipe his greasy fingers on toilet paper. He says toilet paper's cheaper than paper towels, and I understand that—I do, I really do—but it's *toilet* paper; it belongs near a toilet, not on the kitchen table. Every time I mention it he gets all red and flustered and shouts, "Do you wanna buy paper towels?" What kind of question is that? Do I wanna buy paper towels? Show me a kid who actually wants to buy paper towels. Seriously, bring him to me. He's ruining everything.

I move my backpack on top of my unmade bed. I still have the same green and white football sheets and covers I used as a kid. The field is green, the yard markings are white. On the fifty-yard line, a player in a blue uniform holds a football under his armpit. He's not moving. He's just standing there. Ramrod straight. His knees aren't even bent. I mean, I know it's a sheet, but the player in the blue uniform isn't moving at all, not even backward or to the side. He's just standing there, like a bump on a log. I think it's sad, that's all. I know it sounds dumb.

But even though my sheets are juvenile, they're very comfortable. I throw them over my face when I want to disappear. Some days, when I feel *really* lousy, I build my old G.I. Joe tent, grab the sheets, and go disappear in there. But it takes energy to do that. "I think I'll get some rest!" I holler down the hall. "Had a long day."

"Right, uh, okay then," he stammers. "Let's talk when you're feeling better."

That's what he always says. "Let's talk when." If I see him later, he'll pretend he never said it. The most he'll do is hand me my one dollar allowance. One measly dollar. You can't even buy paper towels with that. Not a single roll. At least not the good kind.

I *appreciate* my allowance, don't get me wrong. I know there are plenty of starving children who aren't fortunate enough to wipe fried chicken grease on toilet paper. But, come on . . . *one dollar*? That's been my allowance ever since my mom got sick. My allowance—like the laundry room, my football sheets, and everything else in my house—sort of got frozen in time.

I don't even think of spending my allowance anymore, but I used to. I'd have to wait two weeks to buy a pack of gum, five weeks to buy a five-dollar foot-long turkey sandwich at Subway—but then there's tax, so I really had to wait six weeks.

But try telling that to my dad. He's not exactly a natural schmoozer. Doesn't like to sit down and talk things out. I don't blame him a whole lot, though. I'm kind of glad he's like that. I'm *not* glad he's ballooned to over three hundred pounds the past few years, but I'm grateful he doesn't talk a whole lot. I mean, even if my dad tried to talk to me about Mom and asked me why I kept talking to her on her old broken phone, I'd probably ask him if the Phillies will make it back to the play-offs this year, if Chase Utley is still his favorite player, if hot dogs are better on the barbecue or at a ball game.

I don't mind talking about baseball, because when you talk about it, you don't have to worry that one poor choice of words will make the other person run away. Like one time I told my dad I was glad Mom died. I didn't mean it. What I meant was I was glad she wasn't in pain anymore. I just wasn't used to talking about important things.

I know that what happened in Mrs. Q's class is important—to her, to me, to my dad—so of course I don't want to talk about it. I don't even want to think about it. Surfing on an armrest desk? Falling in the trash can? Seriously?

I pull at a metal chair, drag it over the stained carpet to my desk, where I sit down and jot,

Dear Mrs. Q, I'm sorry my inappropriate behavior got in the way of the Learning Zone. You're a good teacher, a very good teacher, ~~and very good-looking~~.

I cross off that last line because it sounds terrible. The whole thing sounds bad. I crumple the letter into a ball and throw it across the room toward a small wastepaper basket and miss, of course. Air ball. Like the rest of my day.

I start over:

Dear Mrs. Q, Sorry for interrupting your very fascinating lesson on mathematics. I can't wait to use these tools in the very near future. You deserve many awards: teacher-of-the-year, rookie-of-the-year, and best-looking-lady-of-the-year. You are an inspiration. You're my inspiration.

So keep up the good work. I really am sorry.

I think of walking into the kitchen to show my dad the note. Maybe he'd be proud of me for manning up and apologizing. Maybe he'd tell me I used sound judgment in apologizing and that I should do the manly thing and give it to Mrs. Q. No, he'd probably just nod his head, which I hate because I'm not a mind reader, and hand me back the note. And then later, if I eat with him and he works up the courage to ask me questions, we'll do the same song and dance we've done so often I've memorized it:

Dad: "Uh, hello, Denny."

Me: "Greetings, Dad."

Dad: "Yes, uh greetings."

Me: "And salutations. Greetings and salutations."

[Dad fiddles with his thumbs.]

Dad: "Right, salutations."

[Two minutes of silence.]

Dad: "So, what'd you learn today?"

Me: "Nothing."

[Dad drops silverware on his plate. The clang hurts my ears.]

Dad: "Why didn't you learn anything today?"

[I shrug.]

[Dad glares at me. Then stares at his plate.]

Me: "How was your day, Dad?"

Dad: "Fine."

[Two minutes of silence. Cycle repeats.]

So, yeah, I'm not showing the letter to my dad. For these reasons, and another: The second letter is just as inappropriate as the first one. *Best-looking-lady-of-the-year?* I'm about to rip this one up, too, when the phone rings. An actual working one. It rings four times before my dad answers it, which means he's showing wonderful social skills in wiping his hands on toilet paper instead of rubbing grease on the phone. My dad hollers down the hall: "Denny, it's Manny. Let's talk when you're off the phone."

Sure we will.

I put the phone to my ear.

"Donuts, prepare yourself. We begin tomorrow. Key word being 'we.'"

"Manny, wait, what—"

He hangs up and doesn't call back.

My dad must have schooled him in how to have a conversation.

THE PLAN, REVISED

Aloha, goddess of mathematics! Your earlobes look magnificent!"

I can't say this because I'm banned from class. As Mrs. Q puts it, "You can return after a parent comes in for a conference." In other words, I'm banned for eternity. (No *way* the Natural Schmoozer's coming in. No way will I let my ~~friends~~ colleagues see him and hear him and . . . no thanks.)

Mrs. Q breaks the news to me outside her door the day after my desk surfing.

"But, Mrs. *Q*," I protest, "I wrote you a letter of apology. I really did. I'm sorry."

She clenches her teeth. "Give it to me at the parent conference."

"But, Mrs. Q, what will Mr. Softee—I mean, Mr. Soffer— say to this lifetime ban from the Learning Zone? I am a willing and able learner who has got to get in my zone.

What would he say to you stunting my academic growth and banning me from my zone?"

"He needs to—he will support it. The decision is final." You can tell she's trying to sound tough, but her voice lets her down. It shakes like branches in a storm, rustles like pom-poms. "Come back, Denny, when we have arranged a parent conference. Bye, now." And shuts the door in my face.

Dear Mrs. Q, Good for you.

That should be the letter I give to her. It's short, concise, and it rhymes. And it'd be the most work I've submitted to her all year.

No matter, there's still a great deal to learn at Blueberry Hills Middle, and Manny is eager to teach, as long as the coast is clear and the air is filled with fries.

Having downed his thermos, Manny sips a carton of chocolate milk at a café table for six but seating two. After asking him what's *so* important that he called my house, I rip open my own chocolate milk as Manny gets down to business: "In order to make this happen, Donuts, and to do it right—and by 'right' I mean host and sponsor the hippest of after-parties for only the hippest of hippopotami, or offer a helicopter ride or a sports car—we are going to require money. An overwhelming amount. I mean . . . look at us." He points at my french-fry-oil-stained T-shirt and torn jeans, then points to himself. "And I am underappreciated as a male commodity. While I have recently increased in value, I remain undervalued. I mean, my compatibility quotient, our compatibility quotients are, well—"

"You mean we're both losers." It's not a question.

He rubs his chin. "You more than I, but precisely. That is why I am examining business strategies. Are you following me, Donuts?"

"Whatever." It's hard to focus on Manny. I just got dumped by a teacher and the warm air is making me woozy.

Manny presses on. "I have studied food-selling methods for some time now. It is a popular tradition with many models worth emulating. I have followed Girl Scouts as they knock on doors and pawn their Thin Mints and—"

"Wait, you *followed* them?"

"Indeed I did. I am not a creep or anything, but I did creep behind trees so they would not see me. And let me tell you, Girl Scouts are a force, they are bulldozers. They do not even have to bang on doors anymore because their whole organization is a bulldozer. Uniforms, order forms, cookie variety, cookie freshness, cookie uniqueness, years of reliable service. I envy them, plain and simple."

"So . . . you're gonna become a Girl Scout?"

"Negatory, I am just saying that I have studied their business model and think we can borrow from it. They are not the only model, though. I have also examined candy sales by rising young entrepreneurs such as myself. My mom recently sent me to stay with relatives in the Bronx for the weekend and, turns out, kids can make $150 per day selling candy on the New York City subway. They pardon the interruption, very polite, you see, and say, 'I ain't sellin' candy for no basketball team; I'm sellin' candy to put money in my pocket so I can buy more candy and make more money in a positive way.'"

I steal a peek at Allison. She's twirling Anna's lacrosse stick like it's a baton. She just dropped it again. Allison may be a cheerleader, but she's not a very good one. That's okay. I forgive her.

"The point, Donuts, is that we need to up our sales if we will have any shot at attractive dates. Like the one you cannot divert your eyes from."

I shoot him an innocent look.

"I *see* you staring." He takes a sip of his chocolate milk. "Okay, here goes. Remember yesterday, when that sixth grader—"

"Had no fear and bought a Three Musketeers?"

"Indeed, it *is* a catchy jingle, which I tailored to test-taking clientele, for it is common to turn to candy to steady one's nerves. But there are other groups of potential buyers whom I have ignored. Allow me to present my plan." He reaches into his backpack, pushes past his secret compartments, and pulls out a piece of paper and a pen. "Let us make this interactive, shall we? Okay, when do people eat candy?"

"When they're hungry."

"Excellent. You are smarter than you look."

Level 1, he writes. *Hungry people.*

"Now, when are people the most hungry?"

"During lunch."

"Precisely, which means I need to be a more active sales-man during lunch. But people also crave food—and lucky for us, they crave junk food—when they are stressed, such as that kid before his big science test. But there are other stressors that we teens face on a daily basis. Not you and me, Donuts, but a lot of teens."

Level 2, he writes. *Breakups.*

"As I have discussed previously, I am an integral part of the social pipeline, so I have access to copious quantities of information, which I can use to my economic advantage. For instance, when there is a recent breakup and the girl is alone, I will walk up to her and say, 'You look like you are in pieces. How about a Reese's?' Catchy, yes?"

"Very."

"And if the girl is surrounded by her friends, I will waltz up to the whole group and offer candy. How can they pos-sibly turn me down? I will be like that guy who walks into restaurants selling roses to anyone who looks like they are on a date. Good luck saying no to *that* guy. Guys cannot possibly turn down the rose peddler in front of girls, so they grudgingly make a purchase. So, too, will girls be un-able to say no to me when their friend is in a time of need."

"Genius, Manny."

"I am aware. Now these are just a few ideas. We do not

have much time to waste. The dance is in less than two months. Let us, together, begin selling this instant!"

My stomach tightens. "Together? What about the airplane? You know, help yourself first and then—"

"Look, even I cannot do this on my own. You will need to be an active salesperson and business partner. It will be good for you, beneficial for you, trust me, it is the distraction you need. Besides, from what I hear, you now have some time on your hands, considering your ban from Mrs. Q and all."

"How did you—"

"Social pipeline, Donuts, social pipeline." Manny raises his carton of chocolate milk. "You can do this. You have nothing to lose and you can do this! A toast, to a successful business venture. And date-filled adventure!" His eyes are aflame. The intensity is frightening. It gives me goose bumps. "This will only be a successful distraction if we go ALL OUT! Selling candy is our oxygen. It is our everything. And we must work together. Now raise your glass and toast with me!"

"We don't have glasses."

"Your milk carton. Raise your carton and toast with me!"

His plan is bonkers. Or genius. Either way, it makes me smile. And Manny's right about at least one thing: What do I have to lose? A night of disappearing under my football covers? A night of watching my dad rub fried chicken grease on toilet paper?

I need to change the narrative. Manny was right. I need a distraction. Something life-changing. And he'd be proud of me if I pulled this off. My dad, I mean. He'd ask questions and I'd *want* to give the answers. We'd have something to talk about. Always.

I raise my chocolate milk carton and bump it against Manny's. Our excitement is so powerful that it erupts and overflows. I mean, what really overflows is a wave of milk that spills over the top and, as if in slow motion, rises in a tight blob, reaches its peak before my eyes, spreads itself out like an octopus flaring its tentacles, and comes crashing down on my shirt. I can feel the wetness against my stomach.

"Your tableside manners are flabbergasting," Manny says, shaking his head. "We are not off to such a stellar start. But fear not, we will rally. It will get better."

"Not soon enough . . ."

LIFE

And I am correct. Which is more than I can say about my current English teacher and hero and role model, Mr. Morgan, who offers great wisdom when it comes to writer's block and all other matters of writing and literacy, but gives blatantly false, wrong, incorrect information on each work sheet, as part of the heading. "Life is good!" it says, right there smack at the top underneath the date. Life is good! Well, he's wrong and inappropriate for spreading this message. Propaganda is what it is.

Since it's frowned upon to argue with teachers and thus get banned from (more than one) class, I haven't said anything. To him, I mean. To his work sheets, I've said plenty: Life is ~~good~~ a rare baseball card, a rare coin, a rare diamond because it is rarely good. Life is ~~good~~ a rare piece of meat that is edible only if you have a strong stomach or are a lion or a tiger or a bear or a dog or another thing that barks or roars and is lucky enough not to be human. Life is ~~good~~ a drink or food or medicine that can only be swallowed in small doses. Life is ~~good~~ the sun or another bright thing that makes you want to turn away and go inside and put on sunglasses.

Life is ~~good~~ a roller coaster with a few ups and a lot of downs and a long boring line with annoying people in it that say annoying things like "essentially" and "it is what it is" and talk about things you don't have. Life is ~~good~~ a roller coaster that has a really long line but you wait anyway and stuff your face with clouds of blue cotton candy and when you get to the front they close the ride because it's broken. Life is ~~good~~ a loop-de-loop roller coaster that makes you smile even if you don't want to because it's fast and thrilling, but then you get off and go home and turn on the news to see it's been swept into the ocean by a hurricane, washed out to sea.

I hate to be Denny Downer on my work sheets, but someone needs to tell the truth: that one day your mom is beside you laughing at home movies while eating ice cream sandwiches and the next day you're hoping for another chance, begging for another year, and then you're watching Judge Judy tell you your case is a poor one, buddy, it's all over, say your goodbyes. Life is ~~good~~ a rigged game of cards. Life is ~~good~~ a vending machine that only accepts other people's quarters. Life is ~~good~~ a friend named Manny with big ideas and promises but no guarantees. Life is ~~good~~

a candy scheme that's dangerous and desperate and wrong but is the only distraction big enough to keep me from ripping my hair out and crossing off "Life is good!" on every single work sheet I get.

And life is ~~good~~ a bucket of your dad's fried chicken that looks and smells delicious but isn't fresh and is still on the kitchen table when you walk into your house. Life is ~~good~~ hearing your dad flush the toilet and walk into the kitchen without wiping his hands, and when you throw your bag down on the floor, you realize your bag isn't zipped, probably hasn't been zipped in a while, and all of your papers suddenly come tumbling out on the floor. Life is ~~good~~ watching your dad see a whole stack of papers with the heading "Life is good!" scratched out and replaced with more accurate headings like life is ~~good~~ a roller coaster and life is ~~good~~ a candy scheme and life is ~~good~~ a bucket of fried chicken. He finds these edited handouts strange and touches them with his wet, quivering hands and wants to talk about it but you know he doesn't want to talk about it but he's already *said* he wants to talk about it so he figures he'll give it a try.

"What are you DOING?" he roars, waving his arms, flinging beads of water in the air. "Why are you DOING this?"

Because it kills time. Because, like the candy operation, it's a distraction. Because someday I'll sell these work sheets on eBay for fifty years of allowance. Because I can and nobody cared until now. Because it makes me feel better. Because why not?

"Is this what you write during class?"

Usually, yes. Sometimes I draw pictures. Sometimes I list my favorite athletes. Sometimes I just write my name and practice my signature, again and again and again, which makes no sense whatsoever but I do it anyway. Sort of like why I go to school.

"Is this what you think life is?"

Not all the time. I mean, if there are fourteen waking hours in a day, I only feel this way for ~~half of them eight of them twelve and three-quarters of them~~ thirteen and one-quarter of them.

"Do you know what life is, Denny?"

Yes, Dad, I do. That's why I've written on these work sheets, see. But why don't you tell me anyway, because when adults ask their own questions, you know they have an answer that they're just dying to give since they think it's right but it probably isn't.

"Life is getting up every day and playing a game that you've already lost," he says, and I don't know how to respond because when people tell you the truth, or at least their truth, and what feels like my truth, it's hard to make a comeback, even in your head.

"I'm trying, Denny," he says. "I'm trying to get through it." He eyes his bucket of three-day-old chicken. "It may not look like it." *No, Dad, it does look like three-day-old chicken.* "But I am. You should do the same. You still have time."

Before I can respond, which is probably his plan because he never wanted to have a conversation anyway, he grabs his chicken bucket, storms into the living room, turns on the television, parks himself on the couch, and stays there in the glow of movies and shows and commercials until he falls asleep. And when I wake him early in the morning, his breath smelling of chicken, I'll lead him down the hall to bed, where he'll sleep for a couple more hours before he wakes up and plays a game he can't win.

But thinks that I still can.

CHARITY WORK

Manny walks beside me as we head from school to his apartment. Because, as he puts it, "we have not a second to spare in our preparations," he's walking at a blistering pace that is so blistering it must be giving him foot blisters. His arms are at his sides, his eyes dead ahead, his jaw clenched.

It's necessary at this point to explain that there are two sides of my town and Manny and I live on the wrong one. It's still the suburbs, which means malls and movie theaters and mini-golf, but there aren't any country clubs or swimming pools or fancy cars, which would make it that much sweeter to drive in a Rolls Royce or a Bentley to the dance. Have someone drive us, I mean.

No matter which side of town you live on, if you don't have a license or a car in the 'burbs, either you have a smiling parent as an escort, or you graze like cattle behind a fence, watching everyone else whiz by in their popular, mobile little lives.

I can't even go "down the shore" when I want to, even though it's less than an hour away. Not that summer's anywhere near, and not that the shore is so special or anything. I mean, the water at the Jersey Shore isn't even blue. It's brown. Even at the end of July, on the sharpest, most glorious day of summer, the best it gets is light brown, or if you're lucky, brownish green. Still, it'd be nice to go once in a while to check out the boardwalk, maybe eat an ice cream cone or funnel cake. Maybe fall asleep in the sand until a middle-aged hippie waves a metal detector over my body and rummages through my pockets for change . . .

If only that hippie knew how much more money he'd make selling candy in middle school. But it'd be weird for a middle-aged hippie to sell candy in the middle school hallways.

Manny takes a shortcut through a crowded shopping center with a giant Shop-Rite. Kicking stones softly through the parking lot to avoid hitting the cars, I can't help but think we're doing something terribly wrong. That we're attempting to disturb the natural order of what *naturally* becomes popular and not popular. That this experiment is immoral and just plain wrong. That my mom would be embarrassed, my dad, too. And that I should probably apologize to Mrs. Q and everyone else and call this off ~~before~~ when it goes terribly wrong, but Manny grabs my shoulder—hard—and pulls me behind a parked car. It's a Honda, not a Bentley. I notice these things now.

"Look at this," he says, pointing.

He doesn't mean the Honda. I rub my shoulder through my coat and look ahead where eight Girls Scouts have set up shop in front of Shop-Rite. In green uniforms, all well-ironed with sashes from their shoulders to their belts, they sit daintily at a table with boxes stacked above their eyes. Overseeing their sales to the side is a chaperone, or escort, or troop leader, or whatever you call a Lady Scout. Probably a Lady Scout.

"Flabbergasting," Manny says, shaking his head. "Bull-dozers."

He's right. Their smiles as sweet as candy, their labeled boxes and those fancy uniforms . . . customers don't even need a sales pitch! They just see those uniforms and—bam!—here's four dollars. There's no denying their efficiency.

"Genius," Manny mutters, stroking his chin.

"I know, right? Those Girls Scouts are really smart."

"I mean me, Donuts." Manny tugs me on the arm and lifts me upright. "In due time, we will be a well-oiled machine. But first we must prepare."

Manny sits next to me on the cracked beige couch in the middle of his living room as he stacks his candy stash across the carpet. Nestlé Crunch, Snickers, Sour Patch

Kids, Swedish Fish . . . every variety in neat little piles. The only thing neat in his apartment.

His place has a staleness to it, and I don't mean the tortilla chips in the cabinet. The kitchen table covered in junk mail, the bathroom strewn with magazines and hairs on the tiled floor, and in Manny's room, a brown futon in the corner instead of a bed. The air, the smell, is like an old shopping center.

His piles in order, Manny turns to me. "Tomorrow morning, we begin." He reaches for a Snickers and raises it high. "Like all generals and space invaders and lovebirds about to enter into battle, we must prepare. Before our candy invasion, we need to stock our ammunition, as well as confirm and rehearse our strategy."

"Wait, why do we need to rehearse? Haven't you been selling for a while?"

He huffs. "Yes, but not in public like those Girl Scouts. That is what we need to discuss. We will need to adopt a strategy that I am *not* altogether familiar with. Until now, I have sold candy in secret, or as secretly as possible while still pulling in over fifty dollars per day. But my underground operation, like any scalper's operation, takes too long. It will not fit our needs. It will not fit the massive scope of our endeavor."

Manny must sense the confusion on my face. "Scalping, Donuts, is a covert business. It is illegal. Money is slipped under the rug, exchanged via sleight of hand. Due to the hush-hush-ness of the business model, sales are not maximized. No ticket scalper sells thousands of tickets outside a venue. The risk is too great: getting handcuffed and tossed in a cop car. Merchandise can move, but it jogs; it does not sprint, does not fly. The only way to have our social status truly blast off is to let our merchandise fly. In the open. Legally."

"How do we do that?"

"We fund-raise. Like those Girl Scouts."

"But it's not a fund-raiser."

"Sure it is. If you give something a name, everything changes. For instance, how is dating life since I dubbed you Donuts?"

I freeze. "Fantastic," I mutter.

"So you concede the point." He chuckles. "Names mean everything, my good friend. Why do you think I obsess over an old wrestler and wear this perfect T-shirt?"

"Because you don't like to do laundry."

"Well, yes, but the real reason is because nicknames can be controlled. Now everyone knows me as Mr. Perfect."

"Not really . . ."

He puts out his hand. "I admit that everyone does not recognize my name—yet. But it will pay off by the time we reach high school. The same is true of our candy sales. It is best not to wait until eleventh grade to decide that popularity is suddenly important and ditch your old friends. Too much controversy, too much phony bologna. But now, while there is still time for our reputations to season, to bloom, to marinate—"

"I get it."

"Good. Now, as long as we name our candy operation, we are in. The name does not even have to mean anything; it just needs to exist."

"So what will we be called?"

"It does not matter, that is my point."

Borrowing from those bulldozing Girl Scouts, the first thing we do is make our business look more official, an official fund-raiser for the good of the community, and nothing's more official than a business name: M & D's Date Foundation.

"M & D's Date Foundation is a fine name," he says, "but it is reckless and irresponsible. We cannot have our names or initials attached to this in any way. The name does not matter, only this." He gestures to his candy stash. "Now, Donuts—and we are not selling donuts, just so we are clear—we must organize our inventory and make an official color-coordinated order form, like the Girl Scouts. The last thing we want to project is disorganization. Reflects badly upon the whole business."

"Roger that."

"This is business, not a spy mission, so easy on the 'Roger that.' And in business, feelings get put aside for the good of the company. Are we clear on that?"

"Ten-four," I tell him.

He takes a deep breath.

"I'm kidding, Manny, it's not a spy mission. Over and out."

He shoots me the stare of death. "This is serious, Donuts. And this probably goes without saying but I will say it anyway: you are not permitted to tell anyone about our operation. Nobody. Not a single soul."

"Wouldn't dare. Too embarrassing."

Aside from that, and what I don't tell Manny, is that I don't think you should tell anyone about anything big you're working on because when you fail, they know. Someday, if I ever get a job interview, or plan to write a book, or decide to take over the donut business nationwide, I'll just do it, without telling anyone. I mean, I'd rather live an incognito life where no one knows me, what I want, or who I want. I want to be a masked man—but one who doesn't draw any attention for wearing a mask.

"Seriously, I need you to focus. Your job is to quantify our merchandise. Can you handle that?"

I nod.

"Good, now count up everything on the carpet and mark it down on the sheet. From there, we shall devise our order form, inventory on the left, with pictures for those too lazy to read, and on the right a grid with boxes to either check off or X out. We must be consistent with the markings, so which do you prefer: a check or an X?"

"I'd say an X, but I've never had one."

Manny squints, then groans. "Ah, a joke: you have never had an ex-girlfriend."

"Good one, huh?"

"This is business, hardly a time for laughing matters. And not usually a time for gifts, either, but . . ."

A brief smile, the beginning of a blush. Manny darts for his room and returns with green Christmas wrapping paper haphazardly taped to a large box.

"It is nothing special," he says, now fully blushing. "Well, *I* think it is special and I hope you do, too. I hope you are intelligent enough to appreciate it."

"Manny—"

"JUST OPEN IT!" He covers his mouth with his hands. "I did not mean to yell. The suspense of this moment seems to have bested me."

I tear away the paper to find a large white box.

"I made it precisely like mine," he says. "Same care. Same craftsmanship."

I pull open the box. A backpack. He got me a backpack.

"Go ahead," he says, "test it out. The code is on the back of the lock."

I throw him a puzzled look, but I soon see what he means. The backpack has all the trimmings and trap doors one can expect out of an Emmanuel "Manny" Templeton creation: a combination lock at the zippers, newspaper separation at four levels, Velcro, fasteners, pouches, and a key lock for the bottom compartment . . . It's not a backpack; it's a vault. Unsure whether to hug him or punch him, I settle for a thank you.

He nods. "This will come in handy during our candy sales. And we have quite a bit of selling to do. Our goal will be to make two thousand dollars."

"Two *thousand* dollars!"

"Indeed, one thousand for each of us. Not in sales, but profit. We must hurry. With the dance less than two months away, quite a few of the babes, honeys, beauties, sweeties, and/or sweetie pies are already committed to groups and are thus off the market. So back to work. We must clean this up before my mom comes home."

"She *still* doesn't know about your candy sales?"

"Negatory, kemosabe. And I plan on keeping it that way."

"Does she know about your grades?"

"Another negatory."

"Your attendance?"

Manny ignores me and gets up to go to the bathroom, leaving me with my new backpack and a carpet full of candy to count. As I pile pouches of M&M Peanuts on top of one another—sure to be a bestseller, especially in winter when they're less likely to melt—I can't help but think how it was supposed to be different for Manny. Given his math skills and mile-wide vocabulary, he was supposed to earn straight A's and a free ride to a private school and fancy college, join their debate team, and then become a slick business-man or lawyer. But Manny is not even on track to graduate from middle school. Out of the 180 days of school, he shows up for 90. Not a day less, certainly not a day more. His magic number of 90 is just enough to keep him on the school roster, just enough for Manny to pass his major tests, just enough to keep child protective services away. Not enough, however, for him to earn many credits.

When I said that I don't do homework, I meant that I rarely do it, like once every other week. Manny, though, *never* does it. Ever. Our English teacher a few years back, the one who introduced Manny to the concept of formal versus informal language in essay writing, was so sick and tired of Manny wasting his potential that he told him, "If you don't do your homework, I swear I'll pull off your fingernails with the back of a hammer and nobody will be around to hear you scream." He was fired.

Manny was promoted, even though he failed the class. Manny didn't pass many of his classes last year either, but Mr. Softee doesn't believe in holding kids back if they lack only eight or fewer credits. So he pushed him through.

In order for Manny to graduate, there'll be after-school and summer school and makeup projects and parent meetings with the social worker. And when they get home, there'll be punishments and threats of grounding Manny for life, but what'll that do? He never wants to leave the house anyway, except to go with his cousin Kenny to Costco to load up on food merchandise. (The same cousin Kenny who has now volunteered to make color copies of our order form. For a price. For a profit. Some swell family he's got. And some dent in my wallet *I've* now got. Adios, two years of allowance . . .)

I stare at the Snickers bars in front of me and count them as fast as I can. No way I want to be here when Manny's mom gets home. I hate to be Denny Downer, but I've seen her entrance before and it ain't pretty.

In elementary school, when Manny smelled, which was fairly often since he almost never washed his favorite "Nobody is perfect. Except me" T-shirt, his mom held her nose and walked to another room. When she came home and found him lying on the couch, she kicked the couch, which meant that Manny should do something more constructive or else get off the damn couch so that she could lie down. When Manny's report card arrived in the mail, she took one look at the D's and F's before she ripped it to shreds and ordered Manny to pick it up. I saw all of this go down as far back as preschool, when Manny used to pee in his pants so often that when he woke up from a nap and his pants *weren't* wet, he threw his arms in the air, jumped up and down, and yelled, "Yes, I never pee myself! NEVER!" On most days, his mom had to come drop off clean clothes, and when she saw him sitting in a pool of his own urine, she gave him an ice-water stare and wouldn't leave until hot tears ran down Manny's bony cheeks, until his face turned fire truck red, until he begged for forgiveness and swore that it would never, ever happen again. Our teacher, Mrs. Shaffer, suggested that Manny's mom store a pile of clothes at the school so that she didn't have to come in all the time.

But she wouldn't hear it. "The last thing I need is a child who thinks it's okay to urinate on himself. This boy needs to grow up and he better do it soon. No more diapers, no more change of clothes, and no more night-lights. My boy is still afraid of the dark. Can you be*lieve* that?"

I could believe it. I'd seen it. Not for a few years now, but Manny used to sleep at my house, especially after Manny's dad left. His mom used to drop him off for days at a time. For a break. That's the only explanation she ever gave. She needed a break.

"Well, are all of the goods accounted for?" After Manny emerges from the bathroom, and after he checks my candy count (twice) to make sure I haven't pocketed any merchandise, he wipes his hands on his shirt, pushes my new backpack to the side, and sits down next to me. "You should depart," he says. "My mom will be home soon. You should not be here when she arrives. The candy, too, must go. She cannot see this."

"Probably a good idea, Manny."

He nods. "My mom, unfortunately, is not like yours is. I mean, was. I mean . . ."

His sentence lingers there for far too long. "She's not a *tense*, Manny!" I don't mean to get so upset but I'm at her

95

funeral again, listening to the priest's CliffsNotes, his references to her in the past tense, and my shirt is getting sweaty and my face is red and the paint-chipped walls of Manny's apartment are closing in like a vise and my mom isn't a tense. Never was. Never is. I mean . . . is, present, present tense, presently . . . Manny is making this hard for me, and I know I'm probably overreacting, but I can't help it and don't want to help it and I'm already stuffing armfuls of candy into my new bag.

"I am sorry," Manny says. "Really, I am, I did not intend anything by it. She was good to me, too, you know." You can tell he means it. His face is scrunched up and he's shaking his head, but my eyes are about to leak—not cry, just leak—and I don't like letting other people see when they do that. I scramble for the front door and open it. I don't want to turn around but it's rude not to say goodbye.

"Thanks for the bag, Man—" I tell him. It's all I can get out.

THE LADYBUG

We are nine years old. Manny's mom is on her first break.

A camouflage shirt, a strip of black paint under each eye, a walkie-talkie in one hand and binoculars in the other, Manny is ready for battle, is ready for our mission: to spy on my neighbor, Allison Swain.

Standing beside me, he orders, "You go around back and I will stay in the front. Call me when you see the Ladybug."

"Right, Ladybug... Wait, who's the Ladybug again?"

"You forgot already! You are such a boogiebrain! Allison Swain's code name is 'Ladybug.' We agreed on that, remember?" He doesn't wait for a response. "Now go around back and make sure your walkie-talkie is turned on this time."

"Roger that."

"You do not have to say 'Roger that' until we start."

"Oh, right. Roger that."

"What did I just say!"

"Not to—sorry, Manny."

He shakes his head.

"Manny, wouldn't it be funny if your name was Roger. You know, Roger that . . ."

He shoves me in the back. "Move, soldier!"

I race around the side of Allison's house, toward the backyard. The latch on her gate is old and rusted, and the grass in her backyard is thick and sharp. The plants, all vines and garter snakes, are alive and breathing. They slither from the porch to the back fence. Thankfully, they don't eat me as I pass.

The high grass makes my legs itch. I want to scratch them but I can't because Manny gave his orders, so I dive behind a bush. And land on a pinecone. It digs into my knee like shards of broken glass and I can't help but scream. My walkie-talkie booms with static. "Come in, Eagle One! This is Fox Three, over!"

"Roger that, this is Eagle One," I grunt, rubbing my knee. It looks deformed.

"I think I heard a girl screaming!" he shouts. "Was that the Ladybug?"

"Uh, yes, I think so, yes."

"Confirm your location, Eagle One."

"Uh, behind a bush, on top of pinecones, over."

"Any sign of Ladybug?"

"Not yet. What about you, Manny?"

"My name is Fox Three," he grumbles.

"Right, sorry."

"No sign of Ladybug from my present location," he says. "Let us rotate counterclockwise. You should be at two o'clock in fifteen seconds. Over."

"Wait, what? What time?"

Manny sighs loudly into the walkie-talkie. And then again. It sounds like this: "Haw. Ha. Haw. Ha," which reminds me of Darth Vader. I tell him that.

He sighs again and, in his best Darth Vader voice, says, "Eagle One." Haw. Ha. Haw. Ha. "I am your father." Haw. Ha . . . Loud, hacking coughs and then Manny's voice: "Move to your left, quickly, Eagle One, and keep your head down. Run to the side of the house and call me when you see something. MOVE, EAGLE ONE, MOVE!"

"Nothing is happening," I grumble into my walkie-talkie. "It's getting late, Manny, and I don't see her."

"Her name is Ladybug, and mine is Fox Three."

"Well it's almost time for dinner, Fox Three. My mom's making chicken with bread crumbs and the Ladybug isn't here."

"My mom's—I mean, your mom's chicken is delicious. She is quite a force of good in the kitchen. Perhaps you can stow me away in one of your kitchen drawers. I shall be a stowaway, stowed away in your mom's kitchen."

I don't answer because I don't know how.

He continues. "But first we complete our mission. Which rhymes with 'kitchen' but has little else in common." He stifles a laugh. "You see, I brought a secret weapon. It is foolproof, even around you. Heard of a stink bomb?"

"Yeah, but—"

"I call it the 'missile' for short. I brought it just in case. So we can smoke Allison out of her house, like in cowboy movies. Whoever sees her first, wins."

"I'm on my way, Fox Three." I sprint toward the front of the house.

"That is preposterous, Eagle One!" he shouts. "You will not come near me."

"Already on my way, Fox Three." I leap over a bed of yellow flowers, running as fast as I can.

"Retreat, Eagle One. I am warning you."

"I can see you, Fox Three."

"You are standing right in front of me, you ignoramus."

Manny pulls out a glass vial, small and yellow, from his side pocket. "All I need to do is break this sucker and then, like the doctors say on television, CLEAR."

"Can I touch it?"

"You lack the necessary coordination to handle such a toxic device. Besides, I have a straight shot through the front window." He squints his eyes and puts his hand in karate chop position. "Preparing to take the shot. Stand by . . ."

"Wait—"

"Listen to me, Eagle One. There are two exits to Ladybug's house. The front door and back door. I recommend you position yourself in the backyard so you do not compromise our mission. Proceed with caution, Eagle One."

"But she'll probably come out the front door," I tell him.

"That is why I am staying put," he says. "Ten seconds until launch, which means you MOVE, EAGLE ONE. THAT IS AN ORDER FROM A SUPERIOR OFFICER."

I jump to my feet and race around the side of the house, pumping my arms and legs as fast as I can. The walkie-talkie buzzes in my hand. "Five seconds until launch."

The gate is only a few paces away.

"Four seconds until launch."

I reach for the latch but it doesn't budge. I pull on the latch. Pull on it and pull.

"Two seconds until launch." I shake the latch free and the gate swings open and I dash through the grass—"One second until launch"—and leap behind the bush.

"BLAST-OFF, EAGLE ONE. BLAST-OFF. THE MISSILE IS LOOSE."

I bury my face in my lap and pinch my nose shut.

"Remain in position, Eagle One. The Ladybug should be coming out. Keep your eyes peeled and your head down. Wait—listen, Eagle One. Shhh."

Screams. That's the first thing I hear. And then accusations. "What is the . . . why did you . . . call the . . . I can't . . . need to . . . breathe."

The back door bursts open. I curl into a ball and peek through the gray branches.

"Come in, Eagle One!" the walkie-talkie booms. "This is Fox Three, come in." I grab hold of it and turn the volume down. Allison Swain walks out on the back porch. She's wearing a pink shirt and *shorts. She has pigtails with a pink scrunchie. Her skin is the color of sand and she doesn't see me. Allison sits on the stoop and coughs into her hand. I can't do this. I need to help. I reach into my pocket for a tissue and almost come out of hiding to hand it to her. She dabs her eyes with the back of her arm and looks in my direction. I hold my breath. She can't see me because I'm invisible. I'm invisible. Aren't I invisible?*

FULL OPERATION

It never happened. Manny doesn't mention my eyes leaking or my mom's tense, and I don't mention my family's tense or his family or anyone else's family, and he doesn't ask about me or mention anything else about my mom, which is great and wonderful and what I'm used to and pretty much what everyone else does.

Teachers try every few weeks, but once they've reached their quota and gotten the answer they want (that I'm fine and merry and basking in a field of joy), they back off. Barely anyone talks about her because they don't know how and I don't know how, but they *really* don't know how. Don't want to step on my toes and say the wrong thing at the wrong time. The ol' let's-talk-about-everything-except-the-one-thing-you-want-to-ask-me-about-and-the-only-thing-I'm-thinking-about. Instead, let's talk about sports, TV, weather, girls, cars, teachers, food, movies, and actors better than myself. I know I shouldn't think of all of this now given that I was the one who ran away from the conversation and out of Manny's apartment, though sometimes it's hard to stop.

And sometimes, it's hard to start. Anything, I mean: homework, a day, a morning routine, a phone call, an exercise, a meal, a conversation, a candy business . . . So I tell my brain to shut up, shut up, shut up, and focus on our task at hand because all that matters is here and now. Because our mission is a go.

Order forms in hand and matching oversize, eighty-three-pound backpacks across our chests, Manny and I scout out the morning terrain of Blueberry Hills Middle, preparing for Day One of International Monetary Prudential. His words, not mine. I still prefer to call it Manny and Denny's Date Foundation, or M & D's Date Foundation. But Manny's the boss. It's his business. His company. (Which is exactly what I'll tell Mr. Softee ~~if we happen to~~ the moment we get caught.)

Allison "Ladybug" Swain isn't in the hallways. Or Chad. Barely anyone is because school hasn't started yet. Manny and I review the plan one last time before taking out a few boxes, which is no big deal because the only people who can hear us are a few rookie teachers scurrying like squirrels to make copies. Mrs. Q, one of those scurrying teachers, tries not to look at me, so I try not to look at her.

If I had the apology note I'd written for Mrs. Q with

me, I'd hand it to her. But I left it at home, crumpled in a paper ball, and I don't trust myself to say the right words without it.

It's 8:25. Five minutes till game time.

The back of Manny's neck is a pool of perspiration. "Remember the order form, Donuts, which *you* hold on to. If customers insist on filling it out, make sure you get it back. We cannot under any circumstances leave a paper trail. And no receipts, remember. It is an order form, not an invoice. Do not lose the order forms; we will use them to get a quick count on profits. Do not get caught. Remain vigilant for teachers and the principal, Mr. Softee—do not let his name fool you—but if you do get caught, do not give me up."

He eyes me carefully, peering so deeply into my eyes it feels like he's staring into my soul. I'm not sure what he'll find in there. "Manny, you think this'll actually work?"

"Of course it will, I am a human lie detector. I can tell when someone is lying just by looking at them. I can decipher someone's motives by looking in their eyes."

"No, I mean, this whole . . . candy thing. Do you think people will actually buy candy for twice the price we got it for?"

He takes a step back. "Of course. Everywhere you look these days, there are stupid people. Especially at school. Stupid people at school make me sick, literally sick. That is why I barely come. All these idiots floating around our atmosphere, you know?" He doesn't wait for an answer. "Your inventory—"

"Is arranged alphabetically, Snickers in my bottom pouch."

"Good. Now, Donuts, this is the moment of truth. It will be 8:30 in twenty seconds—now in nineteen seconds—those doors will burst open like a tidal wave and our operation will be in full operation." He gestures to the red double doors at the end of the hall. "Ten seconds. Now nine short seconds until we fill their eager mouths with chocolate and begin our compatibility crusade. Oh, I can barely stand it." He covers his mouth. "The anticipation is too much. I cannot—in three, two, one, NOW!" Manny inhales. "Follow my lead, Donuts. Follow my lead and stay as one."

The doors open.

They don't *burst* open, but they open. See, I forgot to mention that Blueberry Hills students are usually late. It's not really our fault. I mean, we don't drive, remember? We rely on other people for rides. If they're late, we're late. If they don't care about being on time, then we get yelled at by teachers for not being on time.

Anyway, so the doors open. Slowly. People trickle in. By "people" I mean mostly sixth graders. Seventh and eighth graders are fashionably late. By "fashionably late" I mean "sort of late on purpose." By that I mean their parents are sort of late on purpose because we can't drive.

Manny smacks me on the arm. "Watch this," he says,

lugging his backpack to the first sixth grader through the door.

"Candy is a dollar!" Manny hollers. "Help support I.M.P."

One order form checked. One sale.

And another. "Support the I.M.P. foundation. It is for a good cause."

Manny can't resist turning to me and whispering, "It is for a good cause be*cause* the money is going to me."

Back and forth he goes, announcing his product and whispering to me:

"Here you go, candy is a dollar. You have made an excellent investment.

"[An investment in *my* future.]

"Support I.M.P., part of the United Adolescent Foundation.

"[*I* am that adolescent and I am united with this box.]

"It is tax deductible.

"[Not that you have even the *slightest* idea what that means.]"

Nobody questions Manny or says a single word, until the seventh and eighth graders stroll in. "Buy your candy here for a good cause!" Manny shouts. "Support I.M.P."

Reaching for his wallet, some smart-aleck puffs out his chest and says, "Oh yeah, what's I.M.P. stand for?"

"International Monetary Prudential," Manny answers, unblinking.

The kid freezes.

"I assume you *have* heard of it," Manny adds.

The kid nods his head slightly. "Well, ah, whatever, give me a Snickers."

Once he passes, Manny chuckles. "He has no idea what International Monetary Prudential means."

"Manny, I don't even know what that means."

"Neither do I. But I.M.P. does stand for something." He stifles a laugh. "It stands for In My Pocket."

As the crowd continues to shuffle in, I take a deep breath and make an important public service announcement: "School draggin' you down? Eat a Mounds! Tired of the school's laws? Suck on Sour Straws! Candyman, Candyman here. Just your friendly neighborhood fund-raising Candyman who won't linger, so get at that Butterfinger!"

Even Manny has to give me props. "Catchy," he says, "now make a sale." Well, he *means* to give me props. And soon he has to.

A minute later all I see is a blur of desperate fingers and dead presidents on green paper. A tap on my shoulder, a tug on my backpack, dollar bills waved in my face—"No, I don't have change for a twenty"—"but now I do"—a poke in my arm, tap on my head, Skittles, Skittles, Skittles, two fingers in the air, now four, Milky Way, Snickers, no *two* Milky Ways and *four* Snickers.

Snap your fingers. I just sold four more candy bars.

Snap them again. I sold another five.

I love snapping my fingers but I can't now because they're busy. Order forms in my right hand, candy in my left, an X, another X, an X in the right box, an X in the wrong box that's okay here's your candy, fund-raiser, candy, candy, candy, support I.M.P., Candyman is here and wanted and ready and willing and able to seize this school by its sweet tooth. X, another X, hello yes I have what you're looking for no need to look any further you understand, yes you do, pats on the back, smiles, crinkling wrappers, tearing wrappers, it's for a good cause, good cause, wrappers twisting to the floor, at my feet, I step on them, they're everywhere, "hey clean up after yourselves, you monkeys!" I'd like to say but all I hear are wallets, zippers, freezing firm cash, three Sour Patch Kids, two Swedish Fish, three X's, two X's, no *three* Swedish Fish, *two* Sour Patch Kids, two X's, three X's, another Swedish Fish and I ditch the order forms. Way too slow and my wrists are on fire and my hands are tired and my trapdoor backpack is getting more complicated and my fingers are losing their grip, but the end product—someone to dance with, reach my arms around, and kiss?—pushes me forward.

"It's morning, as stale as a fart. Buy a bag of Swee-Tarts!" I announce . . . and now SweeTarts sell like hotcakes. I don't know about selling hotcakes or pancakes or flapjacks or whatever you want to call them in the middle of the halls, but I know this much to be true: candy is the new hotcake. Manny was right about selling in public. The candy flies out of my backpack so fast it must have wings.

I couldn't get my clients to stop buying even if I tried.

By 8:40, I've raked in $47, Manny $33. I must admit, I feel good.

With adrenaline and good vibes running through my veins, I tell Manny my next plan of action. "I'm going to sell in the bathroom. In the stalls."

"What! Flabbergasting!" His eyes bulge. "First, that is a downright strange and convoluted idea. But, more important, that is a highly ineffective use of time, for as everyone knows, you never know who is actually in the stalls."

"Some people may not know but I always know. I like to stick my head under the door to see. Sometimes attach a mirror to my shoe, like in spy movies. And sometimes I do a pull-up on the stall door, peek down, and yell, 'Spell ICUP! Spell it!' And if they don't spell it, I help 'em out: 'It's spelled: I SEE YOU PEE!'"

"You must be kidding. Tell me you are kidding."

"I am. Sort of."

I may be kidding about selling inside the stalls, but I'm not joking about moving merchandise outside the bathroom. So, first period, while Manny's in math class and I'm still banished from the Learning Zone, I waltz up and down the halls near the bathroom, feeling good, scouting out potential buyers.

Bathroomgoers, it turns out, are a reliable clientele.

Do I sell candy in the stalls? Heavens, no. Don't be ridiculous. I just wait outside, and when they approach the bathroom, I go in for the kill.

"Taking a pee? Buy candy from me."

"Dropping a deuce? Buy Starburst, the juice is loose." That one's a stretch, but so is our whole operation. How we'll ever convince girls to be our dates is beyond me, but why worry about such things when business is so good?

How good? In ten minutes, I sell thirty-three candy bars outside the boys' bathroom. *That* good.

Nearly as predictable as a bathroom break is Manny's *Level 2: Breakups*. You can hear them from down the hall, sniveling, pulling tissues from their lockers, blowing their noses like foghorns. A big breakup involves a support group, circling around the victim like a moat around a castle—cue Manny's rose-peddler strategy—but a smaller one, such as that involving this girl leaning on a locker on the right side of the hall, is a solo operation.

Above the girl's head, a reminder of my mission: a poster, written in purple glitter—SEVENTH GRADE DANCE, APRIL 3RD—which means that if I want a date but don't raise enough money to entice one with fast cars and after-parties, I have less than two months to ask a blowup doll if she'll go with me, convince Manny to wear a girly wig, or move to Canada where they don't have dances.

Anyway, the girl is maybe four feet tall, wearing a baggy red shirt and sweatpants. She looks like a sixth grader, but with girls you can never be too sure of anything. Except the obvious signs of heartache. Nothing screams breakup like sweatpants and boogers.

A big ol' wipe and she stuffs a palmful of wet tissues in the pockets of her sweats. Might as well tattoo "Property of the Neighborhood Candyman" across her nose.

I comb my fingers across my eyebrows and slink up to her, smooth as silk. In my most sympathetic, soothing tone, I say, "My heartfelt apologies for the interruption. I don't mean to startle you, but if there's any way I can help, please don't hesitate."

I hold up two packs of SweeTarts.

She dabs her eyes, pouts her lips, but there's a smile under that blanket of sadness, I can see it. "You're better off without him," I say. "Look at you, your beauty could move continents."

And there it is, like a rainbow after a storm, a smile behind a string of braces as she says, "You really think I could move the United States?"

No wonder she got dumped. "Absolutely," I say. "The United States is a fine continent. You could move it for miles. Across the American Ocean."

She giggles—at me, at herself, at her breakup? Hey, all that matters is that this geography whiz pulls a five out of her wallet and cleans me out of Snickers.

Of course, I'd personally recommend SweeTarts, but who am I to argue?

As she unwraps the first of her purchases and gives me a thankful smile, I feel an urge to keep her company, eat a candy bar by her side in this time of need. I haven't eaten breakfast yet, didn't even eat dinner last night, passing on another leftover fried chicken meal with the Natural Schmoozer. I *could* eat a candy bar—I mean, one of the great things about being the Candyman is instant food access—but Manny says it's incest to dip into your own candy supply. He also says it's flabbergasting to steal from yourself. Manny's warnings aside, a candy bar sounds about as appetizing as a cotton swab right now because I've never been this thirsty. All that advertising, those shouts to calm down and be civil and wait in line for my autograph. Being the friendly neighborhood Candyman has its side effects, and I certainly have a newfound respect for the many food men out there—Pretzel Man, Hot Dog Man, Bagel Man, Cotton Candy Man—because my throat is as dry as peanut butter.

I need a drink, not candy, and that's when I come upon a new level. *Level 3: Those who aren't thirsty.* And where can the least thirsty people in school be found?

Around the corner from the geography whiz's locker is the water fountain, which unfortunately for my thirst but fortunately for me is currently being used by a female with black leggings and a checkered purple top. I haven't practiced slogans for the water fountain yet and unfortunately it shows. "Your thirst is now erased, so how about some

Skittles for your face? You know, for your mouth, which is part of your face."

The girl picks her head up from the water fountain and brushes her hair from her eyes. Seeing that it's Sabrina, I decide not to waste my time making a sale. "Never mind," I tell her. "I thought you were someone else."

She looks me up and down. "Do people really buy those lines?"

"No, they buy the candy. Gladly from the candy. Man."

She smirks. "Take your time on those rhymes."

"Nice!" I tell her. "A poet, I like that in a woman."

"Getting banned from Mrs. Q's class so I can learn. I like that in a man."

"Wow, you *are* a poet. You just rhymed 'banned' with 'man.' I believe that's called off-rhyme. Mr. Morgan taught us that. We have him next period."

She closes her eyes and takes a deep breath, like Mrs. Q. "If it's poetry you understand, then run away, play in the hallway—just stay away so I don't waste my day."

"Noted. But first, might you care for a Milky Way?"

She grunts past me.

I really gotta work on my water fountain sales pitch. A perfect rhyme, a catchy jingle: *Now that your palette is refreshed, how about a Nestlé Crunch?* So close.

Skipping Mrs. Q's class due to banishment is one thing, but I never, ever—I mean *ever* (unless it's on a Friday)—skip

Mr. Morgan's English class. Mr. Morgan isn't like the other gods or goddesses of the school. He wears jeans, rarely shaves, and rocks aviator sunglasses even when we're watching a movie in class with the lights out.

Mr. Morgan is more than the god of English. He is the supreme and unmerciful and omniscient god of English, or for short: S.U.O.G.E. I don't call him S.U.O.G.E. or supreme and unmerciful and omniscient god of English to his face because that would be long-winded, ridiculous, and inappropriate. And he told me not to. Many times.

I've also tried calling him "hero and role model"—or for short, H.R.M., pronounced "Herm," which would be perfect if his first name was Herm. Or Herman. But it's not. When I asked him what his first name was, he said it started with an "M."

"Michael?" I guessed. "Matthew? Mitchell? Marc? Manny? Marvin? Melvin?"

"Mister," he said. "My first name is Mister."

"Homey don't play that," it says above *Mister* Morgan's chalkboard. He told our class he borrowed the line from some television show that he used to watch before we were born. Which makes him sound old. Because he sort of is. Older than Mrs. Q anyway, but unlike her, Mr. Morgan is a grizzled veteran, as grizzled as the grizzliest middle-aged grizzly bear in the grizzliest middle school forest in Grizzlyland. He said he was 138 years old, but nobody believed him.

(I think he's that minus 100.) He also said he was a ninja warrior sent back through time to save the human race from children who don't do all their homework. I always know when he's making a joke because we're both skilled comedians and all skilled comedians know that timing is everything.

He tries sometimes to have good noncomedic timing by asking me after class how I'm doing, and if there's anything he can do for me. "Eliminate homework. And all other work," I've told him, "ban it forever." Lately, I've been telling him that more than anything I want him to make me strong.

You see, the best part about Mr. Morgan is that he's a strong dude. But he doesn't like when you call him dude. (He is really very particular about nicknames.) Fortunately, he doesn't mind that much if you tell him he looks strong. Or ripped. Or jacked. One time, he wore a red and black flannel shirt to school and looked like a lumberjack. Like Paul Bunyan. He even had Paul Bunyan's beard. I was so excited to tell him he looked like a lumberjack that I handed him a piece of paper and a pen and said, "Wow, you cut down trees to make this paper. Can I have your autograph?" He didn't sign the autograph. He understood the joke, but he just didn't want to show off, which makes him a very humble lumberjack. Much humbler than Paul Bunyan, anyway.

Unfortunately, Mr. Morgan doesn't call me "lumberjack" during second period. He doesn't call me any nicknames.

He calls me Denny, as in "Where's your homework, Denny?" . . . "Write it in a planner, Denny" . . . "Do some work, Denny" . . . "Do you really want to get held back, Denny?" . . . "Do you like summer school, Denny?"

He has no problem putting people on full blast. Because of my mom, I don't think he's ever put me on *full* blast, but regular blast, or almost full blast, or a-second-away-from-full-turbo-blast . . . yes, I've been put on that. Always violating, that Mr. Morgan. I never said he was a pushover; I just said he was different from other gods and goddesses. And unlike the Natural Schmoozer back home, at least he doesn't skirt the tough issues, doesn't say, "Let's talk when you're finished with your homework." Instead, he says, "DO IT! Do it NOW or I'll give you triple homework and tell everyone you've got a crush on the school secretary. Write your homework in your planner! Now!"

He makes far too big of a deal out of writing the homework down in a planner. Sometimes he won't let students leave until he sees everyone's planner. "Nobody's leaving until I see everyone's planner!" Like that. And he gets real bent out of shape when students don't do the homework, as if it's some grave personal affront. "I'm shocked," he'll say, "floored, disappointed, wounded. You let me down." This is all very confusing, though, because when a student says, "Mr. Morgan, I did your homework last night," that just about makes him breathe fire. "You didn't do MY homework," he shouts, "you did YOUR homework!"

Another confusing thing about him is that even though he's a goofy guy, he makes a big deal out of student laughter in class. It really bothers him. He only laughs when *he* wants to, which is confusing and unnerving and downright unfair. Plus, he laughed on the first day, which completely skewed our expectations. If he didn't want us to laugh, he should've refused to smile or laugh until Christmas like the rest of my teachers.

I imagine Christmas for most teachers is one big laugh fest. A real "brouhaha," as Mr. Morgan once said. I bet they all sit around an open fire roasting chestnuts, sipping eggnog. At first they talk about Christmas vacation and favorite students and least favorite students like Denny "Donuts" Murphy and that bag of a principal and teacher romances and a new super-duper online grading system that's really "high-tech"—oh, and a new lunch spot near school whose spinach wraps are supposedly *fabulous*.

And then it happens. Someone laughs. Maybe it's about the way Barry called that Web site "high-tech," or maybe it's the eggnog, but suddenly everything is so bellyachingly funny and everyone is laughing so hard they fall over themselves and knock over each other's glasses. It's not funny, not in the least bit—I mean, *someone* has to keep the place tidy—but it's the funniest thing they've ever seen. Their laughter spills on the hardwood floors and they follow. Middle-aged bodies in blouses and sweaters sloshing around in eggnog. It looks like they're swimming. One-handed. They clutch their stomachs because they're laughing so hard it hurts.

Carolyn finally comes up for air, recapping all those *classic* classroom scenes she wanted to laugh at but couldn't and now she finally can, thank you Lord, she finally can, which is even more hilarious because Carolyn now has eggnog in her nostrils. Someone suggests they make a movie called *Eggnog in Carolyn's Nostrils* and everyone laughs so hard a few of them begin to worry about their health, which is a legitimate concern given Murray's history of chest pains, but even *that's* suddenly funny: "Murray's chest pains, HA! He's got some chest all right!"

Everyone agrees that it's one of those classic evenings they'll be talking about for weeks to come. But a few weeks later someone, probably Murray, realizes in the shower or wherever he does his best thinking that nothing, not a single thing that anyone said that Christmas night, was even the least bit funny.

Murray calls Carolyn who calls Barry because she needs to "talk about that night, that they all may have a very serious problem, and it's high time they change strategies."

Halloween, they promise. It's a pact. Everyone must laugh by Halloween.

Mr. Morgan's class isn't like that Christmas eggnog scene. It is orderly and structured with clear limits and laws. We wait in lines inside and outside of the room. We are prisoners and he is the gatekeeper. For the most part, we're willing prisoners, because, for the most part, he's an effective gatekeeper. We're not allowed to talk in line. Or laugh. Or roll our eyes. Or suck our teeth. No noise. No movement, especially once he's greeted the class in the hall with a welcoming "Good morning, readers and writers" and a stern "Leave the hormones in the hallways."

On our way in, we pick up a handout on which I plan to revise the "Life is good!" heading, especially if the class gets boring and once it's clear he's not collecting it. Inside, the desks are straight and the room smells like cleaning spray. Mr. Morgan stands at the front, sunglasses down, and proclaims today's law: "We have a project." *Crap.* "It is worth two hundred points." *Crap.* "It is about a play." *Crap.* "You must select a scene and perform it in a creative manner." *Okay.* "It is a group project." *He might as well say it's Christmas.*

Group projects, gotta love 'em. You get to meet new people, learn new material, do no work, and get good grades. Plus, talking isn't only allowed, it's encouraged! Where do teachers come up with this stuff? Gods and goddesses, I'm telling you.

Mr. Morgan likes to choose books above our level because he claims he teaches a high school course. I think he's in the wrong place, but nobody has enough nerve to tell him. We're reading excerpts from *Death of a Salesman*, a real inspiring, uplifting play by Arthur Miller about an old salesman who kills himself. A real Sunday morning picker-upper. I sort of like it, though. I mean, Willy Loman, the salesman, gets frustrated by everyone around him, which reminds me of my dad, and not just because he's a sales-man. But unlike my dad, Willy Loman crashes his car on purpose so his son gets an insurance payout. I'm not saying I want my dad to crash *our* car for insurance money or any-thing. I'm just saying.

Anyway, Mr. Morgan starts every class with a Do-Now, which is what everyone is supposed to DO NOW (hence the creative name), RIGHT NOW, and today's Do-Now is to pair up for our group project. Pairing up is the only bad part because my reputation for group projects is battered, bruised, and busted. Stay away, that's the general feeling.

Quietly and orderly, in line with class laws, students stand up and arrange their partnerships. I also stand up, but there's nowhere to go. I count: twenty-seven students, thir-teen pairs, and me. *Where are the Rockafellas when you need 'em?* Come to think of it, even *they* wouldn't pair up with me on a group project. Too much of a risk. Can't say I blame 'em.

"Looks like I'm riding solo this time, Mr. Morgan!" I holler, so everyone can hear. Best to draw attention to yourself in times likes these. "I guess everyone forgot what an intellectual powerhouse I am at English!"

Mr. Morgan shakes his head.

"Why are you shaking your head, Mr. Morgan? You don't think I'm an intellectual powerhouse?"

He shoots me a stare that says, "Homey don't play that." So I don't play that.

"Denny, get started," he says, even though he hasn't finished giving directions. Turns out, I don't need them because the door opens and in walks Sabrina, my poetess, of course with an excused late pass, and a grade point average that could batter mine in a fight, which is relevant to the scene at hand because after Mr. Morgan nods in my direction, Sabrina looks about ready to fight. "We're partners!" I scream. "Welcome to partnership. Aren't you so happy!"

Some people have a hard time displaying their happiness. "Mr. Morgan, you've got to be kidding me," Sabrina counters.

"It's a group project," he says.

"Not with *him* as my partner. Mr. Morgan, he doesn't even know what *Death of a Salesman* is about."

This is my cue. "I beg your pardon! I do so know what it's about." *I* may know what it's about, but Donuts the Entertainer doesn't have a clue. "*Death of a Salesman* is a fine play about the Grim Reaper trying to convince people to die. He's a salesman who goes door-to-door asking if anyone has had enough and wants to join him on the Dark Side. It's a chilling play. So cold it belongs in the freezer."

Again, Mr. Morgan's stare. He knows I'm kidding because he knows everything. After all, he *is* the omniscient god of English. "Work with him, Sabrina," he says.

"Yeah, work with me, Sabrina."

"*With* him, not *for* him," he says, but I wasn't listening when he said that.

Sabrina sits down in a huff.

"Oh, and Denny," Mr. Morgan adds, "your partnership will work better if you stop staring at her. She doesn't like you."

CHECKING IN

Hello. This is Mary Quentin—Mrs. Q, Denny's math teacher. I'm concerned about your son, Denny. He hasn't come to my class in—a while now. I know he's going through a lot. I was so sorry to hear of his—your wife's passing. I'm hoping you could come in for a meeting as soon as possible. Perhaps this afternoon? That would be great."

Beep. "You have no more messages." Beep. "Message erased." Beep.

No way I'm gonna let my dad hear that one. He'd have a heart attack and collapse right on the kitchen floor and I'd have to give him mouth-to-mouth resuscitation, which would be the first time I put my lips anywhere near his face since . . . well, I don't remember the last time. Maybe at my first baseball game. One other time he kissed me in the ear. He had tried to peck me on the cheek after I gave him a birthday present but I moved at the last second, as if a bee were buzzing on my face. It was bad, but not as bad as it'll be listening to Mrs. Q's message and then having to bring my dad back to life. And unlike Willy Loman's kids in *Death of a Salesman*, I don't stand to benefit from his departure. And don't want him to go anyway. So I erase it.

The next morning before the sun rises, with my backpack so stuffed and weighed down it feels like I'm carrying a hippopotamus, I arrive at school ready for Day Two of I.M.P. But with the hallways so empty, I definitely don't feel like the hippest of hippopotami. Manny isn't here. Isn't anywhere. Despite the boulders on my shoulders, and my ability to rhyme about it and maybe become a professional poet who doesn't have to sell candy to be liked, I peek down every hallway. No sign of Manny and it's already sixteen minutes past our meeting time. I start going through my list of reasons he didn't show: he overslept, his cousin Kenny lost his Costco card and he and Manny fought about it and Manny got beat up, he skipped town and joined up with pirates who liked his business savvy because it gave them reason to say "savvy," he decided to keep all the candy profits and never show his face again, his mom took another break, Mr. Perfect came back from the grave and recruited Manny to go on tour . . . and that's when I start hearing voices. Yikes, that sounded bad. I mean, from down the hall, and I realize Manny must not have gotten to *his* answering machine on time.

I take cover, and by "take cover" I mean that I scrunch myself into as small a ball as possible in the corner of the hallway, perpendicular—as Mrs. Q would say—to the on-coming voices.

"Thank you for coming in so early, Ms. Templeton. I'm Mrs. Tice, the school social worker."

Mrs. Tice's soothing voice gives me comfort and stresses me out. Always has. She helped me talk about my mom at the beginning, but then I didn't want to talk about her any-more.

"It's not like I had a choice," Manny's mom says. "This was the only time I could come in."

"Well, thank you, and nice to see you, Manny."

"Look, I don't know what to tell you, Mrs. Tice. My son Manny just lies around the house doing nothing. I don't know why he doesn't come to school more often. He says he doesn't feel well, but who knows? He stays at home all day long. A bum, that's what he is, like his father."

"Let's step into my office, shall we, Ms. Templeton? It's down the hall but it's private. We can talk more there."

As I peek around the corner with one eye, my body as crouched as humanly or hippopotamus-ly possible, Manny comes into sight. He looks smaller and shorter and skinnier than usual. With each step he takes toward me, it looks like he's shrinking, leaking his body weight on the cold hallway floors. Or maybe his backpack is just *that* much bigger than he is. When he sees me, his face drops, like it, too, is losing fluid, but then instead of running away or shielding himself from view, his eyes go big. He mouths a few words to me that I don't understand. So I mouth back, *Huh? What?* He gives me a thumbs-up with one hand, and with the other, he points to the merchandise on his back. *Still a go,* he mouths. *Still on.*

"Look, I don't need to sit down or anything. I don't need to stay long. I gotta get back to work, you know? I mean, I know Manny's got nothing to do, but I gotta work. Gotta pay the bills. Somebody's gotta do some work, you know?"

Manny's mom, skinnier even than her son, is walking faster than anyone, her arms in full swing, her face full of makeup twitching with every rapid step she takes.

"I really can't stay, Mrs. Tice. I wouldn't even be here in the first place if the school hadn't threatened to call the Administration for Children's Services, or ACS, or whatever you people call it. Like I don't have enough to worry about. I can't take much more of this. I got a heart problem, you know? This isn't good for me. I just want to go to work. I'm sick of this. I feel like washing my hands of him, you know?"

"I know you're frustrated, Ms. Templeton, but let's talk in private in my office, if you don't mind."

"Look, I really gotta go to work. They make the schedule when you get there. They got some people working overtime on one day, and other people working overtime other days. There's no consistency. And the traffic on the turnpike . . . you gotta be kidding me. Twenty minutes to drive one mile!

I could walk a mile in less time, not that I would, given my heart problem."

"I understand. It'll be quick, I promise. Let's just get into my office and—"

"I'm trying to be nice here, I really am, but I gotta go to work, you know? And Manny's gotta—well, he's gotta whole lot of nothing to do today, so he's got some catching up to do . . ."

That's the last thing I hear, as their voices fade down the hall. The last thing I see is Manny turning around with a thumbs-up, a silent laugh, and a wide cartoonish smile that I know from plenty of personal experience he's faking.

HUNGRY PEOPLE

This morning never happened," Manny says to me, wiping his eyes on the way to lunch. I understand him not wanting to talk about it, so I don't say anything.

"It is just—" he starts, "she is not like your mom," and now *I* don't want to talk about it. Don't want to hear him talk again about how he misses my mom and how she was a better mother than his and how lucky I was, still am, and how he's still sad, too, and how we need to distract ourselves with our candy scheme. Instead of answering his comparison of our moms, I get missile-straight to the fund-raising operation when we enter the lunchroom by telling him, "The mission is a go." He doesn't say "Roger that" like I want him to, but at least he nods, takes off his backpack, and gets down to business.

* * *

In this, our second GRAND OPENING lunchtime extravaganza bonanza fund-raiser, I feel like a wanderer, a nomad, going table to table with a message and a murmur: "Yo, I got that Reese's" . . . "I got that Heath Bar" . . . "Y'all better believe I got that Butterfinger." And then, slowly but surely, like the Girl Scouts dreamed it up when they invested in uniforms, our lunchtime customers come to me, keeper of the candy flock, local shepherd and conqueror of *Level 1: Hungry People*. Never, in all my almost thirteen years of existence, have I been so wildly popular, in demand and on demand. DONUTS ON DEMAND. You can have me whenever you want me, as long as your favorite snack is still on the shelf. The shelf being my book bag. And halfway through the day, the shelves are empty. I've completely sold out. In a good way.

Day Two profits: $126 from me, $112 from Manny.

Dear February: In case you didn't receive the memo, you have been asked to leave. Instead, you have brought rain and darkness by the time I approach our front door when I come home from school. My dad, as usual, is at the kitchen table. "No more," he says, biting his lip, and I know what's coming: *Cut the act, you junky food dealer. No more candy conquering.*

Someone must have called home again. Mrs. Q again, Mr. Softee—

"I came home today and I could have sworn there was

more chicken"—his hands are shaking now—"but there wasn't. There wasn't any left."

On the tiled kitchen floor, I let my backpack drop, which doesn't take a whole lot of effort. Eighty-three pounds at the start of the day, now down to five. Thankfully, none of my English papers spill out this time, which makes life ~~good~~ bearable for the moment. "Dad, it's fine," I tell him.

"It's *not* fine. I wanted a relaxing night after a long day and . . ."

He bobs his head up and down like a chicken. He must really miss his chicken.

"How about Chinese?" he asks.

We squeeze into his old green Buick—well, *he* squeezes, I just sit—and as soon as he turns the key, National Public Radio is already cued as loud as it can go, which isn't that loud because the hosts sound like they're reading the newspaper on a snowy Sunday morning with a mug of hot apple cider by their side, but it's still loud enough that my dad doesn't have to talk to me and I can look out my window without him getting angry, or lonely, or impatient.

The car smells like last week's lunch gone sour. I'd look around for a lunch box, a paper bag, moldy Tupperware, but he never packs a lunch. "Tomorrow," he always says, "I'll pack it tomorrow." On the backseat, a mess of take-out menus, tissue balls, tissue boxes, bent folders, two umbrellas, and a black dress shirt crumpled into a ball.

On the radio, a soothing voice, so soothing it sounds like a whisper—*I'm Kai Ryssdal, and this is Marketplace*—then a choir of flutes. I bet that Kai Ryssdal has a swell life. I bet he wakes up every morning with his pillows nice and fluffy. I check to see if my dad is still awake, not that he has a history of passing out behind the wheel, but I'd understand if he did now. Those flutes and Kai Ryssdal's melodious voice make me want to close my eyes and look around for a few sheep. So I do.

There are thousands and thousands of sheep. In the meadow, on the farm, grazing through high grass, munching on hay. There are too many sheep and not enough space. They pile in tightly, squeezing up next to one another. The sheep get mad, really mad. *Baaaaaa,* they cry. There are newspapers on the ground. The sheep look down and read the headline. It's bad news, really bad news. A new shipment of sheep is on its way. The sheep don't like this news. *Baaaaaa,* they cry, and stomp their hooves in protest. The other sheep join in. Newspapers are dirtied, shredded, destroyed. But the shipment arrives on schedule. A thousand more sheep. They fight over space, but it's no use. *Baaaaaa,* they cry. There's no more room on the ground; stacking is the only option. The sheep stand on top of each other. There are piles and piles of sheep to count, all over the green meadow. Hundreds of sheep piles. Another shipment of sheep comes in. The piles get bigger. They approach the sky. *Baaaaaa,* the sheep cry. There are hundreds and thousands of sheep, and no sign anywhere of sleep, which isn't a bad thing because the restaurant's only five minutes away from our house and we're already here.

Hunan Palace. Against a black misty sky, a pink sign buzzes with missing letters. Or maybe they meant to advertise as Hunan Pal. Friendlier that way, more chummy: *You got a pal at Hunan Pal.*

I hope not. I really hope there are no pals here. You see, I've never been part of the United States Secret Service, but going out to dinner with the Natural Schmoozer can't be much different. Climbing out of the car in the wet cold, it swallows me: the paranoia, the fear that someone at my school is lurking, watching, waiting, dining with their friends and family, strolling through the parking lot, swapping tongues in a parked car. The exhaustive searches, scanning the premises—someone will be here already, will suddenly appear, a drive-by, a drive-through, a driver with a big mouth, a sniper with a smartphone, a classmate with a computer, a familiar face from Facebook. I need a suit and sunglasses, Secret Service–style, a baseball hat, makeup, a fake mustache, a fake dad, a motorcycle for a quick getaway. I look left, I look right, I look down, I look up and say a prayer that the coast is clear, that there is no threat—yes, I am a scared member of the Secret Service, but my dad is too big, too unpredictable. If he loses his cool, the gig's up. All those carefully timed jokes, pranks, and performances. My public persona, so carefully chipped and carved and crafted, will crumble into pebbles, and all I'll have left is just Denny Murphy, an eternal life of loserdom, and my dad. I must be vigilant, be vigilant, c'mon, be vigilant. I peek through the restaurant's frosty windows, past a bubbling tank of pink and yellow fish. As a Secret Service agent, I fight an urge to protect the fish. Would I take a bullet for them? Silly question. Small fish don't get shot. Would I take a net for a fish? As long as it got me out of having to dine with the Natural Schmoozer.

I continue scanning. A man in a blue shirt and yellow tie at a corner booth, eating with his wife and two young sons. One looks eight, the other six. They're strangers. Green light, they're safe. A family of eight at the middle table. A grandmother in a flowery blouse, her husband in a black button-down shirt. Green light. Their kids all over forty. Green light. Three grandchildren still too young for Blueberry Hills. Green light. One grandchild is a teenager. Hooped earrings. Stranger. Green light. A young couple in the back, slurping hot and sour soup; the girl is a green light, the guy's a yellow light. His back is turned. His hair is gelled to the side like no one I've ever seen, but Secret Service agents can never be too sure. There, now he turns around for the waiter. Green light. An older man walks back from the bathroom to his family. He doesn't teach at my school. Green light. His daughter has long, flowing blond hair and that's all I can see. Yellow light. I bend down to tie my shoes, my head tilted to the side for a better view.

"Denny, what are you doing?" my dad grunts.

I see her profile. Green light.

"Nothing, Dad, good to go." It's safe to enter, so I do. A string of bells on the door signals our entrance. The restaurant smells of fish and soy sauce.

The manager, a thin man with a thin black mustache and thinning black hair, is smiling behind the counter. Then he sees my dad enter.

He is no longer smiling. His face drops—sagging cheeks, heavy eyes, like Mrs. Q sensing impending doom upon my arrival, or Sabrina walking into an unwanted group partnership.

We have a history here. My dad does. It's not a good one. But a customer is a customer. "Welcome," the manager says. Such a pal. Everyone is a pal at the Hunan Pal.

The host guides us to an empty booth. Cue the stares, the double takes, the whispers about my dad's weight. At the middle table a grandson in a blue turtleneck doesn't whisper: "WHOA, LOOK AT HOW FAT HE IS, MOMMY!"

His brother elbows him. "Shhh, don't say that so loud. But that guy sure is fat."

They both laugh.

The girl with the long flowing hair turns her head. "Yikes," she says.

From the back of the restaurant, the guy with gelled hair turns around and fights a smile. He doesn't fight hard enough. *Soon, WE'LL have to fight,* I want to shout, but I don't want to draw any more attention than we already have and I don't want to fight him unless I really have to because he'd ~~probably~~ definitely beat me up.

Seated, my dad and I gaze at the pandas on the walls, avoiding each other until a waiter balancing a tray full of water glasses hands us two menus. He must be new here.

"No, no, *no*," my dad growls, "I want the Chinese menu."

"Sir?" Eyebrows raised. "I'm sorry?"

"I want authentic Chinese food, what *real* Chinese people eat."

"I'm sorry, sir," he says, "I don't understand."

(I don't understand either, though we've been through this before.)

"Just bring me the Chinese menu!"

The whole room is closing in and I am trapped. I feel like a mouse locked in a cage. Of Chinese food. The waiter blinks. Water glasses rattle on his tray. He throws me a desperate glance, but I can't help him. I am a mouse.

The Natural Schmoozer smooths out his napkins, mumbling to himself. All I catch are the words "ridiculous," "damn," "quit," "broccoli," "service," and "can't."

In the kitchen someone's blasting a fast-paced Katy Perry song, and it's hard to tell which one it is because they're all exactly the same and I want to shut it off, shut it off, shut it off, stop, stop thinking about it, but it's better than looking at my dad, and *way* better than listening to National Public Radio, especially that Kai Ryssdal.

The waiter returns with two red menus with Chinese writing, even "Hunan Palace" is in Chinese. He tentatively places them on our table.

"Do I *look* like I speak Chinese?" my dad huffs.

"But, sir—"

"I need you to translate."

"But, sir, I don't speak Chinese."

"Just bring us what Chinese people eat!"

The waiter's face turns powder white. I watch him turn around and power walk to the manager at the front of the restaurant, and that's when I notice I've failed as a member of the Secret Service.

A girl walks in with her parents.

She's wearing a black hooded sweatshirt and her hair is parted over her right eye. She has a stud on her nose and a Batman bracelet on her left wrist.

Red light.

Sabrina can't see me like this. Can't see my dad like this. I toss my napkin on the table. "Dad, we need to go."

He's breathing harder. "As a paying customer, I demand— Denny—I've gotten it here before and—they need to—it's not fair and I know—you know—I—"

"Dad, it's okay. Here, take a sip of water."

The manager smiles at Sabrina and her parents. They smile back. Her dad removes his black coat and helps his wife out of her beige one. He hangs them up on the rack. "Right this way," says the host.

I look away.

"Dad, I'm going to the bathroom."

Before Sabrina can see me or my dad can tell me to sit back down, I hustle to the bathroom and lock the door. I wish this were a movie and I wish I were a trained member of the Secret Service, but I'm not. I try to make out an exit strategy through the bathroom, but there is no air-conditioning vent to pop out. No escape behind the paper towel rack, or behind the cracked toilet and out through the pipes.

Crumpled paper towels on the floor with footprints. Water on the sink. A flickering light. I feel dirty and then dirtier, because above the sink I see the blue sign, EMPLOYEES MUST WASH THEIR HANDS, which is obviously an admission that employees *don't* wash their hands—or at least had a history of not washing them.

How comforting to know the employees at Hunan Pal need a reminder to wash their hands after doing their business. The restaurant should just come out and say it: "Our employees don't always wash their hands. We wish they did, but they don't. Sometimes, after they wipe, they get distracted. They think about the day's errands, relationships gone sour, the score of the game, a new ingredient to add to your chow mein. Hey, they're only human. We'd fire our employees for poor hygiene, but we're all pals here at the Hunan Pal and like to keep it light. Enjoy your meal."

I need to get out of here and I don't just mean the bathroom. I walk with my head down the whole way back to our table. I must look like a pouty kid after a tantrum, but I can't make eye contact. I count seven stains on the green carpet before I plop into my seat. When I look up, the manager is headed our way. A smile is plastered to his face. "Ah, Mr. Murphy, good evening, sir. The Chinese menu again?"

My dad nods.

"Not a problem, sir. How are you this evening?"

Another nod.

"We're good!" I tell him, loud enough for Sabrina to hear. "We're really good. Swell, even. So swell we're swollen. We're swelling swellness. Oozing it, actually. Thank you for asking."

The manager bows and points to the Chinese menu in front of my dad. "Having difficulty deciding what to order?"

I touch his arm. "Hunan chicken is good, Dad. It's spicy and crunchy and delicious. We should get that."

He takes another sip of water.

The manager takes out a pen and pad, his first mistake.

"Something good," my dad grunts. "Give me what the Chinese eat."

"Give me what the Chinese eat isn't *technically* an order," the manager points out, which makes my dad raise his voice and other parents gawk and their kids once again whisper, "Look at how fat he is, Mommy."

"JUST BRING ME WHAT I WANT!" my dad thunders.

I don't want to, but I steal a peek at Sabrina. She's looking at us. Everyone is looking at us. Especially the young grandson with the blue turtleneck. He's having a good ol' time. And I can no longer look up. The napkins on the table are red and the silverware is shiny. I turn them over in my hand.

Ten years pass. We are graying and aging at the speed of light.

When the food arrives, my dad sends it back, telling the waiter, loud enough for the whole restaurant to hear, that the food is too hot or too cold or too burnt or simply not good. I don't know exactly what he says because I've been trying to plan an exit route to minimize humiliation, but I haven't yet come up with any ideas.

"Dad, it's fine," I beg, my eyes fixed on the tablecloth.

"Are you paying? Because if *you're* paying, I'm content to eat what's in front of me, but if *I'm* paying, my food should be the way I want it, understand?"

My dad stands up. *Dad, NO! WAIT!* The words grab at my tongue, but it's too late. My dad stands up. And so does the table.

Glasses tip over, fall over, spill, crash, break. The Chinese menus slide down the table into small puddles of water on the floor. The manager grabs hold of the back of his head. I think he rips some hair out, but I don't want to look—at him, at his hair, the laughing children, Sabrina, or my dad, now storming out the door to a chorus of bells. But as I've said, it's hard not to look when you've told yourself not to, and though my face is flushed and I wish myself a sudden painless death, I could use a bit of assurance that Sabrina won't gab about the night's incidents to anyone.

I steal a glance. She doesn't look angry or judgmental or annoyed. Just, well, sad. *Don't tell anyone,* I say with my eyes, but I'm not sure she understands.

February never got my memo, so why should she?

Outside the restaurant, my dad walks aimlessly across the parking lot. Beads of rain stick to the ends of his wispy hair, like someone sprayed the water out of a bottle.

I jog up to him and put my arm around his wide shoulders. His clothes smell. "Don't worry about it," I say. "The employees don't even wash their hands here."

He doesn't answer.

"Seriously, Dad. They don't wash their hands here. They admitted it in the bathroom. You should've seen the sign. It's a low-down dirty establishment any way you slice it. We're better off without them. Hey, you in the mood for fried chicken?"

He leans over with his arms against his legs, as if he's out of breath. "You okay, Dad? Seriously, you okay? I'm not mad. Are you okay? C'mon, stand up straight."

On his way up, he wipes his eyes with the back of his hand and says, so softly I barely hear it, "I miss her."

Then he looks away from me, across the parking lot. All I can see are one sideburn and the side of his eye, wet and distant. "I—I miss her," he says.

I do, too.

So I tell him: "I do, too."

THE WAY IT WAS

It's spring. Not just any spring day, though. My tenth birthday. Spring Training has ended and the season has started and the Phillies have a home game with over 40,000 screaming fans and I am one of them. It's my first game, so the grass is the most beautiful thing I've ever seen. Greener than the greenest green. Greener than a neon highlighter named "The Greenest Green Ever Invented." The chalk lines are as straight as rulers, the dirt looks clean, and I can't wait to tell everyone about this incredible thing called "the wave," and then spread it to my fourth grade class, and then to other grades, and then to the world. It's that *cool.*

From the second level, the players look bright and important, and their arms have muscles in places I've never seen muscles in before. I'm wearing a red Phillies shirt and a Phillies hat. In my hands, another Phillies hat, this one miniature-size and filled with vanilla ice cream and chocolate syrup. "Nothing better than a sundae on a Sunday," my dad says, diving in for a spoonful.

"Da-ad," I whine, though I know I shouldn't. "Da-ad, that bite was huge! You said you wouldn't take a daddy bite."

He shrugs. "It was a daddy bite. But Daddy's paying." He rubs my head and squishes my hat and I can't help but smile. "It's your birthday—if you want another, we can get another. You can take a daddy bite from my ice cream."

I look up at him. "Thanks," I say, and I don't mean about the ice cream. I mean about the game. I tell him that.

He rubs my head again, then turns back to the game, so I do, too. I'm out of ice cream but it doesn't matter. Chase Utley is up to bat and the bases are loaded and the field is still green. I hope the game goes into extra innings so we can stay longer. Somebody should tell the players that they can play longer if the score is tied. And someone should tell the guy who starts the wave that I'm ready for another round.

It's summer. A few months later. We're watching home movies. My mom is next to me on the sofa. We're sharing a large blanket with a tiger on it because the air conditioner is turned up high. Even though it's freezing, my dad is in the kitchen eating his third ice cream sandwich. He has taken more than a few daddy bites. But he's not joking or laughing about it. "Stupid paper wrapper," he mutters. "Always getting stuck to the sandwich."

My mom fast-forwards to her favorite scene: she's in a red rocking chair, cradling me as an infant, rubbing the top of my head while singing about how I am her sunshine.

I want her to finish the song but my dad is making too much noise *crumpling up his wrapper. My mom presses Pause and we both tell him to "Shhhh."*

He looks confused. "What? I'm not allowed to throw out my garbage?"

"Honey—" she starts, but my dad has already stormed out of the room.

"Mom?" I ask.

"Yes, my sunshine?" She rubs the top of my head and I let her, even though I'm now ten years old, nine years older than I am in the home movie.

"What's wrong with Dad?" I ask.

"He's sad," she says.

"Why is he sad?"

She closes her eyes.

"Mom?" I ask.

"Yes, my sunshine?"

"Do you wanna finish the movie?"

She smiles, presses Play.

It's Tuesday, September 12th, still technically summer, but fifth grade started a week ago and I'm as mad as a fire-breathing dragon. So is my mom. We're both as mad as fire-breathing dragons, and the temperature inside my mom's car is as hot as a fire-breathing dragon's breath.

A gas attendant is sweating through his backward hat, filling up a red car to the left of ours. I'm in the backseat, wearing mesh shorts. My legs are sweaty and stuck to the cracked leather seats. My mom won't turn around and look at me because I'm the one that turned her into a fire-breathing dragon, which makes my legs even sweatier, and the gas attendant won't look at my mom, which makes her breath even fierier, but I don't care that she's angry because I don't understand why she won't listen to what happened to me at school and why I came home late.

My day was going fine, just fine. Manny and I played paper football during lunch, we had a substitute in history class, and my English teacher, who has a great sense of humor, said I have a great sense of humor and announced that I wrote the best and funniest similes and metaphors in the entire grade, but then in science Mike Whitman got assigned as my lab partner, and instead of doing the experiment he flung rubber bands across the room, and the teacher, Mrs. Skidich, kept us both for detention. "You are lab partners," she said. "The key word being 'partners.'" I said that I didn't choose my partner, which I thought was a great point, but Mrs. Skidich raised her right hand, her symbol for silence. "Sometimes, Denny, in life, we have to do things we don't want to do," she said. "Sometimes we have to take responsibility for our actions."

"But they weren't my actions!" I yelled, which I thought was another excellent point, but Mrs. Skidich got so angry—"offended," she said—at the level of my voice that she kept me for thirty minutes longer than Mike Whitman. I said it wasn't fair—I didn't even yell it—but she raised her hand and said, "Sometimes, Denny, life isn't fair."

The gas attendant with the backward hat is finally walking over to our car. His biceps look swollen, like they got stung by a whole family *of bees on a family picnic in Stingsville. The gas attendant doesn't go to Stingsville. He goes to Blueberry Hills High School. It says that on his school football shirt. I wish I were in high school, where students pick their own lab partner and teachers don't raise their hands like queens to silence students.*

Stupid Mike Whitman. Stupid Mrs. Skidich. I hope they're both having miserable afternoons. I hope their cars run out of gas on the side of the road and their legs get so sweaty that they get permanently stuck to the seats. And when the police arrive, they'll say they need to use the Jaws of Life to separate their sweaty, stuck legs from the seats. And when Mike Whitman and Mrs. Skidich put up a fight, the police will tell them, "Sometimes, in life, we have to do things we don't want to do. Sometimes we have to take responsibility for our actions."

"What can I get you, ma'am?" the gas attendant asks.

I wish I were big and strong with swollen bee-sting biceps so that I could pound Mike Whitman's face in. I wouldn't hit Mrs. Skidich because I don't hit females, but I'd yell loud enough to wake a whole family of bees way out in Stingsville.

"Fill it——" My mom's voice is cracking like cracks on the street would if they could talk. "With regular."

I know she's upset, more upset than she normally gets about picking me up late from school, but I don't want to ask her what's wrong because she should've listened to my story before blaming me. She should've asked me what's wrong.

Stupid Mike Whitman and Mrs. Skidich, that's what's wrong. And my mom not listening to my story. Well, now I'm not listening to her. The battle is on, like we're playing Battleship in the middle of an important battlefield and I have the coolest battle scars ever invented, and I will outlast my mom and not ask what's wrong.

My mom is making crying noises. I think it's a real cry, but maybe she's just trying to win the battle. I lean forward and put my ear against the back of her seat and listen closely. It's definitely a real cry. She sounds like a sheep would if a sheep could cry like a human mom, and I'm happy about this because it means that she's probably really mad at Mrs. Skidich for ruining her afternoon, and then my mom will be on my team, Team Mad at Mrs. Skidich, and everything will be okay.

"Do you want your receipt, ma'am?" the gas attendant asks.

I squint one last look at his bee-sting biceps and promise myself to lift weights once I'm old enough for them not to stunt my growth. Sweats sticks to my forehead. The air is so thick I could swim home from here. But I think I'd get lost. I have a terrible sense of direction when I'm swimming and always bump into the ropes or wall or people.

My mom takes the receipt and rolls up the window.

I don't want to lose the battle, but I can't help but put my hand on her bony shoulders. They're shaking—no, shivering, like a ghost after an outdoor shower in the back of a beach house in a season other than summer.

"Mom, what's wrong?" I ask.

She shakes her head. I hope it's nothing really serious, like Dad getting fired from his job and thrown in a pit of fire or getting breathed on by fire-breathing dragons. Okay, I know fire-breathing dragons aren't really real, but in the third grade my classmate's dad was fired and I'm pretty sure he was thrown in a pit of fire.

"Mom, I'm sorry about what happened in school," I tell her, abandoning my battle plan. "I shouldn't have yelled at Mrs. Skidich. I'm sorry."

It's not working and she's starting to scare me because she never cries in public and we're definitely in public. The green car behind us honks and a guy wants us to move the hell out of the way. "Hey, move the hell out of the way." That's what he says. He wants to get gas, too. He sticks his arm out the window and honks again. He has a lot of arm hair. I want to punch him for yelling at my mom, but people with a lot of arm hair can usually beat me up (with their fists, not their arm hair).

"Mom, wanna hear a joke?" I ask.

"Honey—" She reaches for a tissue.

"But, Mom, it's a really good one. It's clean, I promise."

Another honk from the green car and a shout to "C'mon, move it!"

I shoot him the stare of death, and though my eyes are like a thousand daggers rolled into two, it doesn't kill him. It doesn't even make him blink. He honks again, this time longer, much longer, so long that I think his horn got stuck, like how my mom always told me my eyes would get if I rolled them back too far.

"Mom, don't worry about him," I tell her. "He's just having a bad day. Like me. Okay, Mom? Don't worry. Don't worry about anything."

I know it's unfair, like life, to keep the green car waiting, but Mrs. Skidich said that life isn't fair, so he can just stay there all day—

"Denny—" she says, between breaths.

The horn stops, then starts again, like a song or a car or a bicycle *or a motorcycle or an air conditioner or an alarm that stops and then starts again.*

I don't think she even hears the horn because she turns around and looks at me. Her eyes look old. Tired. They don't look anything like a fire-breathing dragon's eyes, unless it's an old, tired fire-breathing dragon with no more fire in her belly or throat.

"Denny," she says. "I'm sick."

THE WITNESS

Manny's absence from school puts a damper on the day's candy sales, but on the bright side, it gives me more of a chance to learn. On the dark side, I am still a middle school prisoner. In line again. This time in the back because Sabrina, a witness to the Natural Schmoozer's latest restaurant breakdown, is the last person I want to see, and she's at the front of the line. But after Mr. Morgan, the S.U.O.G.E., greets us and reminds us to check our hormones at the door, his order comes down fast and swift, like the ax of a lumberjack. In a red woolen sweater, which makes him look even more like a lumberjack, he pulls me aside on the way in and reads me a verdict that smells of coffee. "I know you've been dealing with a lot, but you must work like a contributing member of the human species on this project with Sabrina, in and out of school, Denny, or you will get an F."

"Fine by me, Mr. Morgan. My middle name is Frank. F for Frank."

He tilts his shades down. "If you don't pass English, you *will* repeat the course, probably in summer school."

"That's okay, Mr. Morgan. I wouldn't mind spending some more time with you."

"Wish I could say the same."

"*Classic* Mr. Morgan!"

I force a laugh.

He keeps a really good straight face.

As we enter the room and he reminds everyone to sit silently, I say to him, "You're just playing, right, Mr. Morgan?"

He points to his HOMEY DON'T PLAY THAT sign.

"But, Mr. Morgan, we're homeys, remember?"

Apparently Mr. Morgan is getting old and forgets obvious things such as the fact that we're homeys, which is why, hours after a class full of Mr. Morgan's gentle prodding to do group work—"NOW, DO IT NOW, OR FINISH TOGETHER FOR HOMEWORK"—while I try to avoid Sabrina's eyes the same way my dad and I did at the restaurant, I am standing on her driveway in the freezing cold, looking at my breath. (Dear February, please leave.)

I thank my dad for the ride. He says, "Sure, no problem, it was my pleasure. Glad to help out," and then I stop fantasizing and hear him grunt and watch him drive off, his old Buick coughing a cloud of smoke down the street.

Sabrina's house is a ranch like mine, painted white with blue shutters. There's a white cat on the steep roof that scares the bejesus out of me. It's right in the middle, looking down with its blue eyes, and it's not even moving because it's so scared, and I know what I must do. I'm going to rescue it and save the day like a fireman or a lumberjack who fights fires in his spare time and—

"It's not real," she says, pushing the screen door open.

She's wearing a gray sweatshirt, flannel pants, and blue dolphin slippers.

"Of course not," I say, playing it cool. "Please, don't be ridiculous. Slippers made out of real dolphin? Come on! But we really should hurry because—"

"The cat," she says. "It's not real. It's made of ceramic."

"What—oh, pshhh, don't you think I know? Please, I love ceramics. I love painting ceramics at Color Me Mine. I'm a regular there. I have my own cup of paintbrushes. There's a shelf of my finished artwork displayed as examples."

She smiles and brushes her hair to the side. She has hazel eyes. She's pretty and wearing no makeup. I don't know what to do next but I hope it has nothing to do with breathing.

"Come in," she says, so I do.

Her house reminds me of Mr. Morgan's classroom except I don't need to wait in line. It's neat and clean and smells like chamomile. It feels like a home. The fridge is covered with ribbons and tests with big fat A's, and at the top, a chore chart, with names and tasks and an orange pointer. Today is Wednesday and Sabrina has bathroom duty.

"Hey, Sabrina, I hope there aren't any duties during bathroom duty, if you know what I'm sayin', know what I'm sayin'."

I know it's immature, but the way she looks at me makes me nervous and I've never really been to a girl's house before, alone, and can't help myself. Besides, I'm grasping for anything to keep the conversation away from Hunan Palace.

"Remember, honey, there are cookies in the oven," says a motherly voice from down the hall. So much for the house to ourselves. "And remember, Sabrina, what we talked about. You need to leave your door *open*."

"O-kay!" Sabrina shouts, blushing.

"Just joking," I tell her. "About the duty. As you know, I like to joke. Love it. Lots of people think I'm an expert at it, that I should become a professional comedian."

"Interesting," she says. "I haven't yet met those people."

"Ha! Classic! Sounds like something I'd say."

"This way." She leads me down a long foyer with wooden shutters, past a massage chair in the den, the walls covered in photos. Sabrina as an infant with two front teeth. At Disney World, wearing a Goofy hat, flanked by smiles. At a dance recital in a white leotard and pigtails. Halloween, in a Wonder Woman costume with a bag full of candy. She and her dad at a Phillies game with matching red hats. At a picnic eating an ice cream cone with rainbow sprinkles, children running through grass around a statue of—

"Is that Lincoln Elementary?" I ask, though I already know the answer.

She leans in. She smells of strawberry shampoo. "I love that picture," she says, beaming. "Yeah, school picnic."

"I remember that day," I tell her. "All the moms were there—"

My chest hurts, like someone took an ice cream scooper to it and dug away.

She smiles. "My mom hates this picture because she's leaning over in the background. She never thought that when she leaned over in her mom jeans to pick up that Sprite bottle she'd be immortalized that way."

I squint for a better view. A wide blue butt is right over Sabrina's shoulder. "Classic!" I shout, which makes her laugh. "Now that's what I call *butting* into the picture. It's almost as if she posed for that shot."

To the left of Sabrina's mom's butt, two children throw a ball, and a woman cleans cookies off a small table of food. She has pink glasses, she—

Has on pink earrings, the ones I got for her birthday, and auburn hair, all of it, before the chemotherapy took it away. She—

Is wearing a *Simpsons* T-shirt, with Bart and a cartoon

bubble reading "Don't have a cow, man." The sun is shining. It's a beautiful day and everyone is healthy and playing and carefree and I'm not even in the picture, which means I'm not even near her. I was probably playing baseball, and I just left her alone to clean up after a bunch of sweaty children. I never looked around to see if she needed help and I never took a second to look around to see how good I had it. If I'd known she'd get sick, I'd have glued myself to her Siamese-style and never left her side. I'd clean up after myself and we'd watch movies—no, we'd do stuff together, talk more about our days and interests and dreams and hobbies and fears. She'd come to school with me and I'd get the best grades in the whole class because she's so smart and I'd be smart, too, because we'd read the same books, even the ones that sound boring and lame and confusing in the first chapter. I'd hold on to the books and I'd hold on to her and appreciate things more, *everything*, sunsets and—

"Come," she says. "This is my room."

I breathe in, but it feels like someone slammed the door on my lungs.

"Are you coming?"

"Yeah, I—"

"It's not *that* funny. I mean, I know the mom jeans are great, but— Are you okay?"

I nod.

"You sure?"

"Yeah, just got a little dizzy, that's all."

She doesn't look convinced but ushers me into her room anyway, leaving the door open. The floor is lined with light purple carpet. There are teddy bears on her bed, a desk that's cleaner than Mr. Morgan's, a foldout table with a slice of pineapple pizza, a can of Cherry Coke, and a laptop playing a Bruce Springsteen song. Even *that* doesn't cheer me up, not that it's a cheery song. My dad plays it all the time, which is all you need to know about the mood of the song. But still, thinking of Bruce, I know I need to perform. I can't let her see this side of me.

"Did you know, Sabrina, that my surfing performance in Mrs. Q's room was inspired by Bruce Springsteen? True story."

"Since when does Bruce surf?"

Good question.

She leans on her chair, looking so relaxed, so confident, so at ease in her questioning. Add that to the fact that she also bested Manny in a debate. She should seriously be a lawyer.

I give it my best shot anyway. "Bruce totally surfs. Listen to the song 'Atlantic City.' There are tons of beaches in Atlantic City. I bet you he surfs there all the time."

"How much you wanna bet?"

She puts her hand out. I'd love to touch it, but I need to hang on to all the $339 I've raised so far selling candy. "Not a betting man," I say.

"'Atlantic City' is *not* about surfing. Like most of his

songs, it's about a last chance. Getting beat down by life and trying to get back up. It's about pain."

She's right, I know it, but it's easier to pretend. "He probably fell off his surfboard," I explain. "Believe me, falling off a surfboard is pretty painful. When I fell off that desk and into . . . Here, let me reenact."

"No!"

I look around for something to leap onto, but all I see is her bed, which looks so nicely made I don't want to mess it up. I settle for an alternate performance. I strut up to a long mirror and strike a pose. While I'm here, I might as well strike a few more. "This mirror is a magic mirror, Sabrina. It makes me look really good."

She picks up her *Death of a Salesman* book. "Denny, stop acting."

"Acting? That's a negatory. 'Homey don't play that'—as you know, that's what Mr. Morgan likes to say. I also like to say this when people encourage me to fraternize with thespians on the stage. I'm just keeping it real, Sabrina. Telling it like it is, and the way I see it, I'm having a terrific hair day, wouldn't you agree?"

I wouldn't. My hair is blasting out on the sides.

She peeks down at her watch. "We should probably get started," she says.

"I *would* get started, Sabrina, I really would, but first I gotta dance a bit, loosen up, limber up my limbs—you know, get the blood flowing." I know I should stop but my legs are juking and jiving on her carpet, my hands crabwalking into breakdance position.

"Denny, I can't—please stop pretending. You don't need to pretend around me."

I stop in mid-breakdance, which, you should know, is difficult. "Pretend? I'm not a pretender, I'm a contender. Been training for the Golden Gloves for months."

"Denny, come on—"

"Don't believe me? Here, check this out." I nod toward the mirror. "Watch my shadowboxing skills." I throw playful punches at my reflection. Jab, jab, right cross, uppercut. "Check out these stellar combinations."

She stands up. "Denny, I saw you at the restaurant. I saw the whole thing."

"What thing?" Jab, uppercut.

"Dinner. Chinese. Hunan Palace. Your dad . . ."

"Oh, that? Psshh, doesn't everyone's dad do that?"

"Mine doesn't."

"Well, mine does. Yes, he certainly is very passionate about Chinese cuisine."

"Will you stop boxing for a second. Does that happen a lot?"

"Well, ever since—I mean, ever since he discovered the flavorings of the Orient."

"Flavorings of the Orient?" she mouths. "Sounds like something Manny'd say."

"Who?" Better to distance myself now.

"Your friend, Manny. You know, Mr. Perfect."

"I don't know anyone by either name."

"Denny, stop. Can't we have a five-second conversation without you pretending?"

"I told you, Sabrina. I'm a contender, not a pretender. Been working on my jab a lot lately, though it makes my left shoulder sore. Should probably get it checked out."

She leans closer and puts her hand on my arm. "That must have been hard for you, what happened at the restaurant," she says. "Seeing your dad get so—"

"It's no biggie, really. I mean, *he's* a biggie. But it's no big deal. My mom would've come but she—was at home, rapping to a rap song by a rapper on MTV."

She doesn't dignify that with a response and I don't blame her. There's something about the softness in her eyes and the soft teddy bear on her bed and her soft touch on my arm. "She died," I say.

"I remember, Denny . . . I was so sorry to hear. I still am really sorry. My mom said she was a wonderful lady, said she loved working with her on the PTA. I'm so, so sorry." And you can tell she means it.

"It's okay," I tell her. "My dad's got a real good handle on things. As you saw, he knows where and how to receive the best food in town."

She rubs her forehead. "I remember the whole class wrote you notes after she passed away. I wish I could've done more."

"You don't have to do anything. I don't need a pity party or anything."

"It's not—it's just, I wanted to help."

"It's okay, really, it is. I'm sorry. And with our project, don't worry. I know more about *Death of a Salesman* than I let on in class."

She grins. "I know you're smart, Denny. You just play too much."

"But if you knew I was smart, why didn't you want to work with me?"

"Because you play too much."

"Right."

Behind her, there's a poster with a girl and the words "*Les Misérables*" behind it.

"So what's the secret?" I ask.

"Secret to what?"

I point at the poster. "How do I become less miserable?"

She grins. "It's a play. My favorite one. But it's not about becoming less miserable. It's about how miserable *everyone* is, at least at some point. *Les* is the plural word in French for 'the.' Like, *all* of the miserable people."

I shrug. "Makes sense."

"It does, actually," she says. "Misery loves company, you know?"

"That's why I like this book," I explain, suddenly oozing with confidence. "Willy Loman is miserable and so is his family. They sort of sleepwalk through life until it's over.

For Willy. The whole play feels like a dream that nobody wakes up from until Willy's asleep for good. So what if we . . . hold on, we're supposed to act out at least one scene with rewritten dialogue, right?"

"Right."

"In some ways, it's similar to your less miserable play. We could film it as a dream or as a mashup of the miserable play and *Salesman*."

My ideas may not make any sense to Sabrina, or even to me, but it's the clearest I've felt in a while, talking to her, being honest, not wanting to hibernate. It feels . . . I don't know how to explain it. It feels nice.

"But you haven't even seen *Les Misérables*," she protests.

"I won't tell Mr. Morgan if you don't tell."

"But you really should see the play, it's fantastic."

"Remember, Sabrina, homey don't play that. I am homey and plays are that."

"And to think we were making progress . . ." She smiles. Her lips look smooth, nice. I don't get near them, nor am I a betting man, but I bet they feel nice.

GONE

The phone is warm and greasy. "Hello?"

"Donuts, report your problems."

I think that's what he says. My dad is blasting the TV down the hall so loudly it's hard to hear. "Dad, turn it down!" I shout, and he shouts back, "*You* turn it down!" which makes about as much sense as Chad telling me my meat is sour. "You're not making sense!" I holler. "I don't have the remote for the TV, Dad, and I can't turn the volume on a phone down. There's no volume switch on a phone!"

I realize after I say it that there *is* a volume switch on the phone, but that's not the point. Since his Chinese meltdown last week, the point of our conversations (or lack thereof) has escaped me even more than usual. Sometimes I think one of us is actually speaking Chinese. Hopefully it's me. Everyone knows the ladies dig a bilingual man.

Manny is once again in my ear. "Donuts, you do know there is indeed a volume button on the telephone, right?"

"Yeah, I know. But honestly, Manny, I don't want to report my problems to you."

A pause, and then, "Huh? Do I sound like the school social worker?"

"No, but you told me to report my—"

"Profits, Donuts. I told you to report your profits."

I feel my face go hot. "Right, uh—hold on." As I reach inside my backpack for the latest tally, I notice my dad has turned the volume down a smidge. What a trouper. "As of this afternoon, Manny, including sales on the way home, I've made $414."

Silence.

"Manny?"

No answer.

"Manny, you there?"

"Flabbergasting . . ." He clears his throat. "It seems you have bested me thus far, Donuts, but we are a team. My profit is only *slightly* less than yours—$359—but still an impressive sum between us—$773—especially given the time constraints. And remember, the idea for the company was mine."

"It's not a competition. Your sales are very impressive, Manny." Having to massage his ego is such hard work, but like most things that are hard work, it's necessary. "You are the king of candy sales. All hail King Manny, Master of Perfection."

"Indeed. Indeed." Manny pauses. I hear him take a deep breath and then ask, in a softer voice, a timid one that sounds of sadness: "Is it working?"

"Is what working?"

"Our scheme."

"Well, we have made over seven hundred dollars."

He sighs. "No, I mean is it working? Has—has it been a distraction?"

I take a moment before answering him: "It doesn't bring her back."

"Yeah, but it *has* been a distraction, has it not?"

I give him the same answer.

"I wish I could bring her back," he says.

"But you can't."

"No, I cannot."

We both don't speak for a few seconds, which feels like a few minutes and then a few hours. Silence hangs between us like a heavy curtain until I mercifully, mostly for his benefit, say: "We are so deep in the money that people may nickname us money: Money Manny and Money Donuts."

I can hear him smiling. "Can you believe that in one week we have raised more than seven hundred dollars? At this rate, we shall reach our goal in ten days, which cannot arrive fast enough, given the dwindling number of available babesicles on the market."

"Babesicles? Tell me you didn't just say that word."

"I did. Now back to the issue at hand. I think we need to

get a handle on the market. Perhaps my—*our*—monetary goal was too high, or heaven forbid, too low. That would be quite a travesty. That is why we must do some market research."

Whatever he's talking about, it doesn't sound good.

"Not it," I tell him.

"Au contraire, mon frère."

"Manny, I don't speak French. I only speak Chinese."

"In your dreams."

"Actually I speak English in my dreams. With a thick Jersey accent. Hey, Manny, I'm from Joisey. I like to wawk my dawg to the mawl."

He sighs into the phone and sounds like Darth Vader. *Haw. Ha. Haw. Ha.* "You are such a bundle of joy to talk to."

"Thank you, Manny. You know, according to Marsha—"

"Who?"

"The lunch lady. According to her, the definition of love is the feeling you get when you appreciate another person's virtues. Do you feel the love?"

No answer.

"Of course you do, Manny. Thank you for loving me."

Haw. Ha. Haw. Ha.

From down the hall: "Keep it down, Denny! I'm trying to watch my show."

"Tomorrow," Manny says, "we will ascertain exactly what it will take for us to secure company to the dance."

"Tomorrow?"

"Yes, tomorrow. We need to figure out our angle—what will best attract the babesicles to us. Food, clothes, entertainment, a makeover . . . whatever it is, time is of the essence. Now remember, feel free to stress to all the lucky ladies out there that it is good clean fun we are after. No ulterior motives. We are looking for a pretty face with which to take pictures. Girls like compliments, but do not creep them out. Simply mention that we want to take pictures and dance, and if she wants a smooch or two, well, we shall oblige."

"I hope you don't expect me to use the word 'smooch.'"

"*Au contraire, mon frère.*"

"Remember, Manny, I only speak Chinese."

"Fine, speak Chinese tomorrow. Use whatever words in whatever language you prefer, but tomorrow we move."

"But, Manny—"

"We are done here."

"Manny, wait—"

But he's already gone.

The only sound I hear is from down the hall, where my dad's parked by the television. I'd rather not go near him, but all that blabbering with Manny has made my throat dry. I tiptoe over to the kitchen, so as not to disturb the Natural Schmoozer, and find him in his usual position, lying across the maroon couch, face on the pillow, his eyes half-closed, saliva at the corner of his mouth. He's gone, too.

Not gone as in *gone* from this world, or *gone* out to the store, or *gone* to bed. More like *gone*, here but somewhere else, gone.

And I get it . . . Manny and I distracted ourselves with our candy coalition, and my dad, like the relatives at our post-funeral gathering, distracted himself in the soft glow of television and hasn't looked back since. Whole seasons on Netflix finished in one night. Action, adventure, bank robberies, prison breaks, singing competitions, comedies, comedy specials, standup comedy, thrillers. No dramas. Or trips to the gravesite, to the priest. No tears. No talks. My mom was here and then she wasn't. There was a void. And he filled it with food, a couch, and a television screen until he was gone, too.

I get it but I don't admire it, don't want to be like that. Not now, not ever.

I pour myself a cup of water and walk past the living room. Body odor, hair not washed since last week. A dusty television set, a man half-asleep and less alive. *Coward,* I say to myself. And then I say it out loud. "Coward."

Though I don't know if I'm talking to him or myself.

LOSS

A week after my mom died, teachers organized poster-size sympathy cards from kids that read "I'm sorry for your loss," and a few careless spellers wrote, "I'm sorry for your lost," and one *really* careless speller wrote, "I'm sorry for you're lost." Or, in other words, "I'm sorry for you are lost," which was the most accidentally accurate thing anyone had said to me. Sorry you're lost.

I mean, you don't *lose* a relative. You don't misplace them like your keys. And it's not the opposite of winning, either. You don't *lose* them like you lose a sporting event or a card game. You don't lose them. You don't lose. The only *losing* you do is with yourself. I lost myself. For a while there (and okay, sort of still now, too), I was lost, *so* lost I acted the fool to mask the pain. And one kid—who should seriously apply to write cards at Hallmark—was sorry to hear that.

I'm sorry for you're lost. I'm sorry that you are lost.

Made perfect sense for me. Then *and* now. For my dad. And for me. But making perfect sense—the feeling you get when everything comes together—is as fleeting as a breath. (Unless it's my dad's chicken breath as I'm helping him off to bed. That lingers.) When everything makes sense, it's a good sign that everything will fall apart, crumble, get blown over because life is ~~good~~ a house made of Popsicle sticks with no glue, and life is ~~good~~ a passing cloud, and life is ~~good~~ a sympathy card that only makes sense by accident.

MARKET RESEARCH

C oward." Manny wags a finger at me beside my locker before lunch. He smells of Lucky Charms, which is a great
smell, but he also smells of milk and coffee. The combo
isn't working. And neither are we because apparently I had
an assignment this morning and Manny acts the part of a
disappointed teacher.

"The fact that you have yet to even begin to compile
market research is not only flabbergasting, but it makes you
a coward," he scolds. "If you refuse to further our enterprise, you are a scammer hater. I have warned you many
times against scammer hating." He looks me up and down.
"Look at you. Like a kid on the high dive afraid to leap."

I ignore that last bit, though it's exactly how I feel. Often.
I want to do something bold, but my feet won't follow. I
want to tell Sabrina I like her and tell Mrs. Q it's all an act,
tell my dad he's got to—

"I don't understand, Manny. You want me to walk up to a random girl and see what attracts her? What type of car she likes?"

He grabs my shoulder. "This is not a focus group. We are not approaching just anyone and asking for their opinion. I mean, seriously, who wants a random person's opinion? There is no better market research than from the primary source. We are after the real thing, and in the words of men much more cinematically Italian than I am, we are not after a Fugazi—we are after the gold. By 'gold' I mean . . ."

He doesn't need to finish that sentence. I'm already two steps ahead. Really, I am. I know Allison's schedule better than she does, so I'm well aware that she's behind me in the middle of the hall, talking with a circle of friends. I know who she hugs and who she kisses (Anna, Chad), which books she carries before lunch (science, history), and which ones after lunch (English, health). I know her locker number (175), which pen she prefers (blue, ballpoint), and which gum she chews (Orbit, green).

I know which sneakers she wears every other Wednesday (Pumas, brown), which period she goes to her locker (third), how long she spends there (two minutes, forty-seven seconds), so I know just when to walk up to her and say, "Hello, Allison. I'm Denny. Denny Murphy. We're neighbors. You know that, right? Okay, good. We have a lot in common, like . . . we're neighbors. I already said that? Okay, well, we also both like lunch. We both eat lunch fourth period.

You're in eighth grade and I'm in seventh but we both go to Blueberry Hills, so we also have *that* in common. My dance is coming up. What do you think of Porsches? Why am I asking? Because I can drive you in one. Well, *I* can't drive you because even very mature middle schoolers like me can't drive, but I'll be in there and you'll be in there and we can play all the Justin Bieber songs you want. What—you like the Biebster? Great, we can go meet him after the dance and—of course we can meet him, we're best buds. Homeys, that's what Biebs and I are, best homeys for life. BHFL. We're even tighter than me and the Rockafellas. Who are they? Nobody of importance. Biebs and I have so much in common we complete each other's . . . sentences. That's how he would've finished that sentence: with the word 'sentences.' What? You like his hair? Funny you should say so. I have an appointment at this swank stylist because she swears she can give me the Bieber do. But only if—you do? You'll go with me to the dance? That's super. I mean, flabbergasting. I mean, good. So we're on like filet mignon? Oh, steak sounds good to you? Sure, I'll buy you dinner beforehand. Filet mignon it is. Pick you up at seven? Yuppers, I mean, yup, yes, I'll see you there."

"Go," Manny says. "Get it done. Now."

But now is obviously not the time to approach Allison. I mean, I sorta don't even want to go with her, because Sabrina, well, maybe, hopefully kind of likes me and I maybe kind of like her, and even if Sabrina *doesn't* like me, I can't approach Allison now. With her friends so close by, I'll end up buying the whole group filet mignon, which doesn't quite fit the budget.

"Too many filet mignons," I tell Manny.

"Huh?"

"Too many people, Manny. I'll talk to her later."

"Unacceptable, Donuts. I am disappointed in your cowardice, but also in your lack of perceptiveness. You are not seeing this scene correctly." He looks over my shoulder. "One of them is crying, Donuts. There was a breakup."

"A breakup? Great! Good for business."

"Indeed, it is. And guess where I heard it?"

"Through the social pipeline?"

"You are so very intelligent, dear friend."

"So what's the news?"

I peek over a stream of moving bodies. Allison's crying.

"The news, Donuts, is that Chad is old news," Manny whispers. "Before you get too excited, you should know that as an integral part of the social pipeline, I hear that these things unfortunately fluctuate. Romantic relationships fluctuate. Lovebirds break up. They piece things back together. They break up. They piece it together. They shatter it irreparably. Time is of the essence, Donuts. Find out her interests, *now*. Do market research, *now*."

"So what you're saying is, I should ask her about cars?"

"Sure, that would be lovely. But if your nerve fails you,

as I expect it will, break the ice and sell them candy." He shoves me in the back. "That is your cue, rose peddler."

I remove a box of Snickers from my bag.

"Meet me at the Warehouse," Manny says. "You have three minutes."

Allison has more friends when she's crying than I do when I'm rich. Well, almost rich. Together, Manny and I have raised over eight hundred dollars. But it sounds like pennies considering the name brands in front of me.

Seven girls in Polo sweaters and Diesel jeans clutch Prada handbags while they pet Allison's blond hair.

"You," one of them says, "can I help you?" It's Anna Harden and I only know this because everyone knows this. Like I said, she's sort of the school's Number Two, to Allison of course. She's phenomenal at lacrosse and has a mouthful of white teeth and makeup and dimples that bend in three places when she smiles. Right now, she's not smiling. Right now, she has pink nails, a red headband, a furrowed brow, red sparkling shoes with heels—sharp ones like spears— and right now, she has one hand on her hip, one petting Allison's hair. "Can I *help* you?" she repeats.

"Romantic relationships fluctuate . . . I hear they do . . . I hear they fluctuate." I don't mean to say this. I really don't, but something seems to happen to my filter in their presence. (It disappears.)

"Excuse me?" they all say. At exactly the same time. It's impressive, actually, like synchronized swimmers with matching caps and dance moves at the Olympics. Thankfully, I don't call them "synchronized swimmers with matching caps and dance moves at the Olympics." Instead I say, "I mean, what you're doing, supporting a friend, is so very important and I feel terrible for pulling you away. But, well, I'm Denny and I'm selling candy and I was wondering if you'd like to support your friend and me, by—"

"Giving us some?"

"Well, each candy is only—"

Anna snatches five Snickers from my hands. "Now beat it. Scram!" She makes a peace sign with two fingers and says, "Deuces."

Laughter, not the good kind, and a spotlight, which at least I'm used to. But I don't even know why I'm here. I miss Sabrina. My face flushes. I steal a peek at Manny. *Keep going,* he mouths between clenched teeth.

"I—I'm happy to help!" I proclaim, but then . . . I don't know if it's their reputation or my thirst or my nerves, but I lose my ability to speak. I lose my . . . I pretty much lose everything. I say, "Your Friendly Neighborhood Fund-raising Candyman is always here, all day, every day, from nine to five . . . that's nine a.m. to five p.m. . . . well, more like eight thirty a.m. to three p.m., but I often get here early around eight fifteen a.m. and stay till around three ten p.m., usually three fifteen p.m., to see if anyone from the band needs nourishment . . . and I don't normally sell on weekends, unless you live near my house . . ." I look between the ladies for a glimpse of Allison. "Anything for a neighbor."

"Get lost," Anna says.

I know I've already overstayed my welcome, but I can't pass up the opportunity. As Manny said, there's no better market research than from the primary source. I take a step away from Allison's crowd, then turn around, as if I'm forgetting something. "Which do you ladies prefer: a sports car or limo? To ride in. To the dance, I mean. To *and* from, round-trip. With someone of my age. Which is the most, ah, enticing?"

No answer. Probably because I'm babbling. *Be clearer, Denny, as clear as Windex on windows. Come on, speak!*

"It's only a general survey, ladies, I was just wondering— hey, I couldn't help but notice that you're wearing nice shoes. Lovely shoes. What shoes do you prefer in a man? I mean, on a man. I mean, for a man to wear on his feet. While he's dancing at the seventh grade dance. And while he's *not* dancing at the seventh grade dance."

They trade puzzled looks.

"Only asking, you know, because I shop at all the finest stores and, you know, where would you recommend picking up attractive clothing? For middle school males, I mean. Like me. Well, not *for* me, but . . ."

Prada. That seems to be the general answer. And that's the last word I see as a bag hits me upside the face. Yup, Prada. I see it again. And again.

And again.

FAST AND LOOSE

To make up for my generous donation to Allison's support group and for the time lost icing the side of my face, I gotta do what a man's gotta do. Such is the biz. Fruit Roll-Ups, which previously were only fifty cents, have doubled in price. It takes me all of about seventeen seconds in the lunchroom to make up for the lost money. *Level 1: Hungry People* has never looked so good.

And it better be. Because we've got competition. At least according to Manny we do. "We have competition, Donuts," he says to me at our lunch table, nodding over my shoulder at a crowd around Ronald Latimer, a tall, already-mustachioed seventh grader who, despite his braces, chews gum incessantly, and since I've known him has gone around the school giving out free gum and Jolly Ranchers. Girls have always shamelessly flirted their way to handfuls of sweets—or as Ronald calls them, "sweeties"—and ever since *that* caught on, whole groups of females have swooped to Ronald's locker between classes, like packs of starving pigeons, cooing, "Sweeties, Ronald, sweeties, sweeties . . ." That's what they're cooing right now.

I turn back to Manny. "C'mon, he only deals out gum and sucking candy. You don't need to worry about him. He's not a threat to our business. He's just a . . . well . . . he's just the Gum Dealer."

"The Gum Dealer is indeed a threat to our business. Look closer."

"Manny, seriously?"

"I promise you will be flabbergasted."

I don't even need to turn around. Ronald's flock has already dispersed across the lunchroom, clutching bite-size Snickers and Twix. Yup, chocolate candy. Just like the candy we sell for a dollar.

"Crap," I mutter.

Manny snarls his face and balls his fists. "Gum Dealer!"

Ronald must hear Manny because he looks our way and smiles a chocolaty grin.

"In your braces!" Manny hollers for everyone to hear. "Chocolate in your braces! Old chocolate! Expired, I think! Poisonous! I would definitely go see the nurse!"

Ronald nods but refuses to give Manny the satisfaction of seeing him pick his teeth. Instead, he picks his nose, at least I think he does. Sometimes it's hard to tell the difference between a scratch and a pick. Anyway, once Manny has calmed down, we test the market to see the impact of Ronald's free candy enterprise.

Thankfully, it's minimal. Ronald may be onto something, but the bite-size candies aren't enough to satisfy a whole lunchroom. Ronald makes a dent in our operation, but no more, because the lunchroom is a gold mine, the forty-five-minute period a gold rush. Manny and Denny, Suppliers of Gold. Might as well be our new name. I take the left side of the room, Manny the right. I don't sit down the entire lunch period. Don't have time to. If someone took a leaf blower to a pile of garbage, that's what the scene looks like. A bull rush to the Suppliers of Gold, then a tornado of wrappers. Minus the burden of order forms, my merchandise is fast and loose. Fast in sales, loose in bargains. Five for four? Sure, why not? With the increase in Fruit Roll-Up profit, I'll more than make up for it. Frequent buyers card? Sure, I'll look into it. Anything for a loyal customer, and everyone in the room fits that description. Even Allison's table springs for a few bars. Half-off this time, which is better than free. For anyone else I'd charge more, but I've had enough of Prada and Chad's sitting with them. I guess Manny was right about how quickly things fluctuate in the romance world. They're *already* back together?

I try to keep my distance and ignore their conversation and laughter as I'm walking away. I can't really hear them because I'm a terrible member of the Secret Service, but any moron can guess what they're saying.

"Look at him go," Allison's whispering in his ear.

"Who?" Chad asks, his voice deep and firm.

"The kid with the candy. Do you know him?"

"Of course I know him. I punched him in the stomach."

"Awwww, why'd you do that?" she says, gripping Chad's biceps.

"Because he was walking the halls and said something about my mother."

"Oh, well in that case he deserved it."

"I told you."

"You're my hero, Chad."

"Thanks. Hey, you know what I heard?"

"What?"

"That he wants a date for his little seventh grade dance."

"*Ha!* I heard that, too!"

"You know what else I heard?"

"What?"

"He pretends to be a clown so no one will make fun of him."

"But we're making fun of him anyway. *Ha!*"

"Isn't that funny?"

"It *is* funny! *Ha!*"

I don't hear them too well, but I think Allison adds something about Manny's and my stupid spy mission and her being the ladybug and how we're the biggest loserasauruses on the entire dinosaur and human and nonhuman planet.

Chad agrees and says that we're better off extinct. Then he mentions something about my mom.

I don't feel *too* bad because I'm able to tune them out, which is easier than you might think because I'm selling so fast I'll soon put the lunch ladies out of business, which I *do* feel the slightest bit bad about, so when my four boxes (forty-eight bars each) sell out in under nineteen minutes, I step over a sea of candy wrappers to visit my favorite lunch lady.

It also doesn't hurt that Sabrina's on the line, too, buying a drink. Her strawberry shampoo overpowers the smell of the lunchroom. This is a good thing.

"Hi, Denny." She's wearing a green button-down shirt with a cat at the upper left corner instead of a man playing polo or a sailboat or flag. I point to it and ask, "Is that the cat on your roof?" It's a dumb thing to say, I know it is, but I love that she's not one of them, not a slave to the logo. I love it so much I feel like singing. So I do.

"Too much," she says, "tone it down."

"It's the bass, isn't it? Too much bass in my golden pipes?"

She can't help but laugh because my game is oozing like cheese fries. Speaking of which, Marsha, the lunch lady, beams when she sees me with Sabrina. "So maybe I *do* have to worry about you running off and disappearing with a woman," she cackles, flashing me an exaggerated wink. "Remember that women are relationship beings and that men—"

"Are not."

Sabrina seems impressed. "True story," she whispers.

"Right you are." Marsha scratches at her hairnet. "Now tell me, how are your classes going? Gonna pass this year, aren't we, baby?"

"Yes, ma'am," I explain. "Straight A's. I'm very much looking forward to the honor roll celebration at the end of the year. I hear it's a potluck dinner this time around. I think I'll bring some of my dad's famous fried chicken."

"You tellin' the truth, baby?"

"Told you you're a terrible liar," Sabrina says.

Marsha nods. "Like I always said, it's better to be rather than to seem."

"Can I get some fries please, Marsha?" I reach into my shoe and pull out a wad of twenty-dollar bills. "For safety," I whisper to Sabrina. "Every businessman should have street smarts."

She gives me a stink face. "All that money in your *sock?* That's gross."

"Your wish is my command," Marsha says, filling up two trays. "Here we go, double order of french fries, made with you in mind."

I thank her.

"You got it, sugar, and remember now. It's better to be, rather than to seem."

"Roger that." I tuck the change in my sock.

"I like her," Sabrina says, following me away from the

lunch line. "It's better to be than to seem. You should listen to her and stop pretending. Her advice is spot-on and smart. Your money system on the other hand . . ."

"Sorta gross?"

"Yeah."

"At least it's safe. And it's not all ones or anything. I've exchanged them for a bunch of twenties and a few hundreds because it's all about the Benjamins."

She rolls her eyes. "What do you need the money for so badly anyway?"

"Yes, Donuts," another voice cuts in, "what do you need the money for so badly?" I don't realize the table isn't empty until we're already sitting down.

Manny has a grin the size of Antarctica on his face. "Tell us, Donuts, what do you need the money for so badly?" I try to kill him with my eyes, but it doesn't work. He presses on. "Why go through the trouble we have been going through, buying boxes, organizing inventory, selling before school, after school, between classes, during classes? Why all the trouble? For whom? For what?"

I wish he'd stop talking. I know why he's angry, I get it. I'm sitting next to the person who drove him so mad during their stupid debate. For this, though it sounds stupid, I can't help but feel the slightest bit guilty. I feel like a cheater, which makes me feel weird because I'm not married to Manny or anything, but, well, sometimes it feels that way. And in the case of selling candy, I am married to him—in profits, in I.M.P. We're supposed to get dates. Together. Sabrina isn't part of the plan.

Though I want her to be part of a new one. An honest one. A real one.

Manny's eyes flicker back and forth between Sabrina and me. "What are you—what is *she* doing here?"

"I brought her here."

Sweat sprouts on Manny's nose, a dead giveaway he's about to burst. He wipes his sweat on his sleeve and says, "So, where did you two lovebirds meet?"

Sabrina laughs. "I don't know about lovebirds, but . . ." which sort of hurts my feelings. A better answer would've simply been "In class. We met in class."

"English project," I tell Manny. "We're partners."

"Interesting." He rubs his chin. "I thought we were partners. Business partners. Remember, Donuts? What was the purpose of that business again?"

I look at Sabrina, then to Manny.

"For a car," I say. "To buy a new car. For when I can drive. Years from now."

He slaps his knee playfully. "Ah, that was it. Forgive me, I recently aged another year, became thirteen. My memory is not what it used to be."

Outside of the lunchroom, Manny pulls me aside and pushes me against a locker. Oohs and aahs ripple through the crowd. "Catfight!" someone hollers.

Might as well have called "Fire." The masses swarm, circling around us. The squeaking of sneakers, the clomping of boots. Cheers, fists, a bloodthirsty mob. In seconds, we're trapped like animals inside a cage, which is fitting because the sneer on Manny's face isn't human—until he realizes the scene he's created.

He loosens his grip. "No, no, not a fight," Manny announces, dusting off my shoulders. "Just two growing men disagreeing is all. A friendly, rational conversation."

Grunts of disappointment as the crowd shuffles down the hall: "*Really* could've used a fight today." "Would've been epic." "Had twenty bucks on Donuts."

Once they're out of earshot, Manny's back at it. "Are you serious, Donuts? You are macking with the cheese with Sabrina?"

"Chill out, Manny, she's just a girl."

He huffs. "You sound like a man of the world, a regular world traveler. Tell us sheltered creatures what girls are really like. Why on earth are you macking with the cheese with Sabrina? Have you already abandoned our plan?"

"Of course not. Didn't you see me selling candy in there? I sold out."

"Indeed you have." He looks both ways. "Let me give you something to chew on."

"I just ate lunch."

"Not literally, metaphorically. Are you familiar with macaroni?"

"The pasta?"

He nods.

"I know all about pasta, Manny. Remember, I asked if we could bring tortellini in our Lamborghini."

He rolls his eyes. "How could I forget..."

"So what's your point?"

"Listen, macaroni is a pasta like any other, but it got labeled as a cheese lover. Labeled in households, restaurants, commercials, and fun-size microwavable packets. We cannot fathom macaroni without its mate, its bride, its gloppy yellow cheese. Macaroni and marinara? Macaroni and sausage? Not unless it is out of a Chef Boyardee can or sloppily served by Marsha at your favorite cafeteria establishment. Somewhere along the line, macaroni got caught up in the wrong crowd, rubbed elbows—pun intended, my friend— with its cheesy neighbors, found itself in mixed company and consciously led the cheese on, making it blush, making it melt, and look where it got him: labeled, branded, cemented in history alongside the pasteurized by-products of a cow."

"Wow."

"Indeed you are capable of rhyme. I am very impressed. Sound the trumpets, cue the violins, for you, sir, are a natural poet. A bona fide Bobby Frost, a teenage one at that. And teenagers, as you well know, Mr. Court Jester, get branded. Labeled. Cemented in history as this or that. Popular, or not. Athlete, or not. Musician, or not. Thespian, or not. A mint-condition academic powerhouse such as myself—or not. A donut-swilling, sad, Springsteen-loving, Jolly Rancher—"

"I get it."

"Or not. We cannot take the chance, so allow me to finish. Teenagers get labeled, especially by their relationships. What social pack they belonged to, who they dated, who they squired to a dance (hence our elaborate operation to maximize profits), who they boogied with on the dance floor, who they kissed, who they dated for a day, week, month, year. It stays with them. Forever. That is what our candy operation is about: avoiding a negative label for all of eternity." He pauses. "If you go forth with Sabrina, she will be on your résumé. Not to be melodramatic—which contrary to popular belief, is not the mellow, laid-back version of drama—but thirty years from now, when we are all middle-aged, people *might* forget your antics, your jokes, your grades, your clothes, your hair, your looks. But they will never. Ever. Ever. Ever forget your résumé."

"Are you finished?"

"Yes, Donuts, but understand, that is why I have lacked a date up until now. I have chosen carefully. And now with the vehicular, musical, and other amenities we can acquire with our candy money, we'll have our choice of date, smorgasbord that our school is. But I am only in this if we are in this together."

"Fine, but understand this: I'm not embarrassed by her. I like her." I fight a blush.

"She is your group partner, Donuts. She is supposed to be nice. I bet you think waitresses like you, too. And hostesses, salesladies, clerks, cashiers, managers . . ." He laughs at his own joke. "I bet you think the lady you buy tickets from at the movies likes you, too. And the lady who rips your ticket. I bet she is gaga for Donuts."

"Stop! I don't know what I want to do for the dance. I don't know if Sabrina even likes me the slightest bit, but if she made it to my, what do you call it?"

"A résumé."

"Right, a résumé. She'd look good there. She'd be the only one there."

He sighs. "I need to know now. If we are going to make our fund-raising operation work, I mean truly work, together, we need to find out now. And in order to find out, we need to step up our market research, take a chance with a purchase of some sort, or get more aggressive in other ways. I doubt we have raised enough money for a helicopter yet, but it is time we spice things up. Desperate times call for desperate measures and Lord knows we are desperate. At least I am, and it is time to get spicy. Are you still with me or not?"

"I don't understand what you mean by spicy, but I don't like the sound—"

"All that matters is this, Donuts: Have you betrayed our

partnership or are we still in this together? Are you with me or not? I need to know now." He lowers his voice. "Before we take this to another level that we cannot turn back from." He pauses, then runs his hand through his hair. "Or until it all grows back."

DESPERATE MEASURES

Oh my god, can you be*lieve* what my son-in-law got me for my seventieth birthday? I mean, hel-lo, who in their right mind would turn down a gift certificate for a Swedish massage? Certainly not *this* lady." Though she's on the phone, "this lady" with the nasal voice, sagging cheeks, and pink curler in her hair points to herself with two shaking fingertips covered in orange nail polish. "I've met silly people before in my lifetime, but *this* lady"—again the orange pointers—"is certainly not one of them. My daughter has married a charmer, I'm telling you. He even got me three full tubes of foot cream all the way from the Dead Sea. And, honey, you know me and foot cream. We go together like chocolate and ice cream."

MELINDA'S MAKEOVER, it says on the window. And this lady must be Melinda. Her salon, which smells of hair spray, has eight mirrors with chairs, though no one else is sitting in them because Melinda's the only one here. She's on the phone beside a row of sinks and pictures of boys and girls with all sorts of haircuts: spikes, fades, perms, bowl cuts, afros . . .

"I think we're in the wrong place," I whisper to Manny.

He runs a hand through his mop of hair, now ungelled and with a mind of its own. "This is the right place. It was recommended by one of my classmates, and I did do my research. This hair salon got a five-star rating on Yelp."

"By who?" I scoff. "The shuffleboard club?"

A framed picture of Miami Beach above Melinda's name, a bumper sticker to the side of her station that reads "I [heart] Art Deco." Combs soaked in blue vials, a yellow hair dryer, and a sign that reads NOBODY NOTICES WHEN I GET THINGS RIGHT, which brings me no comfort.

Neither does Manny's elbow in my ribs. "Do not judge this place by its appearance. That is why we are here, after all. The female species has deemed our current appearance unworthy of its company. So we shall work on that appearance."

Melinda looks up. "Hold on a sec, will ya, boys?" Then she whispers in the phone, "I gotta go, Lucinda. I have new clients. Yeah, they're young, too. They look like charmers."

"We *are* charmers, are we not, Donuts?"

"You can't be serious about this . . ."

Melinda hangs up the phone and opens her arms. "Well, look what the wind blew in this aft-a-noon. Hello, boys, how can I help you?"

Manny clears his throat. "We are looking for makeovers. Well, *I* am. My friend Donuts here is a bit squeamish about change."

Melinda nods in my direction. "Well hello, Mist-a Donuts. Funny, I believe I ate you fa-breakfast. You were powdery and had those little coffee cake crumbs on top." She kisses the inside of her orange fingertips. "Delicious!"

To keep from laughing, Manny smothers his mouth. I'm not sure what's so funny or why we're even here in the first place. I mean, I understand getting aggressive with our strategy to improve our compatibility quotient, as Manny would say, but I look fine the way I do. Don't I? And anyway, aren't makeovers for girls?

"Don't worry, Mist-a Donuts, sweetie." She waves an arm in the air, then bends it at the wrist. "Melinda'll take care of yous."

Manny pipes up. "Greetings, Ms. Melinda. I am looking for the perfect haircut and style to attract members of the opposite species and leave them flabbergasted."

"Species? You mean, like aliens?" Melinda rubs the back of her arms. "They give me the heeber jeebers."

"No, not aliens. Females. Though sometimes I get them mixed up myself." He sighs. "They do often confound me. Especially now. We have a dance coming up."

Melinda puts a hand to her heart. "Oh my! Prom season is upon us already! I should redeem my gift certificate now for that Swedish massage before my shoulders get too stiff, all jammed and jammy."

"No, not prom. It is the seventh grade dance."

"Oh my, the seventh grade dance, quite a rite of passage. Like multiple Bar Mitzvahs at your school at the same time."

"Yes, uh, I had not thought of that and, anyway, unlike most spineless students at our school who migrate to dances in flocks of ten and twenty, Donuts and I would like to bring dates to our seventh grade dance."

She raises her pink-outlined eyebrows. "How ambitious you two are. Are you sure you're only *seventh* graders? Oh, honey, you look *much* older."

Manny grins. "Indeed, but we are not necessarily going for an old look. More of a different look. A perfect look. That is it! I want to look like Mr. Perfect, former World Wrestling Federation Intercontinental Champion."

She frowns. "Unfortunately, sweetie pie, I'm not quite familiar with wrestlers. Do you have a picture?"

"Only in my locker. At school."

"Oh, that's too bad. Can you describe it for me?"

"He has curly blond hair, oily, that falls from his head in spirals, curlicues . . . like oily curly fries hanging on all sides of his head."

"Oh my, that doesn't sound so good, honey."

Dejected, Manny asks Melinda what she recommends.

"Honey, I have hundreds of other styles to choose from. They're all numbered." She hands over a book of hair. I mean, a hair book. I mean, a book of hairstyles. "I can pretty much do whatever you'd like, honey bunches. I'm a very versatile stylist."

"See, Donuts? That is what everyone said on Yelp: 'very versatile.'"

I wish Melinda hadn't called us honey bunches. Too similar to my mom calling me Honey Bunches of Oats, but I have to focus now. On my hair.

And Manny's already in the chair, ordering a blond #45.

THE KITCHEN SINK

Oily curly fries. Now that I think about it—I mean, look at it—it's the perfect way to describe the Mr. Perfect do that Manny wanted. And got. So badly.

"Honey, as the politicians *should* say in their commercials on my television set: My name is Melinda and I do *not* support this message," Melinda kept saying, but Manny assured her it was for a good cause.

Assured me, too. For my hair, I mean.

I *was* tired of the wings on the sides of my head, but . . .

To chop off all the hair on the sides of my head and replace it with an orange Mohawk, hair-sprayed to full attention . . .

This was Manny's idea, which I wasn't on board with, but his chants of "Mo-Hawk, Mo-Hawk, Mo-Hawk" brought me back to the days of "Do-Nuts, Do-Nuts," and I liked that performance feeling, leaping outside myself into another body. Plus, it goes perfectly with my desk surfer persona, if anyone remembers my trash can shenanigans.

"Aloha, new look!" I actually say that in Melinda's chair. "I *do* like the new orange do."

Manny scolds me for embarrassing him with lame jokes, then pulls out a wad of dollar bills to pay Melinda for her "versatile services." Then he tells me to pay for half, so I reach into my sock.

"My pleasure, boychicks. Now good luck boogying down at the dance! Make sure you get a nice suit. You don't want to look shlumpy."

"Shlumpy?"

"That's right. You don't want to look like a shlump. You want to look nice."

We wave goodbye to Melinda.

With my orange hair dye and Manny's perm included, we're still left with over eight hundred dollars but no dates. Until tomorrow.

At least, that's the plan.

What do I have to lose? What do I have to lose? That's what I keep telling my new Mohawk self walking into school today—at 8:30, not 8:15. The less time I have to spend in school in front of other people the better. *But what do I have to lose?*

As usual, I'm supposed to meet Manny in the hallways, but "usual" is the last word I'd use to describe him. Brushing the blond curly fries from the front of his face, Manny struts toward me, orange leather shoes clapping against the hallway floor. A loose-fitting black suit hangs on his wiry frame, a blue shirt and pink tie underneath. In his side pocket, a yellow handkerchief matches his new hair.

For the first time in years, his backpack is behind him instead of against his chest.

"Brooks Brothers," he says, slowly spinning around, modeling his new (and expensive) transformation.

"But, Manny, all the money!"

"Clearance rack." He brushes the lint off his shoulders. "I am indeed a smart shopper—and a sharp one, too, eh? Eh? What do you think?"

"I think we look ridiculous."

He gasps. "I certainly do not, but I admit that you do. You look flabbergasting."

I look down at a red-checkered shirt tucked into dark green pants. With my orange Mohawk, I look like Christmas on fire. I know that because Manny tells me so.

"Okay, Christmas on Fire, listen up. Here is the plan . . ."

Thankfully, Sabrina hasn't seen me yet. Maybe she'll be absent. Maybe she got picked to sing in *Les Mis*. Maybe she's working on our project from home. Maybe . . .

"Are you listening, Donuts? We need to keep selling candy and do our very best to raise our compatibility quotient— and see if we have *already* done so with our new looks. It is my hope that our makeovers, combined with a renewed push to complete our market research, will make for a successful day. 'Successful' meaning a day of dates. From now on, D-Day will be a national holiday to celebrate our Day of Dates. The day perfection was finally achieved by a rising entrepreneur and his pastry-named friend."

The first part of his plan—the selling part—sounds fine. It can't hurt to raise more. If it miraculously works out with Sabrina and I don't need to rent a car or plane or limousine or hang glider for someone else to go with me, I'll give the money to Manny. Or keep it to buy my own car or plane or limousine or hang glider. Or a new food group for the Natural Schmoozer. And top-of-the-line paper towels for him, too.

It's just that second part of his plan—complete market research and actually get a date—that doesn't sound so easy. I mean, Sabrina's not even here.

"You are first," Manny says, nudging me in the back. "Go get them, tiger."

"But where? Who?"

"That one," he says, pointing to an eighth grader with curly red hair and dimples, unloading books at her locker. "Find out what attracts the opposite species. And this time, Donuts, I am watching."

"But I don't even know her."

"Then acquire information for me. Better yet, acquire a date for me."

He hands me a briefcase. It's not heavy but certainly not light. "What's in there?" I ask.

"The kitchen sink," he says.

"A whole sink in a briefcase?"

He rolls his eyes. "It is an expression. The kitchen sink means 'everything,' which in our case means information on everything we can possibly offer. You will find brochures on transportation, a guide to the concert series next month, a spreadsheet of all the hippest after-parties, pamphlets on cooking classes and science museums and formal attire for you and her in hundreds of styles and colors, and coupons for pocketbooks and necklaces, oh, and extra candy bars . . ."

His voice trails off as he nods in the direction of Ronald Latimer, who is handing out candy bars (regular size this time) at his locker, free of charge. The pigeons swoop in for a complimentary snack. "Sweeties, Ronald, sweeties, sweeties, sweeties . . ."

"This may be our last shot," Manny says. "Do not let me down. Make her feel comfortable, inquire about her availability, toss a pickup line in there if you must, but get in, get info and/or a date for me, and get out of there. That is an order."

It feels wrong. But for Manny I'd do anything. Well, almost anything. No way am I asking her to the dance. No way will I bribe her in any way. And no way I'm using any lame pickup lines. Information is all I need. Good ol' safe market research. The redhead is slamming her locker. My hands are sweaty and cold, especially the one gripping the briefcase.

I look over my shoulder. Manny raises a fist. *You can do this,* he mouths.

Do what? I have no idea what I'm doing. But it's too late to turn back now. *For me,* I see him pleading.

I clear my throat. "Excuse me," I say. "Excuse me." But she's already walking away, and though I tell myself not to, I'm following her. "EXCUSE ME!" I say, loud enough for her—and everyone else on that side of the floor—to hear me.

The whispers fill the halls: *Yo, look at Donuts's Mohawk. Dude looks like he got his fingers caught in an orange outlet. Dude lost his marbles, except the orange ones. His hair looks like orange Gatorade froze while being dumped on his head. You'll never believe how many orange icicles Donuts glued to his head . . . Check it out . . .*

I wait until the crowd finishes checking me out before I start speaking to the redhead.

She has fair skin and an easy smile. She looks like an orange daisy.

"Excuse me," I say again.

"Yes, I hear you," she says. "What is it?"

"We have similar hair color, but yours, of course, is better-looking. As are you, compared to me."

"What?!" She's already walking away and I haven't even shown her the brochures for sports cars and helicopters and launching pads and laser tags and I'm failing, failing again.

I've failed Manny and he'll always be alone. Alone. Alone. I'm not cut out for this, any of this, and I've failed myself and failed Manny and I might as well give up, give up on myself, but I can't give up on Manny and—

"Do you know karate? 'Cause your body's kickin'."

I actually say that.

And she must know karate because she knocks my backpack to the floor and I'm apologizing like a madman and she's running away and I'm scooping the brochures off the floor and grabbing candy bars by the fistful and . . .

"I was wondering if we might have a little chat."

I don't say *that*, but I wish I had instead of the guy behind me, whose deep voice feels frightening and familiar. I know that voice. I hear it every day. During morning announcements. He taps me on the shoulder. I turn around and look up.

The principal is wearing a gray shirt and red tie.

"My office," Mr. Softee says. "I think it's time we had a chat."

THE TRUTH

His name may be Mr. Softee, but his office doesn't smell like ice cream. It smells of leather and printer paper. I just hope his softee reputation holds up.

A football rests at the corner of his brown desk. A signed photo of Phillies legend Mike Schmidt hangs cock-eyed on the wall. Pictures with his arm around former graduates. They're smiling and he is, too. These are all good signs.

He tells me to sit, so I do. I place the briefcase at my feet.

"I know what you're up to, Mr. Murphy," he says, staring at me from behind his desk. He peeks at my hairdo and scowls, then scratches his leathery face, folds his hands, and leans back in his chair.

"I'm sorry, sir." Better to play it safe, not to give anything away, though I wish he wouldn't call me my dad's name: Mr. Murphy. Not exactly a compliment.

"It's against school policy, you know," he says, raising his bushy eyebrows.

What is? Harassment? Money? Candy? Bribery? Cutting? Failing classes? Befriending the lunch lady? How many social and school laws have I broken?

"I apologize, Mr. Soffer, sir. It won't happen again."

"You see, Mr. Murphy, that's the thing. I don't believe you." He checks his wristwatch. "I've been doing this for a long time, a very long time."

"And may I add, sir, you're doing a fine job."

"Going on thirty years now. Thirty years of experience has taught me a lot, such as the value of honesty. Level with me. Why are you selling candy?"

I'm tired of lying. He wants honesty. Might as well give it to him. "For a business. I'm selling candy for a dance company. Trying to raise money to get it started."

"What's the name of the business?"

"International Monetary Prudential. Incorporated. TM."

He frowns. "Trademarked already?"

"You know it, sir."

"Well, Mr. Murphy, the name of your business makes absolutely no sense."

"Right, well, ah—"

"Still, I appreciate your entrepreneurial spirit." He grins, leans back again. "You may not know this, but I have a background in business. Graduated from the renowned Wharton Business School."

Pride written all over his face, he points to a framed diploma to the left of Mike Schmidt.

"Wow, Mr. Soffer, Wharton is a great school. Your credentials blow my universe. You're quite a smart man."

He doesn't answer. His gaze is stuck on his diploma. Still stuck. And . . . still stuck. I bet I could sneak out of this office and he wouldn't even notice.

"Jeez, I bet those were the best days of your life."

He jerks from his reverie, chair forward, eyes blinking away the memories. "Right, uh, yes. Since you've leveled with me, Mr. Murphy, I'll level with you. I'm aware of your loss, and as I mentioned to you many times, I am deeply sorry. I really am."

"Thank you."

He nods. "It must have been . . . well, having an outlet for all of that, ah, stuff, is important, and well, I respect your business spirit. Just don't sell in class. Teachers and janitors have been complaining about wrappers in the halls and lunchroom. If you pick each one up at the end of the day, you and me are A-okay."

"Wow, sir, a businessman, a principal, *and* a poet. You're the total package."

He chuckles. "The total—yes, that's nice, Mr. Murphy, very nice."

"I must say that while I am partially responsible for the mess, the Gum Dealer is the main culprit here."

"The Gum Dealer?"

"Ronald Latimer, sir. He just gives away candy all day to become popular. Boxes upon boxes of king-size candy bars free. It's sad, sir, it is. Plus, he has no business spirit like you and me."

"I'll look into it. But until then, if I find wrappers around, I will shut down your operation. And if you don't listen, detention it is. But I don't *want* to give you detention. Thirty years has taught me that it doesn't work and it's time-consuming for teachers and students. We're trying to move away from traditional methods of punishment, and in due time, more progressive consequences such as community service, tutoring, Xeroxing, mural painting, will altogether replace that time-waster named Detention. One of the great things about my school—*our* school, excuse me—is that we all try to respect each other's time."

"Jeez, Mr. Soffer, as a businessman, you sure understand the value of time. And since you do, I must tell you that I have an English class I am eager to attend."

"Ah, yes, of course. How are your grades, Mr. Murphy?"

"Stellar. Fantastic. You pick the adjective." *Hideous. Terrible. Nonexistent.*

"You know, I can easily access your transcript from my computer. Another one of the great things about our school." He raises a finger to the keypad to get me to crack. Won't happen.

"Go ahead, sir," I say, chin up. "I stand by my record."

He puts his hand back on the desk. "A proud student,

such a breath of fresh air. And may I add, your haircut, while not in the least bit stylish or attractive, is as unique as your business approach. You're dismissed." He points to the exit.

I grab my briefcase, leap to the door, then look back. I just can't help myself. "Thanks for the chat, Mr. Soffer. And feel free to call me Denny."

"Will do. Have a great day now, Denny."

Another great thing about our school: the principal is a sucker.

HIGH DIVE

One more good thing about my school: Sabrina goes here.

As I'm on my way out of school, having bested Mr. Softee, Sabrina approaches me at my locker. "Interesting choice of hairstyle," she muses, running her hand atop my spiky dome. "Hadn't pegged you for the orange Mohawk. Figured you'd go green."

"Why green?"

"I don't know, why the Mohawk?" she asks.

"Because I like the name Mo and I appreciate a strong, ferocious bird."

She smiles. "Is that what you are, strong and ferocious?"

If this is flirting, I like how it feels. "Oh yes, very ferocious. Wild, even. Ferocious and very wild, with a very sensitive beak, a helping hand—claw—and heart."

"Is your middle name Mo?"

"No, which rhymes with Mo. But my middle name's not Mo. It's Donuts."

She rolls her eyes, which ends the flirt session. "Seriously, why the Mohawk?"

Because the old look wasn't attracting enough fish in the sea, and Manny and I are willing to try anything to catch those fish. Not that women are fish. I mean, it's just that we thought—he thought—the haircut would look good, but it doesn't.

"Change of pace." I shrug.

She smacks me playfully on the arm. "Hey, speaking of which, if you want to meet up this afternoon to work on our project, I'm free. You could lend a helping claw. I just need to pick something up at the mall first, so if you want, we could walk—"

"Yes! I do!" I don't let her finish her sentence. I know I'm supposed to play it cool, like I'm not all that interested so she gets more interested, but unless I'm reading this scene incorrectly, a girl has invited me to the mall. And unless I'm reading *that* incorrectly, a girl—a live and human one—has asked me on a date.

For the last year or so, I've fantasized about this moment. It looks like this:

The mall is packed. Shopping bags everywhere. The best-looking people in the neighborhood are window-browsing. My girl and I are walking hand in hand. Her palms are sweaty because she's nervous. She's never been to the mall with a man, and I am one. A very manly one. (She is becoming aware of this important fact.) We pass The Gap. I ask her if she wants anything, and she says, "All I need is right here with me." She squeezes my hand tighter. It's her signal for love. I give her hand two quick squeezes, which is my signal that I love her back and always will.

We head to a bookstore. As she browses the shelves for a new novel, I flip through a stack of magazines, rip out a bunch of cologne samples, and rub them all over. Armani Exchange on my neck, Polo Sport on my left arm. If she wasn't aware that she was walking with a man, now she knows. A very manly man, I am. And she—

"Are you ready?" Sabrina's shaking me. "Do you want to go to the mall or not?"

"Uh . . . yes," I say. "Let's go to the mall. Together."

"It's not a date, if that's what you're thinking."

"Of course not. Don't be ridiculous."

Because it's a weekday, the mall is pretty empty. Sabrina and I barely talk as we cover the first floor, passing clothing store after clothing store, nutrition centers and pharmacies. Barely audible music hums in the background, the kind you hear in the dentist's office while he's yanking out your teeth. The errand she needs to run is to a bookstore, perfectly in line with my fantasy. She doesn't find the book she's looking for, but I find plenty of magazines with cologne samples to rub on my arms.

"The best things in life are free," I tell her, wafting my forearms in her direction.

She laughs politely, then tells me the colognes smell terrible.

And then, well, I've passed Victoria's Secret hundreds of times, most of them with Manny. Each and every time, he's said, "Victoria's secret is that she is a man. Her real name is Victor." Manny once dared me to run inside and buy something. I wouldn't, so he lowered the stakes and dared me to tiptoe inside, cross the threshold, and run out. I wouldn't even do *that*. Victoria's Secret is off-limits. Males aren't allowed in. Even *I* know that.

"You sure look like you wanna go in," Sabrina says, chuckling.

"No, no, I don't think so."

"Oh, come on." She tugs my arm and directs me toward the store.

A woman with long black hair meets us at the entrance. She has a headset on. I don't know whether she's a bouncer, hostess, or bra salesperson, but no matter what, the headset is bad news.

"Looking for anything particular?" the bouncer/hostess/saleslady asks, a smile glued to her face.

"No, we're just looking, thank you," Sabrina says.

"Well, let me know if you need any help."

Everything is pink and red and I can't be here. I must look faint and disoriented because Sabrina says, "Are you fainting or acting?"

"Acting, definitely. I could win an Oscar in this place. There's already a red carpet and red . . . dress-looking things."

"They're called nightgowns."

I glance around to see if anyone is looking. Two girls with auburn hair have their backs to me. They talk to each other by the dressing room.

I think of doing something crazy to get Sabrina to laugh, but the two girls by the dressing room turn around. The one on the left has green eyes. *No, please no.* And freckles. *No, please no.* Three freckles. *Three freckles on her left cheek in the winter, six in the fall, nine in the spring . . . Oh, God, no.*

I hit the deck and take cover underneath a table.

"Denny, what's the matter with you?"

The soft red carpet tickles my nose, but I bury my face in it and whisper, "Can't talk now. I'm not here."

"What?"

"Allison Swain," I breathe. "She's here. In the store."

"So what?"

"Guys aren't allowed in Victoria's Secret," I explain.

She chuckles. "What are you *talking* about? Of course they are."

"No, they're not."

"Yes, they are."

"Okay, fine," I murmur. "Even if they are, I don't want her to see me in here."

"You can say you're getting something for Valentine's Day."

"That already passed."

"You can say you're getting something for your girl-friend."

Girlfriend? Does she mean her? Does she mean it?

Allison's feet touch the ground . . . white sneakers . . . marching to a sweet song . . . piano keys . . . saxophone . . . her laughter . . . at me? . . . white sneakers . . . delicate ankles . . . a cushioned landing . . . laughter . . . at me? . . . knees bent back . . . and forward . . . white sneakers . . . delicate ankles . . . footsteps . . .

Before they leave, I think I hear one of them giggle and whisper something about me. I think I heard something about a donut or a nut and then something about a ladybug and they're talking about me and they saw me and I am ruined, forever, ruined for all eternity, like those songs I heard on the radio after my mom's funeral. Ruined, I am— no, I'm not, I hate that word. Nothing is ruined, because I'm still here and not alone. Sabrina is here and I don't mind if they saw me.

For the first time since I can remember, I don't mind what other people think, what they say. She's . . . here, next to me, hiding. And I don't want to hide anymore.

I turn back to Sabrina and look into her eyes. Well, first at the five pieces of red felt in her hair—that swanky red carpet is a pilling mess—and then into her eyes. She looks more nervous than I've ever seen her. She's still here with me. The one willing to hide under a table with me. In an all-female store. Her lips look smooth again.

We're inches apart, the closest I've ever been to a girl. Dreams of Allison and what I've been wishing for my whole life . . . those dreams just left the store with her, and there's no one else I'd rather be under a table with than Sabrina.

I want to kiss her. I want to kiss her. I tell myself, kiss her. And then I shout it, KISS HER! NOW! 3, 2, 1, NOW! 5, 4, 3, 2, 1 . . . KISS HER!

But I'm up on that high dive again and it's cold and windy outside and my legs are stone and my ankles are shackled together. My feet are frozen to the board, icicles between my toes. The fall looks steep, *is* steep: miles below me, a freezing cold stream. Ice cold. I can't jump. No way can I jump, no way. Can't jump, can't jump, can't jump. Okay, 3, 2, 1, Jump! 3, 2, 1, Jump! Jump! I shout. JUMP! JUMP! JUMP!

And then something unprecedented happens on that high dive.

I jump.

It's a softer landing than I ever could have imagined, and I want to stay there forever, or at least more than ten seconds, my lips resting on hers, puckering, then resting, but I don't have time to get the rhythm because it only lasts ten seconds and someone's clearing her throat and it's not Sabrina.

The bouncer/hostess/saleslady clears her throat again, moves her headset mouthpiece to the side. "Um, excuse me, folks? Can I help you with something?"

I hear her and I know Sabrina hears her, but this moment only happens once in a lifetime and last time I checked I only live once.

I jump again.

"Help yourselves." Sabrina's mom greets us at the door with a tray full of warm chocolate chip cookies. I'm not even in the house and I'm already thawed out.

"Oh my," she gasps at my Mohawk, which I had forgotten about until now. "I certainly hope you'll be cutting that. Soon. Very soon."

The only good thing about my hair is that she doesn't seem to recognize me from the Chinese restaurant. Or from my mom's work on the PTA. Or maybe Sabrina just warned her about me. Whatever the reason, I'm glad I don't have to talk about my mom.

"Tonight," I assure her. "I'll cut it as soon as I get home. It was for a fund-raiser."

"I see. Would you like some cookies?"

"Mom, *really*?" Sabrina steps inside and puts her coat on the rack. "I'm barely in the house and you're jumping up on me like a . . ."

Tiger, I want to suggest. *A lion with cookies.* But something tells me it won't go over well.

"Well, you said you were bringing a friend for a project—and my, that is quite a lot of perfume, Sabrina. What were you thinking?"

I raise my hand. "It's cologne, ma'am. My bad." I step inside. "Got a little carried away there. Been testing out a few brands. Gonna surprise my dad for his birthday. They were giving out free samples at the mall."

Sabrina's eyes go wide.

"At the mall! Sabrina, you didn't say you were going to the mall!"

"Denny's just kidding, Mom. He's a real kidder, aren't you, Denny?" She elbows me in the ribs.

"Oh yes, ma'am, a regular court jester. My teachers, unfortunately, don't appreciate my comedy in the classroom."

"But, Sabrina, I thought you said he was a good student," she huffs. "Why are you working with him if he's not a good student?"

Sabrina stomps her foot. "I said he was a smart student, but, Mom, seriously? What do you—what are you—I seriously cannot believe you are—"

Sabrina's mom isn't looking at her anymore. She's looking at me. I'm already backpedaling out of the door when she says, "Wait, did you say your name was Denny? Your mother was . . . Susan?"

I don't feel like talking about her. Especially in the past tense. Besides, I'm not exactly used to working out conflicts with parents, and all the fuss is making me itchy. "It's no big deal, really," I say, backing up. "I should probably head home to do some light reading."

Sabrina's mom reaches for my sleeve and pulls me back in the house. "Forgive me, dear. Your mother was a special lady. So kind, thoughtful, selfless. I miss her."

"Yeah, thanks, I should probably head home. Need to catch up on homework. And you two seem like you have things to discuss."

"Don't be ridiculous. I'm just a little worked up. Caught a bit by surprise. You'll have to excuse me. I'm not used to entertaining boyfriends around here."

"Mom!" Sabrina's face flushes.

Her mom twiddles her thumbs. "Oh no, I meant friends that are boys. Sorry, dear, I guess I'm out of practice, is all."

"Mom!"

Sabrina may be horrified, but those warm chocolate chip cookies look delicious.

"Mind if I take a few, ma'am?"

"Oh, please do. It's what they're here for." She holds out the tray.

I reach in and take two.

"Oh, don't be shy. Take more, *I'm* sure not eating them. If I eat any more, I'll be rolling down the street. Rolling like a big ol' soccer ball."

I look down at her waist, slim as a tabletop. "Ma'am, believe me, you're in good shape. You should see my dad. Really, have a few cookies. They look delicious."

"Well, that's so sweet of you, dear," she says, playfully brushing my shoulder. "You're welcome here anytime."

"We'll be in my room," Sabrina says, pulling me down the hall and into her room.

"Remember, Sabrina," her mom calls, "keep that door open. Or no—"

"Boys, I know."

Even with the door open, I still feel like we're alone as we sit on the corner of her bed. I lock eyes with her and want to tell her everything: I.M.P., the dance, everything. I know it's the right thing to do because females are relationship beings and it's better to be rather than to seem and love is the feeling you get when you appreciate another's virtues—and whatever else Marsha told me that seemed smart at the time but is harder in practice. Love? How am I supposed to leap off that board?

"So I want to get to the group project," she says, "Denny, I do—" and there she goes, saying "I do," and I can hear the wedding bells ringing downstairs or maybe it's the oven buzzer for the chocolate chips cookies, but either way those wedding bells are coming and boyfriend and girlfriend and love and I can hear Marsha's words forming in my head. *A woman will tell you she wants to talk . . . all she needs is attention and love . . . and to be reassured that you ain't goin' nowhere. Oh, you'll see.* And of course I see now but—

"—but first," Sabrina says, "I want to show you the opening scene from *Les Misérables.*" She pulls over her laptop and types into YouTube and voilà. A five-minute break from the real reason we're here: to talk about what happened at Victoria's Secret and whether it'll stay a secret or whether we'll be an item, a date for the dance, maybe. I mean should she, I mean will she, I mean would she like to go with me and be a couple, a married couple with 2.5 children and how will I provide for her and which profession am I considering after middle and high school and college and whether I'll wear a bow tie, or just a tie or a tie and vest to our wedding.

It's actually really good—the opening bit from *Les Misérables,* I mean, which is pronounced *Les Miz* or *Lay Miz* for short, meaning *The Miz,* which rhymes with *The Biz,* like the candy business, which is something I know more about now than I used to and soon Sabrina will, too, which makes my legs shake like a hula dancer's even though I don't feel at all like dancing. The main character is Jean Valjean, which is a cool name. It's like me being named Denny Valdenny. He's this guy with a great voice who is unfairly imprisoned for nineteen years for stealing a loaf of bread. He's forced to do slave labor while looking down. "Look down, look down!" the guards shout as he slaves alongside dozens of other prisoners.

It's dark and depressing, but the action gets really good, really fast—unlike in *Death of a Salesman*, which trudges along until a flashback punches you in the teeth. But there are definitely similarities between the two plays, and I can see how a mashup, like a video montage in which we film ourselves in scenes from both plays and insert modern dialogue and modern music with modern chocolate chip cookies (maybe?), could really work. The feeling of imprisonment, being trapped in a life you hadn't dreamed of for yourself, escaping, sleepwalking through a nightmare, fighting for your life and your love, and children relying on you for food and support, and a flabbergasting ending that she says will leave you breathless.

Sabrina tells me the ending, but I don't lose my breath.

When she kisses me, on the other hand . . .

I mean, when she kisses me on the lips, I lose my breath. Not when she kisses me on the other hand. If she kissed me on the hand, that'd be weird. That'd be like kissing a king or queen. On the hand, I mean. Which is weird. And so is this whole breathing thing because I don't know how to breathe and I think I'm breathing my nose breath on her cheeks which can't be good, and the only reason I'm breathing nose breath on her is because I don't have any mouth breath so it's either nose breath or NO breath and I don't want NO breath because I don't want to die, not now, not ever, but especially not now.

I DREAMED A DREAM

Something about the way the night ended . . .

And what didn't happen. I didn't tell her anything about me. About the dance. Our relationship. Love. Like. Something in between, or something else altogether.

And I walked out in that cold February night as scared as I've ever been. And I've seen some scary movies in my time. Some of the scariest scenes in the scariest movies and I didn't even leave ~~a single~~ more than two lights on to fall asleep.

Sabrina drove me home in silence. I mean, her mom did, in a royal blue station wagon with a MY CHILD IS AN HONOR STUDENT bumper sticker, and after I trimmed my Mohawk and hit the pillow that night, I felt such paralyzing guilt and fear—and thirst. Kissing, it turns out, makes you very thirsty, so I drank a bottle of Yoo-hoo, ate a bag of Doritos, and counted over two hundred sheep before I dreamed an interesting dream.

"I love you," she says.

I freeze up. No, lock up. A zipper across my mouth, locks across my neck, forearms, and I've swallowed the key. The locks are voluntary. I want it this way. I want a force field around me. A moat. A river. An ocean. She's trying to talk to me and speaking my native tongue, but I don't understand a word she's saying. All I hear is my own voice shouting GET AWAY, TOO CLOSE, GET AWAY, RUN, RUN FOR YOUR LIFE!

"Denny, I love you." She leans in. Locks eyes.

Oh, God. Don't look at her. Look somewhere else. Look down. Not up again. Down. Look down. Like Jean Valjean in Les Misérables. *Look down, look down, 24601 . . . Is that a zip code? Maybe it's in Hawaii. I hope it's in Hawaii. Aloha, Hawaii 24601. That's where I belong. Stop looking up, look down. Stare at the . . . dust. Dirt. Candy wrapper. Those ANIMALS leaving wrappers on the ground! Keep calm, keep calm, look away. Look at the . . . paper, hair, shoelaces. My goodness those are some clean shoelaces. I bet they have that new shoe smell. I would smell them if she weren't looking at me. Into me. Into my soul.*

"Denny, I said 'I love you.'"

MY those shoelaces are clean. They sure are clean. Like Mr. Clean. Smooth and clean like Mr. Clean. Clean like Mr.—this isn't working.

Think of something better. Tastier. More enjoyable. Like Doritos. Yeah, Doritos. Think about Doritos.

"Denny, say something. You're supposed to say something."

Cool Ranch Doritos rock. They really do. They're spicy and refreshing at the same time. Like Red-Hots. Like an Atomic Fireball. Like salsa. Zesty salsa. Yeah, Cool Ranch Doritos are definitely zesty. Zestily refreshing. I don't know if "zestily" is a word, but it should be. It really should.

"Denny! Come on! Say something."

Those Cool Ranch Doritos are making me thirsty. Really thirsty. My throat feels like a web. A cobweb. A spiderweb. An old web in a closet that smells like mothballs. If I don't get liquid soon, I'll die of thirst, which is a terrible way to die because all you need is a faucet and even if the water is contaminated at least you won't die of thirst. You might die of contamination, but nobody ever really dies of contamination unless there's lead in the water, and then at least you could sue and score a million bucks, which doesn't go as far as it used to, but a million bucks never hurt anybody except rock stars, who don't drink water anyway. I don't know what they drink, maybe Yoo-hoo.

"Denny, look at me. I care about you. I'm putting myself out there. Denny, I said, 'I love you.' Now it's your turn."

Yoo-hoo, now there's an underrated beverage. Delicious. Refreshing. Almost zestily refreshing. I love Yoo-hoo.

She grabs my shoulders, shakes me. "DENNY, tell me what you're thinking!"

"I love Yoo—"

"Awwwwwww, Denny." It looks like she's melting.

"—hoo. I love Yoo-hoo."

She looks dizzy, disoriented, like I just spun her around twenty times in a relay race. "Denny, what are you talking about?"

"Yoo-hoo. I love Yoo-hoo."

"WHAT!!!!?"

"That's what I was thinking about. You asked me what I was thinking about. I'm just being honest. You always told me to be honest. I was—"

That's when she punches me. (As she should.)

(And I wake up.)

MY DANGEROUS LIFE AS A JANITOR

The weeks that follow are a blur of wrappers and lower back pain.

The good news: *Sayonara*, February. You look much better in my rearview mirror. The bad news: I don't have a rearview mirror. And even when I am old enough to drive, there will be no rearview mirror. My dad's Buick is "the family car," which is a nice way of saying "the only car."

More bad news: that lower back pain I just mentioned. While it's clear that Mr. Softee's name fits him well, it's also clear that business as usual won't cut the mustard, because we don't sell hot dogs or anything else that requires mustard. And more important, our current business model is unsustainable.

Too many wrappers = a shutdown, some type of detention-filled crackdown, and though Mr. Softee may be as weak as the soft-serve ice cream he's named after, that soft-serve ice cream is onto us. He knows my name, my game, even the *name* of my game. I don't tell Manny that I mentioned I.M.P., but I do tell him about the meeting because he saw Mr. Softee lead me away. And because he'd be proud of my nimble escape. (Because it rocked.)

But, to be honest, I don't even know why we're selling anymore, because of Sabrina—a date—maybe I could have a date—with her—I think I—hope I could—be lucky enough for her to go with me—but there's Manny and I promised him and I've already come this far and how often am I going to raise this type of money to rent cars and maybe pay the mortgage and buy dinners other than fried chicken and Chinese food?

But if Manny and I are still selling, we need to do something now, because we're running out of time.

At the Warehouse, Manny draws similar conclusions. "I think we are running out of time and we need to change our methods," he says, slamming his locker.

I hate to say it, but he's right. But because I hate to say it, and because I'd never hear the end of it if I said it, I simply ask how much we've raised so far.

He reaches for a notebook, flips it to the first page, and adjusts his glasses. "At last count, together we have raised $1,438, only a few days from our goal, and two and a half weeks until the dance. Your share of the money is still safe and sound, yes?"

"Of course." I tap my left foot against my right foot so I

can feel the thick roll of twenties against my ankle. "So what's the plan, Manny? What do we do next?"

"Were you not listening? The plan is this: our goal is $2,000. We will only get there if the wrappers are cleaned up, mopped up, picked up . . . however you do it, get it done. We will be increasing our distribution for our last push. The Gum Dealer is a threat, but good luck to him giving candy to everyone at school. We must distribute. Wildly. One last mad dash. But you must be careful and pick up wrappers. This is in your hands, Donuts. Those hands may be sugary, chocolaty, and peanut-buttery. But it is still in your hands."

"Why don't you pick up wrappers, Manny?"

"I believe it was the principal who asked you to do it, yes?"

Eating candy loses its luster quickly. You get that sugar high and you want to swing from the rafters and hug the planet for creating something so delicious and energizing and inspiring, and then you die. Fact of life.

No, that's not true. I mean, you run out of energy, fall from the rafters, crash, hit the floor, smack, crack, and splat.

Turns out, selling candy is exactly the same. At first, it's all fun and games and tens and then hundreds and fistfuls of freezing firm cash. And now, instead of a simple "Thank you, come again," I'm forced to say, "Thank you, come again, but don't drop the wrapper" . . . "Come on, clean up after yourself, man—what do I look like, your maid? Have you no soul? Have you no sense of dignity? Have you no shame, man? You're killing the environment. The ozone is melting and so is the chocolate on your wrapper and you don't even care, spoiled brat!" . . . "Yeah I'm talking to you. Remember not to eat it in class, be respectful, be responsible, you filthy animal" . . . "What, you're never coming back? Fine by me, I just added you to my 'no-sell list.' What's a no-sell list? It's like a no-fly list: you go nowhere and get nothing. Next time you want candy, I'll suggest the nearest corner store" . . . "Hey, seriously? In the middle of class, who *raised* you? How old are you? Don't you think it's about time you act your age and grow up? I mean, really, grow up, man. Grow up. Yeah, you. Grow up. Hey, pick that up! What? No, *you* suck! You're the scum of the earth, you know that? Please come again. My name is Denny and I sell candy."

I am the janitor. I am the manners police.

I am my own worst nightmare. I am a nagging teacher.

With every step I take, I'm back at her funeral, picking up Juicy Fruit wrappers.

They may say Snickers, Milky Way, Twix. But they smell like Juicy Fruit.

Wrappers are like a family of ants: you don't see them until you look for them, and where there's one, there are thousands. Under chairs, on top of chairs, under tables, under desks, *in* desks.

Animals, I tell you, animals at this school!

(And yes, ants, too. Unlike me, they seem to enjoy wrappers.)

Lunch is the worst. The wrappers come down like falling leaves and I can't stop them. I need a rake. I need a broom. I need a leaf blower. I need a new lunchtime activity. Before that meeting with Mr. Softee, each wrapper that fell was a symbol of my success. Now they're proof, evidence, that Donuts was here. All anyone has to do is look down.

It's pretty much all I do, all day, every day.

Look down. Look down. I'm like Jean Valjean in *Les Misérables*, toiling with my bare hands. Look down, and see the animals of Blueberry Hills Middle. Look down. Look down. Mrs. Q, what have I done? I deserve the pain, for I was a pain; I see now what I put you through, and I am sorry. You are the goddess of mathematics and I am trash. A worthless wrapper. I am so very sorry. I want you to know that.

While on the cafeteria floor, before I lose my nerve, I pull out a pen and some paper from my backpack and start writing an apology note:

Dear Mrs. Q, I was an idiot, a ~~maroon~~ moron. I know that now. I am sorry. I hope you are well and that things are ~~peachy~~ okay in the Learning Zone. ~~My hearts and prayers go out to you.~~

I scratch that last line out because "hearts" is a stupid word to use because I only have one heart. And besides, "my hearts and prayers go out to you" sounds like a note you hand to someone who has lost a mom instead of to a math teacher you gotta make up with. "Sorry you're lost" is a much better way of expressing sympathy, but it doesn't fit this scenario. Plus, "peachy" sounds sarcastic, and I spelled "moron" like the color "maroon," so I crumple it up and add it to the pile of trash on the ground and look down. Look down. Snickers, Butterfinger, Milky Way, Twix. This better be worth it. Better be worth it. Better be worth it.

No matter how many I pick up, there are twenty I can't get to. Under tables, under Sabrina's table. She's still wearing blue Converse sneakers, the color fading like our relationship. I look up to tell her I'm now invested in the environment, doing my part for Earth Day, but something tells me she doesn't believe me.

She says it, actually. "I don't believe you."

I don't know what to say to her.

But I do know this: I feel like a moron, a maroon, a moron with a maroon face from sweating and grunting and picking up garbage all day.

And I do know this: I want to tell the truth.

And I do know this: I want to ask her to the dance.

And I do know this: my lower back hurts.

And I do know this: in a few days, when our goal is met, I'll quit this job forever.

Every afternoon from 2:50 to 3:10 is the final sweep. Twenty minutes to do one last desperate cleanup before the janitor clocks in. It's intense, the pace furious. It requires a superhuman burst of strength, exhausting each and every energy reserve. A miracle, a prayer is what's required. Or, what I sell on a daily basis. See, it's in these heart-racing, calorie-burning moments that I find my merchandise to be of assistance.

So, on a Wednesday at 2:48, I reach into the bottom compartment of my backpack, push past all the crumpled stacks of bills, and pull out two Milky Ways. No time for enjoyment, I scarf both of them down in eight bites. I swallow hard.

Propelled by a double dose of chocolaty nougat, I run from classroom to classroom, any garbage, ma'am, any trash? Haven't you heard of global warming? Just trying to do my part . . . A last sweep of the lunchroom: look down, Denny, look down, I mutter, but it's a faster version of the *Les Misérables* song, the techno version, look down look down look down look down look look look look down down down down, look down look down look down look down look look look look down down down down 'cause I'm runnin' on caffeine and runnin' out of time. Gotta get to the bleachers in the gym, the stairwells, the locker room. Don't mind me, dude in the jock strap calling me a perv, dude in the shower cursing me out—just pickin' up *your* garbage. Well, sure, I sold it to you, which technically makes it *my* garbage, but when it became your property it became *your* garbage, so why am I cleaning it up? Ask the principal, yes I'm leaving, shower in peace. My words are fast my heart is fast the cleanup is fast God bless you Milky Way you are seriously an out-of-this-world candy and my sugar high is in full blast—and good thing too because the stairwells are a mess and sure my hands get stepped on but I'm feeling so nougaty good it doesn't bother me and I head to C wing, the last area to sweep, and I'm glad I come to C wing 'cause it's there I stumble into a mountain of wrappers over a foot high in the corner of the halls.

I don't stumble upon these wrappers. I stumble into them, over someone else's foot, and I'm reminded again that sugar highs are only temporary and the fall is steep and I know it has to be Chad because who else mans the halls at a time like 3:08 in the afternoon and who else wears shorts the second week of March and has calf implants and legs as smooth as a snake? He pops a carrot into his mouth and chews it slowly.

"I know what you're up to," he says.

On the ground, with Chad standing over me, I laugh nervously. "You know me, always up to no good. Just trying to clean up the school neighborhood."

"Give it to me," he says. "All of it."

"Sure, more Milky Ways? No problem, they're delicious." Still on the ground, I wriggle my body like a worm and reach into my bag and push past a stack of crumpled bills and fumble for candy bars and that's when he steps on my wrist, his strong right heel pressing down on veins, and I know now those calves are definitely either calf implants or the strongest calves ever placed on a human male.

I know that Chad means business. And that my business is about to crumble.

"The money," he says. "All of it."

No way. Not when we're so close.

He lifts his left foot onto my face. His heel smells like dirt. But feels like concrete. He pushes down—hard.

"Your meat is still sour," he says.

I scream, but it's muffled by his sneaker on my mouth, crushing my lips that were just getting to know Sabrina's and just tasting a bit of success and now they're bleeding, I can taste it, and I just bit my bottom lip and I can't speak.

"I don't want to do this to you," he says. "I really don't. Let's make this easy. Shall we?" He lifts his heel.

I shut my eyes.

"Next time, it crushes you," he says, popping another carrot into his mouth, which sounds strange to me. I mean, with his legs and feet smothering me, it surprises me that he still has arms. I know it's a stupid thing to think about at a time like this, but Chad suddenly feels like an octopus. How many limbs does this guy *have*? And why can't I be a ferocious hawk when I need to be!

My mind is flashing ten things at once and I can't think

straight: money, Manny, Mom, phone, mayday, help, please, please, please, candy, wrappers, bribes, deals, companies, hallways, witnesses, help, help!

He reaches for my backpack and I snatch it and pull it closer.

His right heel pushes deeper in my wrist and I know I'm running out of time.

Time! I've cursed you before (for the record, February, you still suck), but I could kiss you now. "Check your watch," I say. "It's three ten."

"So?"

"Janitors start their shift at three ten. Why do you think I'm buried in wrappers?"

"Because I tripped you."

"Right. I mean, ouch, I mean, why do you think I'm rushing to clean up?"

"Erroneous," he says, which means nothing to me, except that he doesn't seem afraid of the janitor. "I know what you're up to," he says again. Carrot in his mouth, he laughs. Unfortunately, he doesn't choke. *Well, choke on this!*

I maneuver my body to kick him—in the face, groin, stomach—*anywhere*. I've had bad ideas before, but this one takes the taco. As my foot comes up to strike, Chad grabs my ankle and twists. Then he snatches the enormous wad of twenties and hundreds from my sock. All of them. ALL OF THEM!

"Thank you for your donation to the school, Denny. As school secretary, I assure you that your money will not go to waste."

"GIVE IT BACK, YOU—"

He smothers me again with his right shoe. His sole tastes like mud and I bet his soul *is* mud. "If you tell anyone— *anyone*—about what happened here, everyone—*everyone*— will know about your little fund-raiser that's not a fund-raiser." Yup, mud. He grins. "I know about it. Know about how you raised money, you loser, to offer a ride in a good-looking car because you weren't good-looking enough to get a date any other way. Selling candy to get popular, to land a date to the dance."

I need to ask him how he knows, who told him. "MMRRRRR . . . ERRRRARRR . . . GRRRRAAA." Those are the sounds my mouth makes with his shoe in it.

A shoe that he now raises up.

Help! Somebody! Janitor! Please!

And crashes down.

SPEECHLESS

It's spring in the sixth grade. I'm playing soccer, even though I'm terrible at it. Really truly terrible. But my mom likes soccer and I like having her near me and we're running out of time.

One of my teammates passes me the ball. I tap it in front of me, fake left, and go right. The defender slips. "Go, Murphy, go!" my coach shouts. I don't know why he's getting his hopes up. Any second now I'll lose the ball, trip over someone's foot, and eat a faceful of dirt. Like . . . now. It hurts to get up, but my mom is watching and the ball is kicked back my way. I get to my feet and dribble forward, gaining speed.

"Go, Denny!" my mom cheers. Then I hear her cough. It hurts for her to shout and it hurts for her to cough.

I am in full sprint, like a sprinter at the Olympics, who is great at running fast but terrible at stopping. Only one more defender left to beat, the sweeper. I tell him to please move aside so that I can score a goal while my mom is watching. I really say that, "Please move aside so that I can score a goal while my mom is watching," but he's running too fast to hear me. He slide-tackles the ball away from me.

On the sidelines, the coach gives me a high-five. "That was aces," he says.

My mom walks over to me. Her face is soft and beautiful. Like flowers. Like a dozen yellow daisies. She dangles a cup of orange Gatorade, my favorite flavor. "Drink up," she says. "Champions deserve refreshment."

I try to explain that I didn't score, that I didn't even shoot.

"But you did your best," she says, "and that's what makes you a champion, my champion, and champions deserve refreshment."

It's almost summer. My mom's lying on a hospital bed in a long white gown. She's bald.

A television buzzes on the wall. People are in court. A judge whose name is Judy tells a man that he needs to pay a lady forty bucks, though it looks like he could use the money. People laugh.

"Go ahead. Wake her up," my dad says.

I shake my head. I don't want to disturb her. She looks peaceful but tired, like a dozen yellow daisies that are part of a peace rally but wilting after too much rallying.

"It's okay," he says. "She wants to see you."

I take a few steps forward and realize I don't want to see her, because up close she doesn't look peaceful. She looks dead. Her lips are purple. She's as pale as a vampire wearing pale makeup. Plastic tubes are stuck up her nose and I wonder if the tubes are permanent, like cement and permanent marker.

She tilts her head toward me but doesn't open her eyes. The judge named Judy makes people laugh again, asking a guy if he's lying. I turn around and whisper to my dad that I want to leave.

"Hey," my mom whispers. Her breath smells like laundry. "Nice to see you."

"Nice to see you, too," I tell her. I am lying. I hate seeing her like this.

"How's school?" she asks.

"Fine." I am lying again. Since she got sicker, I lie to her all the time, but I don't feel bad about it because this isn't really my mom in front of me. It's a stunt double. A replica. A wax figure at a museum that's so bad it's funny. The artist even got her glasses wrong: they're bigger, goofier, and black instead of her skinny pink ones. (This museum is ridiculous.)

"Glad to hear you're doing well," she says. "How are your grades?"

"Excellent," I tell her. She knows I'm lying because my dad tells her about my detentions. I wish he wouldn't tell her and I wish I wouldn't act up. I take it back. All of it. Especially because my health teacher told the class today that stress can make you sick, which means I'm making my mom even sicker and that I'm killing her. Maybe I already have.

A tube is taped to her hand. The tape is clear. I can see through it. The skin on her hand looks like it's melting.

My mom points to her mouth. "Ice chips," she says. "I'm . . . thirsty. Please tell the nurse to bring more ice chips." My dad runs out to tell the nurse.

"Are you doing your best?" my mom asks me.

"Yes."

"Good," she says. "That's what's . . ." she coughs into her hand. "Important. You can always fall asleep at night when you know you've done your best."

"I am doing my best."

"Stop! This is nonsense," the judge whose name is Judy yells at a man. "I don't believe you. Case dismissed." She bangs the gavel and walks away. Everyone laughs.

THE HORMONE EXTERMINATOR

Wiping the blood from my nose with the back of my hand, I realize I haven't done it. My best, I mean. Not even close. Mrs. Q knows it. My dad knows it. Sabrina knows it. Chad knows it. Or at least his foot does.

And soon Manny will, too. But I can't tell him now. I can't and I don't care that I'm not doing my best by keeping it from him. I can't tell him. I can't tell anyone.

Yes, I'd like to report a robbery. How much? At last count, around seven hundred dollars. What was I doing with that much money? Raising funds. For what? For a fund-raiser. What's the fund-raiser for? A dance, to get someone to go with me. Really? Yes, really, but never mind that. There was a robbery. How did I raise that much money? Selling candy in school. Am I allowed to do that? Sort of. Can I *prove* that the money was stolen? What do you mean, like do I have order forms? No, they were getting too tedious and unnecessary and sales were so good. I was a prolific salesman. Have I told the principal about this? Not exactly. Have I told my dad? Not a chance.

So, yeah, I'm not calling the cops.

Besides, I still have everything I want, anyway . . .

I still have Sabrina. Don't I?

I need to see her, tell her everything, have her tell me everything is gonna be all right. Everything is gonna be all right. Everything is gonna be all right. This morning I had seven hundred dollars. And now I don't. It was stolen. Everything is gonna be all right.

The next day, Sabrina passes me in the halls on the way to English class. "I have a surprise for you," she says, smiling mischievously, tugging me down the hall.

I have a surprise for you, too. SAY IT! *I didn't sell candy for a fund-raiser. Not a real one, anyway. And now it's all gone—my share is, I mean—but it doesn't matter because, look, we need to talk. Now. Say it!* SAY IT!

I want to, I really do, but my high-dive skills have withered away and we're almost to class and I can see Mr. Morgan in his room sipping coffee from a Dunkin' Donuts cup while setting up his TV/VCR. Teachers at Blueberry Hills are the only humans left on the planet who still use VCRs. They don't even have working remotes, which is why he's leaning over, pushing buttons manually on that clunky piece of junk. It looks like it was made a hundred years ago. Mr. Morgan tries to bang the top of it to get it to work. It doesn't. I want to walk in the room and help him, but I don't know a thing about old VCRs and everyone knows better than to burst into Mr. Morgan's class.

"Guess what?" Sabrina cries, leaning against the wall at the front of the line.

"Sabrina, really, we need to—"

"I finished!"

"Finished what?"

"Our project, silly. I filmed myself as Willy Loman's wife, and took video of you picking up wrappers and dubbed the 'Look Down' song to it and—"

"Wait, you took video of me picking up wrappers in the halls?" *I'M SAVED!* "Where'd you film me? Do you have Chad on video?!"

"Why would I have Chad on video?"

"No reason."

"What's wrong with your nose? Was it bleeding?"

I touch the bridge of my nose, now swollen and painful and hopefully not discolored. "Oh that, it happens all the time. It's the dry air. In the atmosphere. Tell me you filmed me in the halls."

"No, I filmed you in the lunchroom. When I got home I put a few sound bites together and rewrote much of the dialogue to fit the footage. I took a few pictures, too.

Not completely done yet, but maybe we can finish after school."

"Yeah, that'd be great. I need to talk to you, Sabrina, I—"

I can't finish my sentence because everyone in line is giving me a stink face. It's easy to ignore one stink face, but twenty-five stink faces . . . that's another story, especially when one of them belongs to Mr. Morgan. His face gets *really* stinky when he wants to make a stink face. Now is one of those times.

"Good morning, readers and writers. You are about to enter a hormone-free zone. No hormones allowed in here, for I am the hormone exterminator."

Normally I'd laugh, but I'm too focused on Sabrina and what I have to say and—

"Are we ready, Denny?" This from Mr. Morgan, owner of said stink face. "For the last time, stop looking at Sabrina. She doesn't like you. Class, you may enter."

On our way in, I'm scared to turn around and look because I'm afraid I won't find her there and won't see blushing and everything will be lost and I'll be left with nothing because she doesn't like me, never liked me . . . I can't help it. I must know . . .

I sneak a peek behind me. Sabrina's cheeks are red and rosy, as rosy as roses, and that's a beautiful thing because she's a beautiful thing—not a thing, a girl, a young lady, a female member of the human species who likes me, or *has* liked me, or doesn't like me at all and is simply embarrassed by what Mr. Morgan said. Or embarrassed of me, like my mom would be if she found out what I've become, what I've done, how much I've lost, what I've said, what I haven't said to Sabrina and Manny and my dad and . . .

Mr. Morgan shuts the door behind us.

"Okay, class, settle down," he says, and of course everyone does. "We've had volunteers to show a few rough sketches of their work thus far. Shelly, care to go first?" Mr. Morgan claps lightly, a golf clap, and encourages us to do the same, like we're all one big polite golf audience. As the first volunteer walks up to meet Mr. Morgan at the VCR, I get itchy, really itchy, like red ants are crawling up my leg, and I know I need to leave this room. LEAVE THIS ROOM I'm shouting at myself but the door is closed and my feet are frozen and I just feel so uncomfortable all of a sudden that I sort of start laughing. Maybe it's because Sabrina blushed earlier, which means she may, she might, she could still like me. Or maybe it's the clunky old VCR giving Mr. Morgan fits. Or the way some girl named Shelly says, "So, like, I don't know if it's, like, any good. I, like, think it's, like, honestly pretty *bad*, I mean, I'm like still working on it, and, like, here goes," but I can't stop laughing.

"Denny, stop," Sabrina whispers, tugging on my sleeve, and for a second I gain my composure, but then I notice the word "Donuts" on Mr. Morgan's Dunkin' Donuts coffee and it makes me laugh again.

"Denny, what are you *doing?*" This from Mr. Morgan, and the last thing I want is for *him* to get mad. I try to smile so that he'll lighten up, but he's not getting any lighter. He takes a few steps toward me. "And now you're smiling? You think what you're doing is funny?"

I can see myself in the reflection of his sunglasses. I look like Silly Putty, a stretched out, discombobulated lump of Silly Putty. I look like my dad. That's when I get even more uncomfortable and start to laugh. I don't want to, really I don't, but the more uncomfortable I get, the more I laugh. And the more I laugh, the angrier Mr. Morgan gets. Even through his sunglasses, I can see his eyes are ablaze. "What are you—I can't—believe me—you need to—Denny—seriously."

"Are you on drugs?" he finally asks.

I'm not, so I say I'm not.

"Don't believe the hype," he says. "The dope will make you a dope."

I don't want to laugh, but it's such a lame thing to say, especially for an English teacher, so I laugh. Louder. Longer. It's at this point that Mr. Morgan looks down at the work sheet in front of me with the following headings: Life is ~~good~~ a misunderstanding. Life is ~~good~~ a series of unfortunate events that are stacked like trees, and the stacks are so tall that not even lumberjacks can cut them down. Mr. Morgan's face tightens. And then my hero and model, the good ol' supreme and merciful and omniscient god of English, the S.U.O.G.E., always a quick trigger on student laughter, gives me the boot. The old heave-ho. The ax.

He doesn't actually take a lumberjack's ax to me or physically *boot* me out the door, but picturing him doing either while yelling "Homey don't play that!" is pretty funny, so I laugh harder, longer. Mr. Morgan shakes his head, muttering something about "waste" or "space." He might've said I was a waste of his time. Or a waste of space. A space cadet. A wastebasket. A waste of Silly Putty. I think he called me a waste of Silly Putty. And then he removes his sunglasses for the first time ever and his eyes look like the eyes of white owls, like someone at the slopes after a week with goofy ski goggles, and he's staring at me so intently that I laugh some more. Then he says, "I'll see *you* in detention," and the way he stresses "you" as if it was unclear if *I* was in trouble or someone else, like that girl Shelly who, heavens forbid, got, like, worried, she was in, like, a lot of trouble, and was in, like, detention, so I laugh some more and glance one last time at Mr. Morgan. For some reason, I start thinking of that Christmas eggnog with those teachers who hadn't laughed in months and now can't stop laughing but don't even know what they're laughing about. I want to stop, I really do, but I can't, and Sabrina is blushing again and not in a good way, and I don't want to embarrass Sabrina more than I already have, so I leave and don't look back.

MY BEST

Hello? How are you? That's good. Dad? Oh, he's not here. I'm in school. I'll tell him you said hey. Not much. Yeah, just wanted to hear your voice."

This time, after I put the phone away I don't feel better. After getting the heave-ho from Mr. Morgan and wandering the halls, I've settled at the front entrance of the school, where the doors are freezing cold from the outside wind. I feel, well, cold, but also naked, sort of like how it is in a dream, where you're naked in a public place like a classroom or stadium or bus stop and you can't do anything about it. Can't find clothes, can't hide in the bathroom, can't even cover yourself because your hands don't work.

I must spend about a minute touching my coat, my jeans, my hat—anything to convince myself that I really am clothed. Then I rest my face on the cold glass doors. A few small black birds chirp outside, a large black crow squawks, and it just seems that everything is in black and white all of a sudden. The street, the cars, the birds, the mat, the clouds—everything is in black and white, like I'm in an old movie. I realize maybe I *am* in a black-and-white movie, like I've traveled back through time, but then I remember that even in the days of black-and-white movies people lived in color, and I notice the sign for Blueberry Hills Middle School has mold on it, the first sign of color. The tops of the B, H, M, and S are dark green, like month-old mashed potatoes.

I throw my bag on the ground and all I want to do is lay my head down. Somewhere. Anywhere. Just tip over. Timberrrrrrrr . . . But it's the same feeling as the high dive. I can't tip. I want to, but my body screams, "NO, STOP, YOU MORON! YOU MAROON! DON'T BUST MY FACE!"

I don't know where to go. I don't want to face Mrs. Q or Mr. Morgan, and I know none of my teachers from the previous year will let me in their classes. They won't even let me stand outside their door. I could go to science or history, maybe get kicked out again, but not going to class is so much easier. On everybody. The more I think about it, the more I think it's actually noble of me, heroic even, to cut class instead of bothering my classmates. I'm sacrificing my playtime for their education. You're welcome, fellow students. You don't have to thank me now, but one of these days you'll recognize my contributions.

I picture myself going to an awards show, dressed up in

a tuxedo. The show will be filmed in black and white. Mr. Morgan will be the presenter, and after telling a few corny jokes, he'll say, "And now, the moment you've been waiting for: The winner of the sacrifice award is . . ." and he'll announce my name and everyone will cheer "Do-nuts! Do-nuts!" and with a rose between my teeth I'll strut to the stage, where Mr. Morgan will hand me a plaque that reads:

This recognizes Denny "Donuts" Murphy for his selfless acts of courage in humbly accepting his lack of a future, and the heroic choice to further the advancement of more talented, better-looking individuals than himself.

So I walk the halls.

I peek into the lunchroom, looking for Marsha. The lights are off and the tables are stacked, but I can see her in the back, wrapping up some food. I don't have anywhere else to go and I could use a bit of advice, and, strange as it is, she's the closest thing to a relationship expert I can find.

I walk to the lunch counter. Marsha is still in the back, now scrubbing pots, her hairnet swaying from side to side as she sings a Disney song about wishing upon a star.

My mom liked that song and I open my mouth to tell Marsha that, but another lunch lady hustles over to me, waving her arms hysterically, yelling, "Lunch is over, honey! We closed three minutes ago!"

"But wait," I plead. "I—"

"Sorry, kiddo. Maybe you'll come on time tomorrow."

"Yeah, maybe. Look, can I talk with Marsha?"

"She's busy. Doing her job. See, honey?" She points at Marsha, who wipes her brow with her forearm.

"Marsha!" I shout, leaning over the counter. "Hey, Marsha!"

"Hey, baby!" She puts a pot down in the sink and walks over to us. "It's all right, Gilda," she says. "He's no stranger. This here is one of our best customers."

"Make it quick," Gilda snarls. "The both of yous."

As Gilda storms to the back of the kitchen, Marsha asks me, "What's a matter?"

I take a breath and come out with: "Remember how you said women are relationship beings and that guys aren't?"

She chuckles. "Yes, sir, never seen a better quote than that."

"Quote?"

"Yeah, it's on a piece of paper behind the lunch counter. That's where I keep all my favorite quotes. Come around the counter, baby, and I'll show ya."

Something feels wrong, like hearing some old guy tell you he's got something special for you waiting in his car. Still, I let her direct me to the other side where, at the top of the lunch counter, she has pasted a whole slew of typed quotes, written quotes, and fortunes from fortune cookies.

She gives me the grand tour: "Okay, baby, let's see, 'It's better to be, rather than to seem,' 'Made with you in mind,' 'Women are relationship beings,' 'Whether you think you can or you think you can't, you're probably right.' Henry Ford said that last one. You know, like Ford trucks. Built Ford tough. Henry Ford." She sucks her teeth. "He wasn't a nice man but he had a nice quote. Oh, and over there, look over there." She points to a piece of gray construction paper with black writing. "'Same, same, but different.' That's from Thailand," she says. "My niece went there. It's on the other side of the world and some of them still speak English. Crazy, right? Yeah, I've collected a lot of good quotes over the years. My favorite one is about—"

I've heard enough. "Let me get this straight. All that stuff about relationship beings . . . that was just a quote? You mean it wasn't your own idea?"

"Heck no, sugar."

"So you really don't know how relationships work?"

"Ha! If I did, I wouldn't have been divorced three times!" She slaps herself on the knee in a brief fit of laughter. "But it's better to have loved and lost than to never have loved at all. That's a darn good quote, too."

"So you—you lied? I can't believe that you—"

"Your horses," she says. "Hold on to 'em. I didn't lie or plagiarize. I put quotation marks on them, see?" She points to a few squiggly apostrophes. "But I suppose I should have told you. Lies always catch up to you eventually, see. You should always tell the truth. Always."

"So you think I should tell the truth? I mean, to my girl—a friend, a girl who is/was a friend of mine?"

"Just do it," she says, chuckling. "I got that quote from Nike, but it's a good quote. Smart man, that Nike. Wish I had thought of that. Oh, and 'the truth will set you free.' Wish I thought of that one, too."

She smiles crookedly and adds, "Now we both know why you *really* came up here . . ." She runs into the back and returns with a tray. Beaming, she hands it to me. "French fries, made with you in mind."

I don't want to eat. All I want to do is lie down, but last time I checked, lying down in the back of the lunchroom wasn't the most socially acceptable thing to do.

I find the nurse at her desk, flipping through fashion magazines. As usual, her lips are pursed—decades of smoking have left them permanently in that position. Even though she can't possibly be a day over fifty, she looks eighty.

With my arm, I wipe my nose, which still feels painful and red and puffy. But the nurse doesn't notice. She never notices anything. When I ask her if there are any empty beds, she peers up from an article in *Vogue* and, looking really put out, says, "Didn't your mother teach you any manners?"

"Pardon me," I say, smiling weakly, "are there any free beds?"

She slams her magazine on the desk. "Why don't you see a doctor?"

"I didn't know you had one."

"We don't." She grins. "You don't listen very well, do you?"

"But I thought you said—"

"I *said*, 'Why don't you see *a* doctor?' If *we* had a doctor, I would have said, 'Why don't you see *the* doctor?' or 'Why don't you see *our* doctor.'"

"Right. Sorry, nurse. Don't know what I was thinking. Now can I lie down?"

"Only if you promise to go see a doctor—your *own* doctor—when you get home."

"I promise."

"Third bed on the right," she says. "Don't forget to close the curtain behind you."

My head feels heavy enough to break a bed. Or the green cot in front of me. I lie down and I close my eyes and look around for some sheep. I count sixteen before the nurse nudges me in the back.

"You're snoring. It's bothering me. Now get up." She grabs my arm. "I'm not leaving until you get up."

Like I said, you can't hibernate in middle school.

I roll off the green cot and try to stand up. The room spins. Once the nurse walks away, I sit back down, crouch into a ball, bury my head in my lap, and breathe through my nose so I don't puke. I pull open the curtain and head toward the exit.

The nurse is back at her desk, flipping through a fashion

magazine. I try to think of something nasty to say to her for waking me up, but you have to have energy for that. As I stagger out of the nurse's office, I feel homeless. I mean, I know I'm not, *really*, but I just outstayed my welcome on the only bed in town. I can't stay in the bathroom because that's gross, I can't go to any classes that I don't belong in (gods and goddesses of every subject seem to care about that sort of thing), I don't want to talk to Manny, I can't roam the halls because of Chad . . .

I figure that since I can't keep my eyes open any longer and I have no place to go, I may as well go nowhere. So I stay put. I remain standing. I lean a little bit on someone's locker, but I don't actually move.

I feel like that football player on my sheets, the one with the blue uniform who is just cradling the football in his armpit, the one who isn't pumping his arms or legs. I'm not moving either, not even to the side or backward. That's what I've become: that frozen blue football player. The funny thing is, I sort of feel jealous of him. I mean, I know he isn't real or anything, but when you think about it, he gets to spend his whole day on somebody's bed, sleeping the day away. And because he's frozen, he doesn't have to worry about anything. I pretend for a second that I, too, am frozen and incapable of thought, but when you try not to think about something, that's all you think about.

I try to sing a song to keep my mind off my mom, but every song reminds me of her. Even joyful tunes like that old-school Kokomo vacation song from the Beach Boys makes me feel like crap. Sure, Bermuda and the Bahamas sound nice, but then they have to go and ruin it by mentioning a pretty mama. So I try another, and another, and some songs don't mention mothers but even the word "son" reminds me of her. And "son" sounds like "sun," so any reference to the sun or a sunny day or "here comes the sun" or "the sun will come out tomorrow" is more than I can handle.

The longer I lean on that locker, mumbling old songs, the more I feel like the only man left on the planet. I really do. I even invent a game called "The Only Man Left on the Planet," the point of which is to prove that I really am the only man left on the planet. Every time somebody passes by and doesn't look at me, I give myself a point. If someone looks at me funny, I lose a point. If someone speaks about me, I lose two points. If someone speaks *to* me, I lose three points.

After what seems like an hour but is probably only a minute or two, I'm winning the game, but I don't want to. I don't want to be the only man left on the planet. I want someone to talk to me. The longer I lean on that stupid locker, the more awkward I feel. I convince myself that I've been standing or leaning there for twenty years and that my social skills have withered away. Any minute now I'm sure that someone will pass by and I'll stumble and blurt out the lamest thing ever said.

And then it happens.

Two girls walk past me talking about the dance. Actually, only one of them is talking, but she's talking enough for the both of them: "You should totally come with us. Well you can't actually come with us, because our group is already, like, *way* too big, but you should ask around. Soon. OMG!" She doesn't have a chance to finish because, being the only man left on the planet, having been on the corner without talking to anyone for twenty years, I stagger forward and yell, "The dope will make you a dope!"

The loudmouthed girl puts her hands on her hips. "Excuse me?"

"Don't believe the hype," I say, bracing myself on the locker. "The dope will make you a dope."

She scrunches her face. "Um, excuse me, are you crazy?"

"No, are you?"

"Um, excuse me, does your head hurt?"

"No, does your nose hurt?"

The quiet girl tugs the loudmouth on her arm. "Maybe we should help him."

"That's Donuts," Loudmouth explains. "He's just being funny."

"Ohhhh," the quiet girl says, obviously relieved.

They both start laughing, so I laugh too, and the harder I laugh, the more I stumble. And the more I stumble, the harder I fall. The more I try to get up, the harder I fall back down. And the harder I fall down, the more I feel like the only man left on the planet. And the more I think about it, being the only man left on the planet doesn't feel so bad. So I laugh.

"He really *is* funny."

I laugh.

"Um, excuse me, are you okay?"

The way she says it makes me laugh even more. And thinking again about that scene with those laugh-deprived teachers makes me laugh harder, and I feel like rolling around on the floor in the eggnog with them. I mean, I know they're not there, but rolling on the floor sounds pretty fun, so I do it.

"Um, excuse me, you're freaking me out."

My face hurts from laughing so much. No, it hurts from smiling. I don't *want* to smile because I'm not happy, but you can't laugh without smiling unless your jaw is wired shut. Chad should've stepped on me harder so my jaw could get wired shut and I could laugh all day without cracking a smile.

"Um, excuse me, are you crying?"

Maybe it's the air, like the way the air at the mall makes you tear up because of all the perfumes and colognes, but I start crying, which *is* funny because I don't cry, ever, not even at my mom's funeral. I want it to keep coming, but I haven't cried in so long the pipes are jammed up and only a few tears come out, so I laugh—loudly. Not as loud as a fire alarm, but louder than the guys on National Public Radio, and the more I laugh, the more my face hurts.

"Um, excuse me, do you want me to get help?"

Then I get really tired suddenly, probably from all the laughing and smiling. I shut my eyes and look around for some sheep. Some of the sheep are tired like me and some of them are beautiful like Sabrina.

"Um, excuse me, I'm going to get help."

I try to think of happy things and start to hum that song my mom used to sing to me. The one about me being her sunshine. My eyes are heavy and I couldn't stand up even if I wanted to, which I don't, because the sheep look so warm and fluffy. It's getting dark outside, or inside, which makes the sheep hard to see. I try my best to count them, I really do, but my best isn't good enough. It's never good enough. The sunshine goes away like it does every day and my eyes are closing and it's getting too dark to see anything and the skies are gray and then dark gray and soon I can't see anything at all.

HOMEY DON'T PLAY THAT

How do you feel?"

The sunglasses are off. His eyes still look like a white owl's. About to feast on whatever owls eat. Hopefully not donuts.

"Denny, knock it off and get up. How do you feel?"

"Tired."

"Up," he says.

"Up?" Right, still on the floor, Roger that.

"Get up."

I do as I'm told. "Detention," he says.

"Oh."

"And I'm calling your parents—your dad, I'm calling him."

I want to remind him that it's not on my dad's afternoon agenda to visit me at school, but Mr. Morgan is already helping me up with hands as strong as a lumberjack's, and

I'm too tired to argue, especially with Sabrina standing beside him.

The windows are closed, but the shades are open. It looks cloudy outside. Not partly cloudy, completely cloudy. And cold. The whole room is cold, including the armrest desks, but I don't say anything because he's got an index card on his desk with my dad's contact information in my hand-writing and he's on the phone.

"Mr. Murphy?" He isn't talking to me.

The conversation doesn't last long. Nor will this deten-tion. My dad says he'll be here in five minutes, which means at least ten, but it's still not a lot of time.

"Get some work done," Mr. Morgan tells me, as he turns the newspaper page from Leisure to Local News. I lean forward and squint to see if our upcoming dance has made it to Local News yet. Negatory, no dance, but I see an ad for a local production of *Les Misérables* at the Forrest Theater. *Great.* And an article about the economy crip-pling schools. *Even better.* And Mr. Morgan's impatient eyes. "Work, Denny," he says. *Splendid.*

I take out my math book and turn randomly to page 239. The directions spill to page 243. Five pages of directions for one problem.

Mr. Morgan flips to the comics. Then he unwraps a turkey sandwich on white bread and takes a bite. A Three Musketeers bar is on the table next to him. He didn't buy it from me. The whole scene depresses me and I get this black-and-white feeling back again, for good reason. The gray weather. The cold air. Cold desks. Cold Mr. Morgan. Pages 239 to 243 of my math textbook. The sound of Mr. Morgan's newspaper crumpling. The comics I can't read. The black-and-white lunch I can't eat. I feel like the only man left on the planet. I gotta get outta here.

The newspaper crinkles as Mr. Morgan kicks his feet up. "Get some work done," he says again. "Mrs. Q and your other teachers told me there's plenty to catch up on."

"They're lying, Mr. Morgan. Just like Mr. Softee and his detention thing. He said teachers hate detention because it's time-consuming."

Mr. Morgan chuckles. "Well, *he's* lying. I like the free time."

"Told you he's a liar."

He shakes his head, muttering, "I can't believe Mr. Soffer said that teachers—"

"I wanna get outta here. I need to get outta here."

"Calm down," he says, turning a page of the newspaper. "Use this time wisely."

"I feel like I'm in prison. This is torture. We learned in government class that torture is illegal. Seriously illegal. Are you aware that what you're doing is illegal?"

He yawns. "I'm not aware of that."

"You should be. I can sue you for war crimes."

"War crimes? This isn't a war, Denny."

"We'll let Mr. Softee be the judge of that."

"Well, *that* sounds like a fine plan," he says, folding up the paper.

He has a point—my idea is terrible, because as Judge Judy would say, "It holds no water"—but I don't appreciate his sarcasm. "You know what, I wish they'd fire you."

He smirks. "For what? War crimes?"

"And other stuff. For one, you're not—what's that word Mr. Softee used—oh yeah, *progressive*. You're not progressive enough."

"You don't even know what that means."

Another good point.

"Listen, Denny, your project, it could use a bit of touching up, but it's well done. I'm proud of the work you did with Sabrina."

She did the work, not me. Sabrina did it all.

Sabrina. I find a girl with the type of face you want to come home to, and I ruin our home. I have to tell her. And I have to tell Manny. I have to tell them everything.

"Can I go to the bathroom, Mr. Morgan?"

"Your dad should be here any minute."

I hope the traffic is bumper-to-bumper, as heavy as he is. I hope he gets stuck in the middle of the highway and doesn't show up. Then he'll get blamed instead of me. I'll tell Mr. Morgan that my dad never even *meant* to come. That cutting class and cutting meetings runs in the family. That it's a proud and storied tradition dating back to the days of those mischievous Pilgrims, but I hear his heavy breathing all the way down the hall.

"He's here," I mutter.

"How do you know?"

"Those wheezing noises aren't coming from the heater."

"Well, great, let's go then."

"Go where?"

"Mrs. Q's room."

"What? Why?"

He shrugs. "Change of scenery; I get tired of being in the same room. It should be a nice change of pace for you, too. I hear you haven't been there in a while."

In a black business suit, Mrs. Q doesn't say "aloha" to me, and I don't say it to her, and my dad says nothing. Not "hey" or "hello" or even "thanks for interrupting my day." All he does is nod, which makes me uncomfortable, so I sort of laugh again, but only in my mouth. I'm not sure my dad hears it because I pretend to clear my throat to mask the noise. You know, like when you're in class and accidentally fart, so you slide your chair or cough a few times so everyone will think *that* was the noise they heard instead of the fart.

Yeah, that never works.

And neither does my dad's attempt to sit down. He takes a deep breath, rolls up the sleeves of his wrinkled brown dress shirt, and tries to shimmy himself into an armrest desk, but he doesn't fit.

Mrs. Q offers him her chair. He waves her off and tries to sit on top of the armrest desk, but the desk tips forward and the chair's back legs become airborne until the whole thing almost capsizes. He steps off to allow the chair to come back down, but then he gets right back on until the desk tips forward again. It's like one of those little kid rides in which you put a quarter into a bull or a horse or an elephant and ride it forward and back, up and down, forward and back, up and down.

"I think I'll stand," my dad says finally. A fine idea.

I take a seat, my dad standing over me. Mr. Morgan and Mrs. Q sit across from us. Her room has changed a bit since I last blessed it with a visit five weeks ago. Her decorations have matured, no sign of the Learning Zone; instead, there is a new rules poster—"Three strikes and you're out. Batter up!"—and some new math slogans: "Math is everywhere, math is life. If you say you don't like math, you're saying you don't like life. That's a problem. Solve it!" . . . "If you don't have time to *do it right*, you must make time to *do it over*" . . . "Try math; odds are you'll like it" . . . "Math = Success. Go figure." Get it? Like, in math, you *figure* things out?

Eeesh. She's still got a ways to go.

Mrs. Q calls the meeting to order. "Thank you again, Mr. Murphy, for coming in."

A nod, and then, "Thank you for having me," and it's already sounding too much like a guest on a late-night talk show. *Tell me about your latest movie,* I assume is next. Roll the clip. *Tell me about your love life.* Sip from your mug. Cue the bombshell.

Cue it.

"Well, Mr. Murphy, as you know from the message I left on your machine, Denny has, uh, struggled a bit in math class, and struggled, to a large degree, to show up for class."

I try to switch topics a bit and play the talk show guest for all it's worth: "I *have* struggled in math, Mrs. Q, and may I express my appreciation toward you and Mr. Morgan for organizing this important meeting of the minds and—"

My dad waves me off. "I'm sorry, what did you say about that message?"

"Oh, I—I assumed you got it . . ." Mrs. Q says. "I left it about a month and a half ago."

"About a month and a half ago. A month and a half ago." He keeps tasting those words and it doesn't seem like he likes the taste. "A month and a half ago. A month and a half ago . . ."

He looks down at me like I'm beneath him, which I am, because he's standing.

Given that I'm on trial, I can't help but think of Judge Judy and realize that none of these accounts mean anything without written proof, and I'm just about to proclaim *She lacks evidence* but Mrs. Q reaches for a navy blue attendance book. "Denny is, well, very active and needs a lot of support to excel in his classes. For starters, he needs to *come* to class."

She flips to the back of her book. "He's only been to . . . hold on, let me see here . . . yes, four of my math classes this marking period. This is his attendance record if you'd like to take a look." My dad leans over, nods at her notebook, then nods at me. "And when he *is* in class he has difficulty focusing and he can be a distraction to his peers. I know he's . . . recently been through some difficult times. I was sorry to hear about his loss—your loss. I was—am, sorry."

My dad grunts but doesn't speak, so Mrs. Q continues: "I'd *like* to see him do well, but he hasn't taken the work seriously. He'd much rather interrupt the class and play around."

Once it's clear that Mrs. Q has concluded her opening statements, my dad turns to me. "Well, son. What do you have to say?"

What do I have to say? That's a terrible question. It's not as bad as asking "What do you have to say *for yourself*?" but it's still pretty bad. I mean, what can I possibly say to make anyone feel any better? The worst part is that my dad doesn't even *want* me to say anything. But I know that if I don't open my mouth, he'll keep pestering me just for show until I do. I don't know what to say, so I say that: "I don't know what to say."

He leans over and it looks like he's going to whisper in my ear, but he doesn't whisper, he yells.

"YOU DON'T HAVE *ANYTHING* TO SAY?"

"No."

He takes a breath, lowers his voice. "But your teacher, Mrs. Um . . ."

"Q," Mrs. Q says.

"Right, Mrs. Q tells me you have a lot to say in class. A whole lot to say. You don't have *any*thing to say now?"

"No."

"Nothing at all?"

He's getting pretty worked up and is beginning to sound like a bull, breathing loudly through his nose like a backward sniffle. "Nothing at all, Denny? Nothing at all? We're not leaving here till you say something."

"Actually, I do have something to say. To Mrs. Q." I turn to her. "Mrs. Q, after picking up all the garbage in the hallways like Jean Valjean, I now know how difficult your job is, and how much more difficult I made it for you. I'm sorry." Mr. Morgan furrows his brow, so I explain: "Jean Valjean had a harder life than I do, much harder, I know. Most people do, including Mrs. Q." Now it's her turn to look confused. "It's a play, *Les Misérables*, and there's this guy who—"

"I'm familiar with the play," she says.

"Of course. Forgive me. Anyway, I realize now how hard I've made it for you to teach. I now know what it's like to argue with the animals in this school. I've been picking up trash, you see. It's been difficult, but it was only fair. I'm not complaining about it. I shouldn't have been selling candy in the first place."

"WHAT ARE YOU, A CANDY DEALER?" It seems my dad's volume switch is stuck on loud. "DON'T I GIVE YOU AN ALLOWANCE?"

"Yes, but it's only a dollar and—"

"YOU SPOILED BRAT! YOU HAVE NO IDEA WHAT I—"

Mr. Morgan jumps like a heroic lumberjack savior to rescue me from annihilation, throwing out a two-by-four for me to grab on to for dear life. "In English, Denny has done some good work as of late." Then Mr. Morgan must tire of rescuing me, as he yanks that two-by-four from my hands. "But Denny couldn't stop laughing today in English class." *Okay, that's enough.* "And fell asleep in the hallway." *O-kay.* "And is now in danger of failing my class." *Got it.* "And is in danger of repeating the grade." *Yup, got it.*

"Wait, you're Mr. Morgan?" my dad says. "Mr. Life Is Good, right?"

This is the first time I've seen Mr. Morgan blush. "Well, I—"

"I've seen your work sheets. And what Denny's done with them."

He nods, his face reddens. "I've seen them, too."

"Okay! It's true!" I blurt out. "What's done is done. I'm not proud of it. Any of it. But I promise, Mr. Morgan and Mrs. Q, that I'll bloom in the very near future."

My dad grimaces. "You'll *what* in the very near future?"

"Bloom," I say. "I'll bloom."

"Bloom?"

"Yes, bloom. It's from *Leo the Late Bloomer,*" I explain.

"Leo the Late—what are you talking about?"

I stiffen. What am I talking about? That was Mom's and my favorite book! He doesn't even know what books Mom used to read me. He doesn't know anything.

"I know what I'm talking about," I say slowly, so that I don't seem upset.

His chest swells. "No, you don't know what you're talking about! You haven't said anything at this meeting!"

"Well, you don't say anything at home!" I thunder. "You didn't even mourn for her! You just watch TV all day and night and you never talk about her. You never even cried, not once! You didn't care! You still don't!"

I don't mean to say that. I really don't, especially with Mrs. Q sitting next to us. My dad's face gets really red and he makes this weird noise that sounds like "hul." Then he looks over at Mrs. Q and apologizes for my "inappropriate behavior."

"Inappropriate?" I fire back. "Suddenly it's *inappropriate* to have a conversation? It's ridiculous to open up in a meeting? I'm sorry, gods and goddesses of your respective subjects, but I thought this meeting was about opening up and getting to the bottom of things, was it not?"

"I don't . . . well, yeah . . . but I—" Mrs. Q stammers.

I turn to Mr. Morgan. "I thought we came here to reflect, did we not?"

He shakes his head without moving his head. The movement is in his owl eyes.

"I came here to reflect, Mr. Morgan. I wish the same of my dad." I don't see my dad's hand swinging down until all I hear and feel is a *thump* and my head is a foot to the left. I think I bit my tongue and in front of me there are little white lights that look like stars. Mrs. Q gasps. My hand flies up, but it doesn't know where to go, whether to rub my head or hit him back. So it sorta hangs there, like I'm stretching my shoulder. It's funny, this in-between position, like when you try to shake someone's hand and they want to give you the fist bump so you end up fist-shaking them instead. But right now I don't see the humor in this shoulder stretch, with Mrs. Q touching her face and Mr. Morgan's owl eyes now looking like the biggest-owl-in-the-forest's eyes. He grunts—Mr. Morgan, I mean, like he wants to say something but doesn't know exactly what to say, and I understand because I feel the same way, except my hand is still in the air.

If there was ever an appropriate time to curse at my dad, this feels like the moment. The curse would pale in comparison to his *thump*, which means they'd sort of cancel each other out and I'd still be the victim and we'd both be wrong. But Mrs. Q is here and my mom taught me never to curse around women, so I try a different method.

"You look upset," I tell him, my voice steady despite the storm inside me.

He blinks. "I *what?*"

"It's just an observation," I say coolly. "You look upset."

His mouth twitches. No, his whole face twitches. He looks like some old-school robot about to self-destruct and explode into smithereens. I want to keep watching, I have to keep watching, but Mr. Morgan stands up and yells, "Enough!"

And you know, when Homey don't play that . . . he don't play that.

And my hand is still in the air.

And my dad is crying.

LOSING

I have to tell him in person. It's only fair. A day after the meeting of the minds, I meet Manny at the Warehouse and try to break the news.

"Such a jokester, you are," Manny chuckles. "A regular court jester, this one."

"No, Manny, I'm serious. I'm sorry."

"What is this? Are you scammer-hating? What am I missing?"

"I'm not kidding. Chad took it."

"Chad with the crazy calf muscles even bigger than Mr. Perfect's?"

I nod. "He took it. All of it. About seven hundred dollars."

"Uh-huh. Right. Where is the hidden camera?"

"I promise, I'm telling the truth. He jumped me in the halls and stepped on my face and took it from me. I swear,

I'm telling you the truth. It pains me to say it. The truth hurts and this truth *really* hurts, but I have to give it to you, I have to tell you because we are or were business partners, and I really am very, truly, very, very sorry."

Manny's face tightens as the possibility of the truth sets in. He hits the floor as if a drill sergeant said to "drop and give me twenty," but instead of doing push-ups Manny grabs my shoe, hikes up my pant leg, and tears into my sock. I feel his fingernails scratching against my ankle. There's no money there. Nothing left.

"Manny, I'm telling you, it's gone. I'm so sorry. We've come so far and worked so hard, but there was nothing I could do and there's nothing I *can* do and I'm sorry."

Manny adjusts his glasses. "This is beyond flabbergasting," he mutters, slowly getting to his feet. "Flabbergasting. Simply flab-ber-gast-ing. Flabbergasting."

Shoeless and sockless, I try to give him a hug. A man hug. A chest bump. A *Star Trek* handshake. Anything to prove we're still friends. That we'll survive the dance together. That our friendship will last beyond this.

"You are on your own," he says, shoving me aside.

Friendless and broke, I'd wander the halls alone for the rest of the day, but everyone in the whole school is herded to the gym like a pack of mindless cattle. The basketball team is holding a pep rally in the gym today before their last game against Monroe Middle School. Pep rallies. Really big deal. Like the crowd is really gonna change how the team plays the following day. Like a player's gonna drive to the hoop, leap between two defenders, and realize, *Oh yeah, there were* so *many happy cheering faces at that pep rally.* And only then does he decide he wants to make the shot.

"Flying Dogs! Go Flying Dogs!" Allison shakes her pom-poms as the speakers blast our official school song of "Who Let the Dogs Out?" and everyone barks. Like, really barks. Pep rallies . . . I'm telling you, the worst. A bad use of time. Bad music. Barking. And everything's for show.

Sabrina's standing next to me, leaning on the railing on the top floor of the gym—which the school uses for extra seating but never really needs because nobody comes to games or cares about pep rallies—so we're alone, and she's looking at me, waiting for an explanation, and I can no longer be all for show.

I owe it to her. I can't be as lame and phony as this pep rally.

I watch Allison do three cartwheels and a backflip. Her face flushes as she gains her balance and raises her pom-poms. "Go, go Flying Dogs!" Barking fills the gym.

"Denny, what's wrong with you? What happened to you?"

She tilts her head and looks at me the way my mom did when she knew I was keeping something from her. It makes me feel like I'm walking through a full-body scanner at the airport. Which is fine. Because I need to tell the truth. To everyone.

The truth: I don't drink orange Gatorade anymore because my mom always handed it to me on the soccer field. It makes me sad.

 The truth: "Sabrina. I like you. I want us to romance—be romantic—be partners in a middle school romantic romance. But I'm afraid."

 The truth: "Dad, it's my fault, too. I don't like to talk either. I still don't, but I'll try if you do. I'll need you to go first, though."

 The truth: I used to wish Mr. Morgan was my dad. I don't anymore.

 The truth: "I'm sorry, Mrs. Q. I think you'll make a good teacher. You really will. Your three-strikes-and-you're-out policy is a good idea. If you used that on the first day of school, I never would've messed with you. But it's not your fault. It's mine."

"Sabrina, I need to tell you the truth."

 "That'll be nice," she says.

 "Okay, here goes." Deep breath. "Manny and I had a business."

 "With the candy . . ."

 I nod. "We had a business. To increase our compatibility quotient—"

 "Huh?"

 "Popularity. For people to notice us. Like us. Or at least

want to go with us to the dance. As dates, real dates, instead of groups. We were desperate, we were losers, and then I met you and I didn't feel like one anymore. That kiss under the table in Victoria's Secret, that was . . . my first. I felt for you. I fell for you. But Manny has been my friend since I was two, and this fund-raiser that wasn't really a fund-raiser . . ."

She looks dizzy. More confused than angry.

"We made a lot of money that Manny wanted to use to ask eighth graders—"

"What? Like who?"

I peek down at the cheerleaders. "Allison," I tell her. "And her friend. But I wasn't ever going to go with them anyway, because I like you, I do, I really do, and then I was robbed and—"

"You were robbed?"

"Yeah, but the point is I was going to use the money for us because I want to be near you—I mean, close to you—I mean, with you—and that's why I was acting so weirdly around you and just plain weird in class and why I couldn't stop laughing even though nothing was funny, Sabrina. I mean, we laugh at things together and I hope you think I'm a *little* bit funny, but I'm not being funny now and I still want us to be with each other—I mean, together, if not now, then after the dance—"

I want her to slap me, hold me, hug me, say something—*anything*—but she's walking away, and I want her to turn around and say something but she doesn't, and soon I'm alone on that second floor of the gym. From below, Chad is looking up at me, grinning. And barking so loud it rings in my ears.

I sit down and try to gather myself, but I feel broken, like there are too many pieces to pick up, and I decide that if someone comes up to me and hands me a sympathy card that reads "I'm sorry for you're lost," I will correct their spelling.

It's supposed to read "I'm sorry for your loss."

You *can* lose people.

DAYLIGHT

When I get home from school, prepared for a long night of self-loathing, I try to assemble my old G.I. Joe tent on the side of my bed, but the supports get all tangled and it takes more energy than I currently have. I'm out. Of energy, luck, and friends.

I count 874 sheep before I fall asleep and dream in black and white.

The sound of snapping plastic forces me to open my eyes.

"Your tent. I think one of the legs is almost bent," my dad says, breathing hard. "It shouldn't have even been here in the first place, why are you sleeping, I said that I wanted to talk." He sits on my green and white football sheets, covering at least sixty yards of the football field. The mattress creaks.

"Okay, we'll talk later," I mutter.

"No, I said that I wanted to talk."

"I was asleep."

He wipes his forehead.

"Oops, I fell back asleep again."

"Denny, come on—"

"I'm going to start snoring any second and I'm a pretty loud snorer."

"I told you we'd talk after dinner."

"You always say that. Let's talk when. Let's talk when. Let's talk when. It doesn't mean anything." I don't mean to say that, but I've just woken up, and other than pretending you're still asleep, it's really hard not to tell the truth right after you wake up.

"Dad, you always tell me that you want to talk, but you never do. Why should I have thought tonight would've been any different?"

He looks puzzled, like I've thrown him off his script.

I sit up. "And I can't believe you smacked me during the conference. I know I shouldn't have cut class, but I didn't deserve that."

"I—" he starts. I don't interrupt him; he just stops talking.

"I *what?*" I say, gaining confidence.

Again, that puzzled look. He's forgotten his lines, needs to improvise.

"What?" I say, continuing on the offensive. "What is it?"

He looks down at my bedsheets, rubbing his eyebrows

with his thumb and index finger. I feel sort of bad for him, the way he keeps touching his face. I want to tell him that I'm sorry—for cutting class, for not initiating conversation, for not being a more successful son—but what comes out is this: "You shouldn't have hit me. And you shouldn't eat so much fried food and watch so much TV. And you shouldn't—"

He breathes heavily. "Now you listen to me. I don't tell you how to live your life. Why are you telling me how to live mine?"

"Don't you see, Dad? I wish you did. I wish we spoke about things. Not just the Phillies. And movies. And food. Lots of things. But we don't. I want to ask you about your day and your job, and I want you to ask me about girls and grades and dances and Manny and my gods and goddesses—"

"Gods and goddesses?"

"My teachers, I mean, and my afternoon and my hobbies and movies and shaving and hair and everything else. I want to just . . . I don't know, *talk*. I didn't always, but I wouldn't mind doing it now."

Even though his eyes are open, he isn't moving. Not even blinking. Frozen. Like that football player on my sheets.

I think I see him move his head but it's just the sweat dripping down his face. He doesn't answer me. He's not going to answer me. I've opened up, said what needed to be said, what had to be said, what a parent should say, and gotten nothing. I'm talking to myself.

"Thanks for the talk," I say, scrambling out of bed. I trip over the tent, but he steadies me with his arm against my shoulder.

"But wait—Denny." He leaves his arm there. His face smells of soap. "I'm sorry, I mean, we can talk—another time—another time, that's okay, we can talk." He can't pronounce sentences but at least he's trying. "We can—I mean, talking is okay, another time . . ."

"It's okay," I tell him softly. "I'm glad we talked." He nods his head, which normally would've pissed me off, but not now. Not in the least bit.

"I'm sorry," he says. "For everything."

"I'm sorry, too," I say.

He exhales. Then he turns away, toward my bed. His eyes get cloudy and his nose is running. "I know I haven't . . . been there. I miss . . . your mother. Very much. I miss her very . . ." He slurps snot back up from his nose. "I was sad, Denny, you know?"

I nod.

"I didn't know what to do, where to turn. I wanted to disappear . . . I wanted the days to pass, wanted to fast-forward a few days, a few weeks, a couple of months, a year, you know? All I wanted to do was fast-forward . . . and I sort of did."

"But you never talked about her. You just . . ."

"Don't you think I wanted to? I did, Denny, I did. But I felt that if I let myself talk about her, if I let myself be sad and get down, then I . . ." He touches his cheek and sighs. "Then I'd never get back up again. It was easier to pretend, *is* easier to pretend. Can you understand?"

I can. Now I can. Operation I.M.P. was based on a distraction, based on pretending, based on a lie, based on fast-forwarding time, and I feel bad, awfully bad for pretending . . . with everyone, and for not understanding him, and his body is shaking.

"Sorry you're lost," I tell him.

He looks up, confused.

"Sorry you're lost," I say. "I'm lost, too."

"Denny, I don't even *want* to watch TV and eat and . . . I don't want to disappear. It's just—it's hard to stop. It's hard to start. It's hard to do anything."

I would give him a hug, I really would. I want to grab his wide shoulders and pull him close, letting his snot drip on my shoulder, for there's so much—not snot, I mean, though there is a lot of that—much more to say, but it's buried too far below and I'm afraid to keep digging. I know what I want to say and I can see myself up on the high dive again. The drop is steeper and farther than I've ever seen and it makes me dizzy, makes the world spin around and around, and I need to jump. *JUMP!* I tell myself, and soon it doesn't matter because my dad turns around, nudges me gently out of the way, and walks out of the room. He continues all the way down the hall until he reaches his room and shuts the door.

Hours later, precisely five hours later, my dad and I are yelling at each other. Actually, only he's yelling this time. It seems he doesn't like to be woken up at three in the morning by a phone call from one Emmanuel "Manny" Templeton, former friend, apparently prank-calling as retribution.

"It's for you!" my dad hollers, barging into my room, tossing the phone at me. The way he says it makes it sound as if he's upset the phone wasn't for him, but I know better than to start an argument in the dead of night about his enunciation.

"Hello?" I rub my eyes.

"Donuts?"

"Yeah, Manny, how many donuts would you like? A dozen?"

"My apologies for the phone call at this unseemly hour but I needed to—"

"Rub it in, I know. Get me in trouble. I said I was sorry. I am. I'm really sorry, but there was nothing I could do. Chad and I were alone in the hallways—"

"That is what I am calling about. You see, I played back our conversation from every angle. I played back your story in my head, over and over again—had nothing better to do, really, and plus it *was* a ton of money, my money, sort of—"

"Manny, I said I was sorry."

"Please stop your sniveling. I did not call for an apology. I called to inform you that you may have been recorded."

"What?"

He clears his voice. "Donuts, in most secondary schools, especially ones as busted as ours, there are cameras. In the stairwells, in the halls . . ."

"The HALLS!"

From down the hall, my dad hollers for me to shut up. Then he says "please."

"Yes, the halls. Why do you think I was clandestine in my candy selling in the first place? Our school has eyes. Everyone knows. At least those as plugged into the social pipeline as I am. I should have told you in the first place. Alas, I was blinded by rage and refused to go dateless into the night." He pauses. "That is from a poem, to which I now add for you: 'Now go make this right.'"

The last part sounds a little dramatic and his poem sounds clunky, but I can see, for the first time in a while, a bit of daylight in this long dark tunnel of a year. I just don't know how to get there.

"What—what do we do now, Manny?" I stutter.

"It is your call. All I will say is the following: you have been let go. Fired. When your money was stolen, you compromised our business. You are too much of a liability. Businesses do not want drama. But assuming your story is true, you have been a hardworking employee at International

Monetary Prudential, and like any respectable business industry that treats its former employees with any semblance of decency, I shall offer you a severance package—a going-away present, if you will—of $100 in thanks for helping me turn a rather large profit. A profit so large it is flabbergasting."

"Thanks, but what do I—what do I do? About Chad?"

"I am not the one who got jumped in the halls and I am not the one who has to face him and I am not the one with a reputation of a court jester and I am not the one with a pastry name and I am not the one who has a semi-quasi-ex-girlfriend and I am not the one with a dad that erupts like Mount Vesuvius and I am not the one who is left only with a severance package because I am not the one with the money stolen . . ." The longer he goes on, the more I know, without a shadow of doubt, what I must do.

I know for sure what I must do.

I know what I must do.

I think I know what to do.

I make an educated guess.

I make a not-so-educated guess.

I flip a coin.

I take a wild stab.

I pray for a miracle.

LAST STAND

His desk is cluttered with papers and folders and an old football. His office is cold and smells of leather. He's in his chair, scribbling a note, when he hears me knock.

"Why, ah yes, Mr. Murphy, do come in, won't you?" Mr. Softee gestures toward an empty chair. "Don't mind the mess. How are sales? Come to talk business?"

I take a deep breath. "Mr. Soffer, sir, I didn't want to tell you this in person. It would've been much nobler to leave my name out of it and surprise my teachers, but I've made a donation to our esteemed school."

He leans forward. "A donation? I don't understand. What about your fund-raiser? And your entrepreneurship . . . I thought you had lofty business goals, Mr. Murphy . . ."

"See, that's the thing. I realized that successful businesses need to give back to the community. I'm sure they taught you that at Wharton Business School, right, sir?"

"Well, of course!" He's breathing hard. "Of course they did. Wow, Mr. Murphy, I am very impressed with your generosity! Very, very mature of you!"

"Well, I wanted it to be an anonymous donation, sir, but I worry that my donation hasn't made it to the school's budget."

"Good heavens, what do you mean? Where did you donate?"

"I gave my donation, a rather large donation, sir, to match my enthusiasm and love and respect for our school—"

"Who did you give the money to? You must tell me, Mr. Murphy!"

I exhale. *No turning back. Here goes nothing . . .*

"I gave it to Chad."

"Chad?"

"He's the school's treasurer, yes?"

Mr. Softee touches the side of his face. "Well, yes, of course."

"Don't get me wrong, sir. I'm sure Chad is an upstanding citizen, but the teachers here are first-rate and the sooner they get their hands on better technological equipment, the sooner bright minds such as mine can learn."

"Well, how much did you donate?"

Let's see . . . Chad stole $700, plus inflation, plus "the cost of heartache" as Judge Judy once mentioned . . . that all comes out to . . . well, that Smart Board is a pricey piece of equipment . . .

"One thousand dollars is what I gave him. A cool grand."

His eyes shoot out from their sockets. "ONE THOU-SAND DOLLARS?"

"Indeed."

"Oh my heavens . . . one thousand exactly? Perhaps there was some change?"

"Well . . . how much does a Smart Board run again?"

"On the low end, around a thousand dollars."

"Right . . . I believe it was . . . yes, I donated $1,111. I'm sure of it now because I intended for Mr. Morgan to receive a new DVD player and for Mrs. Q to get a Smart Board to replace her junky overhead projector. And yes, I remember it now, I donated exactly $1,111 because our school is Number One, after all. I tried to use symbolism in my donation. Mr. Morgan taught me about symbolism in his wonderful English class. And anyway, that's what everyone around here says: There's only one Blueberry Hills Middle School and we are Number One."

I do feel a bit bad for going so overboard, but his leathery face beams with pride. "Well, that's just—the nicest—I can't—" He wipes his right eye with the back of his hand. "How can I ever—thank you, thank you, thank you!"

"It's my pleasure, sir. Make sure you get the money from Chad at once. I'm sure he already put it in an escrow or some other holding account and that he was waiting for the right time to surprise you."

"Yes, of course!" He reaches for the loudspeaker: "Will Chad Watkins please report to the principal's office at once. Chad Watkins, please report at once."

"Excellent, sir. Now if for some strange reason—not that I expect this, but if for some unforeseen reason he tries to protect me by refusing to disclose my donation, or denies the amount was actually the very symbolic number of $1,111, I suggest you check the camera hallways, second floor, on Wednesday, around, say, three ten? That's when and where I handed him my donation. You *do* have cameras to keep us safe, right, sir?"

"Why, certainly we do. Safety is a priority around here."

"Great. You'll have to excuse me, sir. I'd rather not be here when he arrives, considering my anonymous donation and all. As someone of your business stature, I'm sure you can understand."

He leaps to his feet, races around his desk, and hugs me. Hugs me tight. "Bless you, Mr. Murphy. You're a saint, an absolute saint. A star. A rock star is what you are."

A rock star...

If only everyone around here thought so.

After my meeting, I camp out at Sabrina's locker. I mean, really camp out. All I'm missing is some marshmallows and a fire, but as I said before, lighters and fires are illegal in middle school. I sit cross-legged on the floor in my G.I. Joe tent, munching on handfuls of granola, and wait until she comes. It's great that I'm already on the ground because if begging is required, I'm willing and able and already in position.

I wave to Mrs. Q, who is on her way to make copies, nod at Mr. Softee walking with a black briefcase, and when I see Sabrina's blue Converse sneakers down the hall, I know it's time. I chew as quickly as I can and scramble to my feet.

"What are you doing here?" she asks.

I reach into my pocket and hand her two tickets and a few granola crumbs.

Her eyes light up, hopefully not out of disgust for the granola—I didn't mean to put it in her hand, but it's everywhere. On my shirt, on my jeans, *in* my jeans, on my fingers.

"*Les Miz?*" She doesn't scream or hug or thank me. She just asks.

I swallow hard. "Yeah," I tell her. "*Les Miz.* They're real tickets. It's at the Forrest Theater in Philly. I saw an advertisement in the paper."

"I don't understand. Why are you—"

"They're front-row. So you'll never have to look down."

I expect a smile. It doesn't come. I hadn't planned for this.

"Jean Valjean may have to look down, Sabrina, but we'll never have to with those front-row seats. We'll be looking straight ahead. And slightly up."

"Thank you, but . . ."

"You don't have to go with me, but the tickets are yours.

I didn't steal them or get anything stolen from me on the way to getting them. Manny gave me a rather generous severance package—"

"What? A severance package . . . what are you saying?"

"That I miss you, Sabrina. I do. I miss you."

"You miss—" She shakes her head.

"I do. I really do. I want us to go, if that's okay, and I'll smuggle some popcorn in and I promise not to make too much of a mess."

"But your business . . . it wasn't for me."

"It *was*, was going to be, and, well, you're my business."

You're my business? It sounds terrible and corny coming out of my mouth. Because it is. I need to step it up. "I was afraid before, but I was getting less and less afraid and leaping off high dives and—"

"High dives? What are you talking about?"

"High dives, with you. Being less afraid, I mean. And now I'm not afraid. I want to sing it from the rafters."

"Please don't sing."

"Fine, I won't sing, but it's not a secret, Sabrina. I don't want it to be. I want to tell everyone." I *do* want to sing it from the rafters, but there are no rafters in the hallways. Still, I need a platform, a podium, a high space . . . and quickly. I step on my tent to climb on top, which for some reason sounds like a good idea, and I snap one of the supports. In half. And I trip and fall, chin to the cold hallway floor, but at least I didn't fall in the trash. Once I'm back on my feet and standing on my broken tent, I raise my voice and tell the crowded hallways: "I HAVE AN IMPORTANT ANNOUNCEMENT TO MAKE. EVERYBODY LISTEN UP. I WANT TO TELL YOU ALL THAT I MET A YOUNG LADY. A GIRL. A GAL."

"You sure it wasn't a donut?" someone shouts.

"You sure it wasn't inflatable?" another cries.

"I MISSED HER. I HEARD A BRUCE SPRINGSTEEN SONG ON THE RADIO AND WANTED TO TELL HER. IT'S A REALLY PATRIOTIC TUNE AND GOOD, TOO. NOT AS GOOD AS 'ATLANTIC CITY,' BUT STILL GOOD."

Sabrina is tugging at my shirt, begging me to be quiet.

"NO, EVERYONE HAS TO HEAR THIS: I SAW A VICTORIA'S SECRET COMMERCIAL AND I THOUGHT OF HER AND WANTED TO TELL HER."

"Awesome!" someone screams. "Tell me more!"

"I MEAN, WHAT I WANT TO SAY IS, I WAS AFRAID. I WAS A SCARED DONUT HIDING ALL MY STRAWBERRY JELLY INSIDE. NO, RASPBERRY, IT WAS RASPBERRY." Another tug from Sabrina, to whom I whisper, "I have to tell the truth: I think the jelly inside a donut is usually raspberry . . . BUT I LIKE A GIRL, A VERY NICE GIRL. A GAL, WHO FOR SOME REASON LIKES ME. I THINK. JUST WANTED EVERYONE TO KNOW THAT I PRETEND. A LOT. I'M A SKILLED ACTOR AND COMEDIAN LIKE

ZACH GALIFIANAKIS. BUT LESS HAIRY. HOPE-
FULLY YOU THINK SO. BUT THAT'S NOT THE
POINT. THE POINT IS THIS: I DON'T WANT TO
ACT ANYMORE. I DON'T WANT TO PRETEND
ANYMORE. THAT'S WHAT I WANT TO SAY: I
DON'T WANT TO PRETEND ANYMORE. SO
THERE YOU HAVE IT. WORLD, TAKE ME AS I AM!"

It feels like an appropriate ending, an inspiring ending, a
final crescendo with which I expect some type of applause
or congratulations or taunt or threat.

But all I hear is "I was hoping for the worm" from one
person and silence from everyone else, and the hallways
are emptying out with everyone spilling back to class.

But Sabrina is smiling.

SOAK IN THE MEMORIES

Flashing lights. Given my transitional Mohawk, my hair is gelled back as best as I can. The sides of my head are no longer flying angels, courtesy of Melinda, and my suit and tie are as nonwrinkly as my dad and I could muster. Flashing lights. My arm is around Sabrina's pink dress. Not just her dress, her, too. She's in the dress—I mean, of course, but I'm afraid to look at her because she's beautiful and she's my date and she's beautiful and she smells of flowers and did I mention she's beautiful? Her hair in curls that fall on her smooth shoulders, my white corsage on her left wrist.

"Over here." "No, over here, you two." More lights. Sabrina's mom smiling. My dad is, too, yucking it up with her mom. Sabrina's dad had to work, which is just fine. I already feel like the whole world is watching me with binoculars on high definition. I don't need him around, too.

"Should I bring out some chocolate chip cookies?" Sabrina's mom asks.

The last thing I want is something in my teeth. Besides, my stomach is doing the butterfly stroke in a pool of butterflies. I want to be out of here, out of parental company and finally alone with Sabrina—and the rest of the seventh grade class.

My stomach does another flip turn.

"No, thank you," Sabrina and I say.

"No cookies for me, thank you," my dad says. "Sort of on a day-by-day diet. Yesterday, no ice cream. Today, no cookies."

"Oh, well then, should I put out some dip, everyone? I could cut up a red pepper, maybe peel a few carrots?"

"Mom, please," Sabrina mutters through her smile.

"Come on, how about some dip?"

My dad cuts in, "Bringing out some dip is a fine idea. Right, Denny?"

I shake my head.

"Sure it is," my dad says. "Let's cut up a red pepper, slice up a carrot . . . maybe a green pepper. Got any green peppers?"

"No green peppers," she says. "Only red peppers."

"That's fine, a red pepper and a few carrot sticks will do the trick. Right?"

"No."

"Aww, come on, Denny," my dad says. "Carrot sticks make a real healthy snack, right?"

"I don't want dip."

"Dip can be delicious . . . well, *I* don't find it very tasty, but with a few vegetables . . . it's still not so tasty, but not bad for you."

"Couldn't agree more," Sabrina's mom says.

My dad claps his hands. "Great, let's get some dip and vegetables out here and truly make this a celebration." *Right, because nothing screams celebration like a handful of vegetables and a cup of dip.*

More flashing lights. "Over here." "No, over here." My arm around Sabrina. "Smile, you two—look this way . . . Beautiful, now it's time for dip."

At the front entrance of Blueberry Hills Middle, Sabrina climbs out of her mother's royal blue station wagon into the warm April air and waves goodbye. My dad, in the front seat, waves, too. "I hope they have real Chinese food here," I tell him, shutting the door. "You know, the Chinese food that real Chinese people eat—when they eat food that is Chinese—in a Chinese restaurant."

(I don't mean to sound so awkward with him. For the first time in a long time I don't feel awkward around him. It's just that my arms and legs and mouth feel trapped in a steel cage of nerves and I'm aware of every slight movement

I make and I hate every single one. I don't know why my hands are balled into fists. I didn't tell them to do that and now they're stuck. Frozen. The April air, though warm, does nothing to thaw me out. *Breathe,* I tell myself, but instead I tug my arms against my body and squeeze, squeeze tighter. It seems my body doesn't understand English. I'd speak Chinese, but I don't understand—even when real Chinese—people—not like me—speak Chinese—to myself. Even my thoughts are robotic and make no sense.)

Anyway, when I mention the Chinese food to my dad, he doesn't yell or get out of the car in a huff. He just smiles and says, "You better ask for the manager."

The station wagon chugs down the street and when the honor roll bumper sticker is almost out of sight, Sabrina pulls me close. "Sorry for the ride. I know you had bigger plans for transportation."

I feel my face go hot. I want to laugh it off, but my body isn't working.

"You okay?" she asks.

No, I'm not okay. My arms are stuck and my voice is stuck and my feet are stuck and you smell nice and I hope I do, too, but I don't think I do and I'd check to see and smell myself but that's not okay at dances and I couldn't even if I wanted to because my arms are stuck to my sides like the way Manny usually walks and I can't unstick them.

"Seriously, what if the money had never been stolen?"

Sabrina says. "How would we have gotten to the dance? In a souped-up limo? A Ferrari? A Porsche?"

I breathe in and spit out the answer in one breath: "We were never going to get a sports car anyway because we probably had to get parental releases, and they were probably out of our price range anyway so it was a bad idea, a stupid idea, it was Manny's idea, really it was, and it wasn't realistic. It was all a dream, JUST PRETEND, REALLY . . ." I feel my words fading, like I have to scream to be heard, and not because of my fleeting breath. They're being drowned out by something around me, over me, on top of me.

"Uh, Denny . . ."

"WHAT? I CAN'T HEAR YOU!" A loud noise is muting everything I say, like there's some new fire drill or music that's all drums and bass, or a plane flying over or something. "I CAN'T HEAR MYSELF! YOU NEED TO SPEAK UP!"

"I THINK YOU SHOULD . . ."

"WHAT?"

"I THINK YOU SHOULD LOOK UP. LOOK *UP*!" She points skyward.

I try to get a good look, but I have to cover my eyes. The air is poking me, blinding me—sand, dirt, a windstorm clawing through my eyelids and suit. My hair is messed up now, I know it, but I can't fix it, and from all around mumbles and groans from other students as the wind whips us from the back and the front and the side, but mostly on top, above, where that bass drum sound, that BOOM, is now a THUMP THUMP THUMP THUMP THUMP THUMP THUMP THUMP THUMP. I reach for Sabrina's hand and ask—SHOUT—if she's all right.

"YEAH! YOU?"

I wipe my face with my sleeve and blink away the sand. Shielding my eyes against the wind, I look up. My jaw drops at the image above me. I'm aware of the bits of sand flying into my mouth, but I can't close it. Couldn't close it if I tried. I do try and I can't close it because I can't believe it. Can't begin to fathom what's in front of me—above me. Can't, can't, just can't . . .

"Can't be," I mutter, but there it is.

And there he is.

Manny, dressed in a tuxedo, beaming—smiling a full-mouthed, openmouthed smile, a smile so wide it looks like it's coming from a dozen mouths, a hundred mouths, and there he is above me, above everyone, waving from the window of a hovering helicopter. Not some toy, or kiddie version. A full-fledged helicopter. Now blowing dust clouds on the way down.

I shake my head in amazement. "Flabbergasting. Flab-ber-gast-ing." I can't help but say it, and if anyone else knew what it meant or what it *really* meant in the scope of Manny's world, my world, our world . . . what it meant, what it all meant, what this meant—Manny in a helicopter, an *actual* helicopter, making a grand ol' entrance at the grand ol' seventh grade dance—they'd say it too: "Flabbergasting."

The chopper descends in back of the school on an empty baseball field and everyone seems to forget the rigidity and anxiety and formality of the seventh grade dance, because everyone, boys and girls alike, in their colorful shirts and ties and pink flowers and dresses and shiny high-heeled shoes . . . like a rainbow running through the wind, everyone makes a mad dash around the school to get a better look. I grab Sabrina's hand, which is warm and awesome, and race around with everyone else to get a good look, too. My shoes are tight, *way* too tight, and I can feel a blister starting at my heel, but it feels so wonderful to run with her, and with each painful but exhilarating step I feel young again, like Manny and I are in my backyard on a secret spy mission and it's a matter of national security and utmost urgency that I run as fast as I can. Sprinting with Sabrina's hand in mine, I just feel light, so very light, like the air is propelling me forward, which is probably due to the helicopter, but whatever it is it feels good. Except for the noise (deafening) and wind (blinding), it feels really good.

Turning at the corner of the school building, I can see Manny giving everyone—dozens of dancegoers and parents, and me—a thumbs-up as the chopper touches down. The pilot, a mustachioed man with a headset on, nods at the adoring crowd.

It takes a good minute and what feels like a good hour—and it really *is* a good minute or good hour because Sabrina is still holding my hand—for the propeller to spin to rest, and it's a good minute or good hour for Manny, too, as he keeps his thumb in the air the whole time, grinning from ear to ear, basking in all his glory. Then he shifts in his seat, gesturing to the back for some reason. And soon I see why.

He's not alone. Him and the pilot, I mean; they're not alone.

The door opens and a redheaded girl in a shiny silver dress climbs out of the chopper, balancing against Manny's hand.

Manny's got a date. An eighth grader. The one who I asked if she knew karate.

"Evening, gents and m'ladies," Manny chirps. He's sporting a slick black tuxedo with a silver handkerchief to match his date's dress. On his head, he's wearing his signature fishing cap. He gives the swelling crowd a presidential wave and raises his date's hand high in the air. As he hops down, Manny's cap flies off his head, but his date snags it in the air. Such excellent reflexes . . . maybe she really *does* know karate. Manny offers to hold the cap and promises not to put it back on.

When Manny's close enough to me, I reach for the shoulder of his shiny tux. "How did you—I don't—how did you do it?"

"The tuxedo?" He gives himself a once-over. "It is a rental. I thought of purchasing it, but my doctor projects my growth to skyrocket in the coming years."

"No, your *date* . . ."

"My doctor does not know the precise date. He does not know exactly when my growth spurt will occur, but he projects—"

I grab both shoulders and point him toward the redhead. "Her! How?"

"Do not hate the player. Hate the game." Manny rubs his chin. "Market research. Market freaking research. Instead of falling over my words like you did, or using corny pickup lines, I just, well, asked. Sure, the helicopter helps, but turns out eighth graders *like* going to seventh grade dances. Who *knew*?"

"You're serious . . ."

"As serious as a karate chop." He winks, then turns to Sabrina and bows. "Evening, m'lady."

"Evening, Manny."

Manny shifts his gaze to the admiring crowd of parents and kids on the baseball field. "I BELIEVE THE SHOW IS INSIDE, CORRECT?" he shouts. Then he whispers to us: "Before we proceed to the dance, a picture, shall we?" He pulls out his camera and motions for the three of us to squeeze in next to him. "Wait, we need to get the helicopter in the background . . ." Holding it straight out and bending it back so we're all in the shot with him, Manny snaps the picture. "Hold on, one more, make it count, and ... priceless." We all take a look. I gotta admit, we look good. We don't even look like ourselves. I certainly don't recognize myself, don't recognize the proud smile on my face, the wide grin on Manny's, or our dates, *real* dates, not the dried fruit. Real actual live human girls who are dates, looking happy and attractive by our sides, happy to be here, happy to be next to us, just plain happy. I don't recognize us and I don't recognize the feeling, but I do like how it feels. I love how it feels.

"A classic, indeed," Manny points out. "Pictures are perhaps the most important part of the evening. Pictures are immortal. They last forever, live forever." I elbow him in the side. His silky smooth tuxedo feels good even on my elbow. "But enough of my blabber," Manny finishes. "Shall we, everyone?"

Walking around the school and through the front entrance, I avoid the gaze of Manny's date. No way I'm looking her in the eye.

Approaching the dance hall, I'm not sure how to look at the guy in front of me, either. In a red and green tweed suit, Mr. Morgan waves us forward. I want to tell him that his suit looks swanky, but I'm not sure if "swanky" is the right word to use and he *is* an English teacher after all, and I want to tell him that I've given things a lot of thought and that I'm sorry, and that the heading on his work sheet isn't entirely wrong, isn't completely wrong; that it should read

"Life is ~~good~~ flabbergasting," but instead I say, "I assume you're the hormone checker. Guess we gotta leave them at the door."

He shakes his head. "Actually, for tonight, but just for to-night, hormones are allowed in. This is a hormone-friendly establishment. In fact, please bring them." He nods at Ronald "the Gum Dealer" Latimer running in place in the center of the dance floor, his arms in full pump, his mustache twitching with every long stride. "If Ronald's the only one dancing, we're in for a long evening."

He pats me on the shoulder on our way in and I can't help but turn around and say, "Turns out Sabrina likes me, Mr. Morgan. I guess you're not as omniscient as I thought you were."

"Don't push your luck."

"She understands what an intellectual powerhouse I am at English."

"I guess so." He chuckles. "By the way, Mr. Anonymous, thank you for the classroom equipment. Mrs. Q thanks you, too."

"I don't know what you're talking about."

He waves me off. "Know it's appreciated. Really, thank you. I admire you."

I think of hugging him—until he says, "But if you don't hand in months of math work by June, you'll be watching her test out that Smart Board this summer."

"Roger that. But you're killing the vibe, Mr. Morgan."

"That's my job. Seriously, it is. That's why they pay me the big bucks and why intellectual English powerhouses call me the Lumberjack and the S.U.O.G.E."

I can't help but smile. I feel another urge to hug him, to throw my arms around him and give him a big ol' bear hug, grizzly bear that he is. But I don't, because students aren't supposed to bear-hug teachers, because bear hugs hurt, and because Manny shoves me forward, barking: "How many times with the 'Roger that'? And how inappropriate for a teacher to engage in conversation with a student at such a formal gathering!"

"Manny, chill out, I engaged with him."

"You are engaged to your teacher? I thought you had a firm grasp of all the rules of social etiquette. You need to be on your best behavior tonight!"

"I was only going to give him a bear hug, Manny."

"*What?* You should never hug people as if they are bears, especially teachers! Not now, not ever, forever and ever, amen!"

I can't tell if he's serious or not. He's so worked up from the helicopter landing that it's hard to get a read on him.

Walking inside, the first thing that hits me, like a basketball or a volleyball or tennis ball or soccer ball or any other balls we use in gym, is that our dance—our monumental and dreaded and fancy and overwhelming and apocalyptic seventh grade dance—is in the gym. Our dance hall is the Blueberry Hills Middle School gymnasium. Like any other middle-size gym in the state of New Jersey that doesn't smell as bad as it usually does. (It smells of cologne and perfume and french fries.) Eighty, maybe a hundred students are already inside, walking in groups, dark clumps like shadows pasted together, like they're attached at the hip for their own comfort, and it looks like it's working because the groups of ten and fifteen and twenty look a lot more relaxed than I feel. But it's hard to be sure of anything right now, and it's really hard to get an accurate count on each group because it's hard to see.

The overhead lights are off; a red and white disco ball sparkles in the back, above a DJ with a strobe-light jacket and long sideburns. The white walls are covered in purple banners and dance posters. "This is a hormone-friendly zone," one of them says. Pink streamers cross the room in all directions, as if it were toilet-papered as a prank. Blue balloons hover above a circular dance floor. A green table-cloth stretches across three café tables full of food.

The DJ begs everyone to come onto the dance floor, but they're all on the outside of the circle dabbling at the tables with all sorts of snacks and a jug of Hawaiian Punch. I feel my body loosening. "Aloha!" I shout, but nobody gets it.

"The punch," I explain to Sabrina. "It's Hawaiian. Aloha!"
She shakes her head.

Still, it's better than the fascinating conversation I hear to my right:

"Are you having fun?"

"Yeah, why?"

"You're not talking."

"Neither are you."

"That's because you aren't."

"No, *you* aren't."

"Okay, I'll start. Are you having fun?"

"Yes. Are you?"

"Yes."

"Great."

"Yes. Great."

"Have you eaten?"

"Yes, have you?"

"Yes."

Manny must catch the tight, cautious vibe because he points to a kid that just joined the dance floor. "He is dancing like the Tin Man. Someone needs to put oil in that guy's armpits. What about you, Donuts? Care to lubricate that tall chap's pits?"

"Why don't *you* dance?"

Instead of dancing, Manny points to the row of candy bars on the food table. "Courtesy of I.M.P," he says. "But do not have too many. Nobody goes to the bathroom at a formal dance because the toilet can overflow and you can slip and crack your head, and you will forever be known as the guy who slipped on his own crap at the dance. Plus, because this is such a formal gathering, you will need to tip some guy for handing you a paper towel in the bathroom.

So, I believe one candy bar will suffice—and one, of course, for the Mrs."

Sabrina fills a cup with Hawaiian Punch and piles celery sticks, peppers, mini-carrots, a spoonful of dip, and a roll of bread on her plate.

"I thought you didn't want any," I say.

She shrugs.

Over her shoulder, I spot Marsha in her hairnet, holding a tray of mozzarella sticks. I wave. Her hands are full so she can't wave back. *Relationship beings,* she mouths. *Relationship beings, remember.* I nod. *Dance. You have to dance.* I nod again.

I want to but . . . I still feel too nervous to dance, too nervous to eat. I fill up a plate of food and push it around, waiting patiently for my song. Something slow, something smooth, something I can rock to. Not rock and roll to, just rock to, from side to side. Or the chicken dance. Or anything by Bruce Springsteen.

The DJ has other plans: techno beats, wailing drums, a strobe light that makes everyone look like robots weaving their arms in and out of figure eights. The DJ, pretending to scratch a record, screams "Wicki, wicki, wicki!" into the microphone, obviously plagiarizing me and the Rockafellas, none of whom seem to notice because they're happily dancing in a group of at least a dozen. And then the DJ plays a song that was ruined. I had heard it on the radio on the way home from the funeral. It still feels ruined, and I feel myself tightening up again, but halfway through the song, I don't know, it sort of doesn't feel ruined anymore—until the DJ groans into the microphone, "Uh . . . yeah . . . uh-huh uh . . . yeah . . . let the good times roll." Then it's ruined. I fight a smile.

"The DJ is an abomination," Manny says. "This music is flabbergasting."

Manny's right, but at least he made me laugh and at least I'm not the only one standing on the sidelines watching the DJ pepper his mixes with uh-huh-yeah sound effects. A few couples within each group gaze at the dance floor, hands in their pockets, until their group pushes them together for a push dance. I call it the "push dance" or "mush dance" because that's really what it is: they mush kids together and say "Dance!"

Reluctantly, the couples oblige. Not that they have a choice.

Sabrina watches the push/mush dances with a sparkle in her eye, sipping Hawaiian Punch. Part of me wants someone to force Sabrina and me to push/mush dance and part of me thinks I'm a raving lunatic for wanting that, and a part of me wants to hug her or kiss her, and part of me just wants to talk to her, show her a good time, but I don't know what to say. Thankfully, the DJ and his music are loud enough to drown out any herky-jerky sentences I think of pronouncing. One song to the next, uh-huh-yeah, I say nothing.

What feels like days later, the DJ leans into the microphone and announces the last song: "I give to you, as voted on by the seventh grade class, your dance song and from what I hear, your *official* school song—" He pauses. "This will be the last song, so make it count. Grab that special someone, escort them to the dance floor, and soak in the memories. Uh-huh, yeah. Soak 'em in, like a sponge. Let the good times roll."

Marsha eyes me from the food table. *Dance,* she mouths, pointing desperately at Sabrina. *You need to dance!*

Dance? With a girl? With my girl? I want to, I do, but my heart is racing and my palms feel sweaty. I reach into my pocket and play with my phone. I want to talk into it, *need* to talk into it. There's so much I want to say, want to tell her, ask her; so much I want to thank her for, apologize, whisper to her. But, I realize, she probably already knows. Because . . . how could I have gotten through the past year without her? I mean, if she weren't with me—if she stayed at her funeral and never left to watch over me at the corned beef fest and everywhere else—then how do you explain the good in this world, in my world: that my dad and I are now speaking—not in long sentences, but still; that gods and goddesses have new technology; that Chad got played; that I have a girl, an actual human female, and Manny has one, too, for at least another hour.

My mom isn't a tense. But if she were, she'd be present. Past, too. But also present. I want to call her, but I get the feeling that she's here with me now, in the present, smiling down on me as the DJ plays the school song and everyone barks in order to let the dogs out. It feels good to think of her like this.

(All of the barking dog sounds in my ears don't feel as good.)

Sabrina asks me to dance. Tells me, actually. "You need to dance." Thankfully, she or anyone else doesn't push/mush us together. But we do lock hands and assume what seems to be dancing position. I know how to ~~surf on a desk~~ fall in a trash can, how to do the chicken dance, how to do the worm, but I've never done them at a dance, an official school dance, with hundreds of barking students and a few barking gods and goddesses—and a girl in my arms, swaying me from side to side.

I don't have a clue how to do this.

But I do know this: the same way I know that somehow I'll get through this night and all other days and nights and months and summer school and the rest of my classes as a student of Blueberry Hills Middle; the same way I'll get through Chad's revenge and all the other issues—and there'll be *plenty*—that come with a flabbergasting age in a flabbergasting school with a flabbergasting friend and a flabbergasting parent and m'lady, m'flabbergasting lady, in this ~~good~~ flabbergasting life.

I'll do my best.

ACKNOWLEDGMENTS

There are many people who helped make this book possible. First, thank you to my wife, who makes everything possible.

Thank you to Hubert for his candy ideas (and candy). Thank you to Joseph for his word. Thank you to all my students. This doesn't happen without them.

Thanks to my agent, Michelle Andelman, for her support. Thanks to Janine O'Malley, Angie Chen, and everyone at FSG for their tireless work.

The book was written for those lost. I hope it provides direction, comfort, a laugh, a smirk, hope, company, a distraction, a conversation starter, and/or a pillow.